CRIM

Ferdinand von Schirach was born in Munich in 1964 and is one of Germany's most prominent defence lawyers. In 2009, his first collection of stories, *Verbrechen* (*Crime*) became an instant bestseller in Germany, and was published in over thirty territories around the world.

Carol Brown Janeway's translations include Bernhard Schlink's *The Reader*, Jan Philipp Reemtsma's *In the Cellar*, Hans-Ulrich Treichel's *Lost*, Zvi Kolitz's *Yosl Rakover Talks to God*, Benjamin Lebert's *Crazy*, Sándor Márai's *Embers*, Yasmina Reza's *Desolation*, Margriet de Moor's *The Storm*, and Daniel Kehlmann's *Fame* and *Measuring the World*.

FERDINAND VON SCHIRACH

Crime & Guilt

TRANSLATED FROM THE GERMAN BY
Carol Brown Janeway

VINTAGE BOOKS
London

Published by Vintage 2012

2 4 6 8 10 9 7 5 3 1

Crime copyright © Piper Verlag GmbH, München 2009
Translation copyright © Carol Brown Janeway 2011

Guilt copyright © Piper Verlag GmbH, München 2010
Translation copyright © Carol Brown Janeway 2012

Crime first published in Germany as *Verbrechen* by
Piper Verlag GmbH in 2009

Guilt first published in Germany as *Schuld* by Piper Verlag GmbH in 2010

Ferdinand von Schirach has asserted his right under the Copyright,
Designs and Patents Act 1988 to be identified as the author of this work

Crime first published in Great Britain in 2011 by
Chatto & Windus

Guilt first published in Great Britain in 2012 by
Chatto & Windus

Vintage
Random House, 20 Vauxhall Bridge Road,
London SW1V 2SA

www.vintage-books.co.uk

Addresses for companies within The Random House Group Limited can be
found at: www.randomhouse.co.uk/offices.htm

The Random House Group Limited Reg. No. 954009

A CIP catalogue record for this book
is available from the British Library

ISBN 9780099549277

The Random House Group Limited supports The Forest Stewardship
Council (FSC®), the leading international forest certification organisation.
Our books carrying the FSC label are printed on FSC® certified paper. FSC
is the only forest certification scheme endorsed by the leading environmental
organisations, including Greenpeace. Our paper procurement policy can be
found at www.randomhouse.co.uk/environment

Typeset by Palimpsest Book Production Limited,
Falkirk, Stirlingshire

Printed and bound by CPI Group (UK) Ltd, Croydon, CR0 4YY

CONTENTS

Crime 1

Guilt 239

CRIME

CONTENTS

Preface: Guilt *1*

Fähner 3

Tanata's Tea Bowl 19

The Cello 45

The Hedgehog 65

Bliss 83

Summertime 97

Self-Defence 135

Green 159

The Thorn 183

Love 201

The Ethiopian 211

The reality we can put into
words is never reality itself.
—*Werner K. Heisenberg*

Preface
Guilt

Jim Jarmusch once said he'd rather make a movie about a man walking his dog than about the Emperor of China. I feel the same way. I write about criminal cases, I've appeared for the defence in more than seven hundred of them. But actually my subject is human beings—their failings, their guilt, and their capacity to behave magnificently.

I had an uncle who was the presiding judge over a court that heard trials by jury. These are the courts that handle capital offences: murder and manslaughter. He told us stories from these cases that we could understand, even as children. They always began with him saying: 'Most things are complicated, and guilt always presents a bit of a problem.'

He was right. We chase after things, but they're faster than we are, and in the end we can never catch up. I tell the stories of people I've defended.

They were murderers, drug dealers, bank robbers and prostitutes. They all had their stories, and they weren't so different from us. All our lives we dance on a thin layer of ice; it's very cold underneath, and death is quick. The ice won't bear the weight of some people and they fall through. That's the moment that interests me. If we're lucky, it never happens to us and we keep dancing. If we're lucky.

My uncle was in the navy during the war, and lost his left arm and right hand to a grenade. Despite this, he didn't give up for a long time. People say he was a good judge, humane, an upright man with a sense of justice. He loved going hunting, and had a little private blind. His gun was custom-made for him and he could use it with one hand. One day he went into the woods, put the double-barrelled shotgun in his mouth, and pulled the trigger. He was wearing a black roll-neck sweater; he'd hung his jacket on a branch. His head exploded. I saw the photos a long time later. He left a letter for his best friend, in which he wrote that he'd simply had enough. The letter began with the words 'Most things are complicated, and guilt always presents a bit of a problem.' I still miss him. Every day.

This book is about people like him, and their stories.

FvS

Fähner

Friedhelm Fähner had spent his whole working life as a GP in Rottweil, 2,800 patients with medical insurance processed every year, doctor's office on the main street, chairman of the Egyptian Cultural Association, member of the Lions Club, no criminal offences, nor even minor infringements. Besides his house, he owned two rental properties, a three-year-old E-Class Mercedes with leather upholstery and air conditioning, approximately 750,000 euros in bonds, and a capital sum life insurance policy. Fähner had no children. His only living relative was his sister, six years younger, who lived in Stuttgart with her husband and two sons. Fähner's life wasn't anything that gave rise to stories.

Until the thing with Ingrid.

★   ★   ★

Fähner was twenty-four when he met Ingrid at the party to celebrate his father's sixtieth birthday. His father had been a doctor in Rottweil, too.

As a town, Rottweil is bourgeois to the core. Any non-inhabitant will be vouchsafed the information, willy-nilly, that the town was founded a thousand years ago and is the oldest in Baden-Württemberg. And indeed you come across medieval oriel windows and pretty antique tavern signs from the sixteenth century. The Fähners had lived here forever. They belonged to the so-called first families of the town, known for their roles as doctors, judges and apothecaries.

Friedhelm Fähner looked a little like the young John F. Kennedy. He had a friendly face, people took him to be carefree, and things always panned out for him. You had to look more closely to detect a certain sadness, some ancient dark shadow in his expression, not so uncommon in this land between the Black Forest and the mountains of Swabia.

Ingrid's parents, who were pharmacists in Rottweil, took their daughter with them to the party. She was three years older than Fähner, a sturdy, big-breasted provincial beauty. Eyes of a watery blue, black hair, pale skin—she knew the effect she had on people. Her voice, high-pitched and strangely metallic, grated on Fähner. It was only when she spoke softly that her sentences found a melody of their own.

She had failed to complete high school and was working as a waitress. 'Temporarily,' she said to Fähner. He didn't care. In another area, and one that interested him much more, she was way ahead of him. Fähner had had only two sexual encounters with women; they had been more unsettling than anything. He promptly fell in love with Ingrid.

Two days after the birthday party, she seduced him at the end of a picnic. They lay in a hikers' shelter and Ingrid did her stuff well. Fähner was so overwhelmed that only a week later he asked her to marry him. She accepted without hesitation: Fähner was what you'd call a good catch, he was studying medicine in Munich, he was attractive and caring, and he would soon be taking his first exams. But what attracted her most was his seriousness. She couldn't put it into words, but she said to her girlfriend that Fähner would never walk out on her. Four months later, she moved in with him.

The honeymoon was a trip to Cairo, his choice. When people later asked him about Egypt, he said it floated free of the earth, even when he knew that nobody would understand what he meant. Over there he was the young Parsifal, his purity that of a holy fool, and he was happy. It was the last time in his life.

The evening before they flew back, they were lying in their hotel room. The windows were open; it was still too hot, the air a solid mass in the little room. It was a cheap hotel, it smelled of rotten fruit, and they could hear the sounds of the street below. Despite the heat, they had made love. Fähner lay on his back, watching the rotations of the ceiling fan, as Ingrid smoked a cigarette. She turned on her side, propped her head on one hand, and looked at him. He smiled. There was a long silence.

Then she began to tell her story. She told Fähner about the men who'd come before him, about disappointments and mistakes, but most of all about the French lieutenant who had gotten her pregnant, and the abortion that had almost killed her. She wept. Shocked, he took her in his arms. He felt her heart beating against his chest and was undone. She has entrusted herself to me, he thought.

'You must swear to look after me. You can't ever leave me.' Ingrid's voice trembled.

He was moved. He wanted to calm her. He said he'd already sworn to do this at the wedding ceremony in church. He was happy with her. He wanted—

She interrupted him brusquely, her voice rising and taking on its unmodulated metallic sheen. 'Swear.'

And suddenly he understood. This was no conversation between lovers, under the fan in Cairo, with the pyramids and the stifling heat of their hotel room—all these clichés vanished in an instant. He pushed her away a little so that he could see her eyes. Then he said it. He said it slowly, and he knew what he was saying. 'I swear.'

He pulled her close once more and kissed her face. They made love again. But this time it was different. She sat on top of him, took whatever she wanted. They were deadly serious, strangers to each other, and each of them was wholly alone. Afterward, he lay awake for a long time, staring at the ceiling. There had been a power cut and the fan had stopped revolving.

Naturally, Fähner passed his exams with distinction, completed his doctorate, and landed his first job in the Rottweil District Hospital. They found an apartment, three rooms, bath, view of the edge of the forest.

When his things in Munich were being packed up, she threw out his record collection. He didn't realise this until they were moving into the new apartment. She said she couldn't stand them—he'd listened to them with other women. Fähner was furious. They barely spoke to each other for two days.

Fähner liked Bauhaus clarity. She decorated the apartment in oak and pine, hung curtains at the windows, and bought brightly coloured bed linens. He even accepted the embroidered coasters and the pewter tankards; he didn't want to put her down.

A few weeks later, Ingrid told him she was bothered by the way he held his knife and fork. To begin with, he laughed and thought she was being childish. She reproached him with it again the next day, and then the days after that. And because she meant it, he took to holding his knife differently.

Ingrid pretended that he didn't take out the garbage. He persuaded himself that these were merely teething troubles in their relationship. But soon she was accusing him of coming home too late because he'd been flirting with other women.

The reproaches became unending, until he was hearing them daily: he was disorganised. He dirtied his shirts. He crumpled the newspaper. He smelled bad. He thought only of himself. He talked nonsense. He was cheating on her. Fähner barely defended himself anymore.

After a few years, the insults began. Relatively measured at first, they then gained in intensity. He was a pig. He was torturing her. He was an idiot. Then came the scatological rants and the screaming. He gave up. He would get out of bed during the night and read science fiction. He went jogging for an hour every day, as he had done when he was a student. They had long since given up sex. He received approaches from other women, but he never had an affair. When he was thirty-five, he took over his father's practice; when he was forty, he had turned grey. Fähner was tired.

——

When Fähner was forty-eight, his father died; when he was fifty, it was his mother's turn. He used his inheritance to buy a half-timbered house on the outskirts of town. The house came with a small park, a wilderness of shrubs, forty apple trees, twelve chestnut trees and a pond. The garden became Fähner's salvation. He ordered books, subscribed to specialist journals, and read everything he could lay his hands on about shrubs, ponds and trees. He bought the best tools, informed himself about watering systems, and learned everything there was to learn with his customary systematic thoroughness. The garden blossomed, and the plantings became so famous in the neighbourhood that Fähner saw people here and there among the apple trees taking photographs of them.

During the week, he spent long hours at his practice. Fähner was a painstaking and empathetic doctor. His patients thought highly of him; his diagnoses set the standard in Rottweil. He left the house before Ingrid woke up and didn't return until after nine in the evening. He accepted the nightly barrage of reproaches at dinner in silence. Sentence by unvarnished sentence, Ingrid's metallic voice laid down animosity after animosity like railroad tracks. She had grown fat and her pale skin had turned pink with the years. Her neck had thickened and begun to wobble, and she had developed a fold of skin at her throat that swayed in time to her outbursts. She became short of breath and had high blood pressure. Fähner got thinner and thinner. One evening when he blurted out that Ingrid might perhaps seek help from a psychiatrist who was a friend, she threw a frying pan at him and screamed that he was an ungrateful pig.

The night before Fähner's sixtieth birthday, he lay awake. He had pulled out the faded photo from Egypt: Ingrid and himself in front of the Pyramid of Cheops, with a background of camels, scenic Bedouins and sand. When she threw out their wedding albums, he had fished the picture back up out of the garbage. Since then, it had found a safe hiding place deep in the back of his closet.

In the course of this night, Fähner was forced to realise that he would remain an eternal prisoner until the end of his life. He had given his word in Cairo. And now, in the bad times, was when he had to keep it; there was no such thing as giving your word for the good times only. The photo swam before his eyes. He took off his clothes and stood naked in front of the bathroom mirror. He looked at himself for a long time. Then he sat on the rim of the bathtub. For the first time in his adult life, he cried.

★　★　★

Fähner was working in his garden. He was seventy-two now; he'd sold his practice four years before. As always, he had gotten up at six o'clock. He had left the guest room—in which he'd been living for years—very quietly. Ingrid was still asleep. It was a glowing September morning. The early mist had burned off and the air was clear and cold. Fähner was using a hoe to weed the ground between the autumn perennials. It was an activity both demanding and monotonous. Fähner was content. He looked forward to the coffee he would be drinking at nine-thirty, something he always did when he took his break. Fähner also thought about the delphiniums he'd planted early in the year. They would blossom for a third time late in the fall.

Suddenly, Ingrid yanked open the door to the terrace. She yelled that he'd forgotten once again to close the windows in the guest room, said he was a total idiot. Her voice cracked—the sound of pure metal fracturing.

Later on, Fähner would be unable to describe exactly what went through his mind at that moment. That something deep inside him had begun to glow with a hard, clear light. That everything had taken on a supernatural clarity under this light. That it was white-hot.

He asked Ingrid to go down to the cellar, and led the way down the outside stairs himself. Ingrid was pouting as she entered the basement space where he kept his garden tools hanging on the wall, organised by size and function, or standing freshly cleaned in tin and plastic buckets. They were beautiful implements, which he had assembled over the years. As she opened the door, Fähner, without saying a word, lifted the tree axe off the wall. It had been hand-forged in Sweden, was perfectly greased and rust-free. Ingrid fell silent. He was still wearing his coarse gardening gloves. Ingrid stared at the axe. She didn't try to dodge. The first blow that cleaved her skull was enough to kill her. The axe, covered in bone fragments, drove itself deeper into her brain, and the blade split open her face. She was dead before she even hit the ground. Fähner had to struggle to lever the axe out of her skull, setting his foot against her neck. With two massive blows, he severed the head from the torso. The forensic expert later identified seventeen further blows Fähner had required to separate the arms and the legs.

Fähner gasped for breath. He sat down on the little wooden stool that he'd always used when planting things out. Its legs were standing in blood. Fähner felt hungry. At some point, he stood up, undressed himself next to the corpse at the garden sink and washed the blood out of his hair and off his face. He locked the cellar and climbed the indoor stairs to the living quarters. Once up there, he got dressed again, dialled the police emergency number, gave his name and address, and said, word for word, 'I've made Ingrid small. Come at once.' The call was recorded. Without waiting for a response, he hung up. There had been no agitation in his voice.

A few minutes after the call, the police pulled up in front of Fähner's house without sirens or blue flashing lights. One of them had been in the force for twenty-nine years and his entire family were patients of Dr Fähner. Fähner was standing outside the garden gate and handed him the key. He said she was in the cellar. The policeman knew it would be better not to ask any questions— Fähner was wearing a suit but no shoes or socks. He was very calm.

The trial lasted four days. The presiding judge was an experienced jurist. He knew Fähner, over whom he had to pass judgment. And he knew Ingrid. If he hadn't known her sufficiently well, the witnesses provided the necessary information. Every one of them expressed sympathy for Fähner; every one of them was on his side. The mailman said Fähner was 'a saint' and 'how he'd put up with her' was 'a miracle'. The psychiatrist certified that Fähner had suffered an 'emotional block', although he was not free of criminal responsibility.

The prosecutor asked for eight years. He took his time; he described the sequence of events and went wading through the blood in the cellar. Then he said that Fähner had had other options; he could have gotten a divorce.

The prosecutor was wrong; a divorce was precisely what had not been an option for Fähner. The most recent reform of the code of criminal procedure has dismissed the oath as an obligatory component of any sworn testimony in a criminal case. We ceased believing in it a long time ago. When a witness lies, he lies—no judge seriously thinks an oath would make him do otherwise, and oaths appear to leave our contemporaries indifferent. But, and this 'but' encompasses whole universes, Fähner was not what you'd consider one of our contemporaries. His promise, once given, was inviolable. Promises had bound him all his life; indeed, he was their prisoner.

Fähner could not have freed himself; to do so would have amounted to betrayal. The eruption of violence represented the bursting of the pressurised container in which he had been confined his whole life by his oath once given.

Fähner's sister, who had asked me to take on her brother's defence, sat in the public gallery. She wept. His former head nurse held her hand. Fähner had become even thinner in prison. He sat motionless on the dark wooden defendant's bench.

With regard to the practicalities of the case, there was nothing to defend. It was, rather, a problem of judicial philosophy: what is the meaning of punishment? Why do we punish? I used my summation to try to establish this. There is a whole host of theories. Punishment should be a deterrent. Punishment should protect us. Punishment should make the perpetrator avoid any such act in the future. Punishment should counterbalance injustice. Our laws are a composite of these theories, but none of them fitted this case exactly. Fähner would not kill again. The injustice of his act was self-evident but difficult to measure. And who wanted to exercise revenge? It was a long summation. I told his story. I wanted people to understand that Fähner had reached the end.

I spoke until I felt I had gotten through to the court. When one of the jurors nodded, I sat down again.

Fähner had the last word. At the end of a trial the court hears the defendant, and the judges have to weigh what he says in their deliberations. He bowed and his hands were clasped one inside the other. He hadn't had to learn his speech by heart; it was the encapsulation of his entire life.

'I loved my wife, and in the end I killed her. I still love her, that is what I promised her, and she is still my wife. This will be true for the rest of my life. I broke my promise. I have to live with my guilt.'

Fähner sat down again in silence and stared at the floor. The courtroom was absolutely silent; even the presiding judge seemed to be filled with trepidation. Then he said that the members of the court would withdraw to begin their deliberations and that the verdict would be pronounced the next day.

That evening, I visited Fähner in jail one more time. There wasn't much left to say. He had brought a crumpled envelope with him, out of which he extracted the photograph from their honeymoon, and ran his thumb over Ingrid's face. The coating on the photo had long since worn away; her face was almost a blank.

Fähner was sentenced to three years, the arrest warrant was withdrawn, and he was freed from custody. He would be permitted to serve his sentence on daytime release. Daytime release means that the person under sentence must spend nights in jail but is allowed out during the day. The condition is that he must pursue a trade or hold a job. It wasn't easy to find a new trade for a seventy-two-year-old. Eventually, it was his sister who did this: Fähner worked as a green-grocer—he sold the apples from his garden.

Four months later, a little crate arrived at my chambers, containing ten red apples. There was an envelope enclosed and in the envelope was a single sheet of paper: 'The apples are good this year. Fähner.'

Tanata's Tea Bowl

They were at one of those free-for-all student parties in Berlin. These were always good for a couple of girls ready to get it on with boys from Kreuzberg and Neukölln, just because they were different. Perhaps what attracted the girls was an inherent vulnerability. This time, Samir seemed to have struck it lucky again: she had blue eyes and laughed a lot.

Suddenly, her boyfriend appeared. He said Samir should get lost or they'd take it out onto the street. Samir didn't understand what 'take it out' meant, but he understood the aggression. They were hustled outside. One of the older students told Samir the guy was an amateur boxer and university champion. Samir said, 'So fucking what?' He was just seventeen, but he was a veteran of more than 150 street fights, and there were very few things he was afraid of—fights were not among them.

The boxer was heavily muscled, a head taller, and a good deal more solidly built than Samir. And he was grinning like an idiot. A circle formed around the two of them, and while the boxer was still taking off his jacket, Samir landed the toe of one shoe right in his balls. His shoe caps were steel-lined; the boxer emitted a gurgle and almost doubled up with pain. Samir seized his head by the hair, yanked it straight down, and simultaneously rammed his right knee into the boxer's face. Although there was a lot of noise on the street, you could hear the boxer's jaw snap. He lay bleeding on the asphalt, one hand over his crotch, the other over his face. Samir took a two-step run-up; the kick broke two of the boxer's ribs.

Samir felt he'd played fair. He hadn't kicked the guy's face and, most important, he hadn't used his knife. It had all been very easy; he wasn't even out of breath. He got angry because the blonde wouldn't take off with him, just cried and fussed over the man on the ground. 'Fucking whore,' he said, and went home.

The judge in the juvenile court sentenced Samir to two weeks' custody and obligatory participation in an antiviolence seminar. Samir tried to explain to the social workers in the juvenile detention centre that the conviction was wrong. The boxer had started it; it was just that he himself had been quicker. That sort of thing wasn't a game. You could play football, but nobody played at boxing. The judge had simply failed to understand the rules.

Özcan collected Samir from jail when the two weeks were up. Özcan was Samir's best friend. He was eighteen, a tall, slow-moving boy with a doughy face. He'd had his first girlfriend when he was twelve, and had videoed everything they got up to with his mobile phone, which earned him his place as top dog forever. Özcan's penis was ridiculously large, and whenever he was in a public lavatory he positioned himself so that everyone else could see. The one thing he was determined to do was to get to New York. He'd never been there and he spoke no English, but he was obsessed with the city. You never saw him without his dark blue cap with NY on it. He wanted to run a nightclub in Manhattan that had a restaurant and go-go dancers. Or whatever. He couldn't explain why it had to be New York, specifically, but he didn't waste any time thinking about it. Özcan's father had spent his whole life in a factory that made lightbulbs; he had arrived from Turkey with nothing but a single suitcase. His son was his hope. He didn't understand the New York thing at all.

Özcan told Samir he'd met someone who had a plan. His name was Manólis. It was a good plan, but Manólis 'was nuts'.

Manólis came from a Greek family that owned a string of restaurants and internet cafes in Kreuzberg and Neukölln. He had passed his high school diploma and started to study history, with a sideline in drugs. A few years ago, something had gone wrong. The suitcase that was supposed to have cocaine in it turned out to be full of paper and sand. The buyer fired at Manólis when he tried to flee in his car with the money. The buyer was a lousy shot, and eight of the nine bullets missed. The ninth penetrated the back of Manólis's skull and lodged there. It was still in Manólis's head when he collided with a squad car. It wasn't till he was in the hospital that the doctors discovered it, and since then Manólis had had a problem. After the operation, he announced to his family that he was now a Finn, celebrated the sixth of December every year as Finland's national holiday, and tried in vain to learn the language. Besides this, he had moments when he was completely out of it, so perhaps his plan wasn't really a fully worked-out one.

But Samir still thought it had some potential. Manólis's sister had a friend who worked as a cleaning lady in a villa in Dahlem. She was in urgent need of money, so all she wanted from Manólis was a small cut if he broke into the house. She knew the alarm code and the one for the electronic lock, she knew where the safe was, and, most important, she knew that the owner would soon be away from Berlin for four days. Samir and Özcan agreed immediately.

The night before the break-in, Samir slept badly, dreaming about Manólis and Finland. When he woke, it was two in the afternoon. He said, 'Fuck judges,' and chased his girlfriend out of bed. At four o'clock, he had to be at the anti-violence class.

Özcan picked up the others at 2:00 a.m. Manólis had fallen asleep, and Samir and Özcan had to wait outside his door for twenty minutes. It was cold; the car windows misted up. They got lost and screamed at one another. It was almost three o'clock when they reached Dahlem. They pulled the black ski masks on in the car; they were too big, they slipped down and scratched, and they were sweating underneath them. Özcan got a tangle of wool fluff in his mouth and spat it out onto the dashboard. They put on latex gloves and ran across the gravel path to the entrance of the villa.

Manólis punched in the code on the lock pad. The door opened with a click. The alarm was in the entryway. After Manólis had fed in a combination of numbers, the little lights switched from red to green. Özcan had to laugh. 'Özcan's Eleven,' he said out loud. He loved movies. The tension eased. It had never been so easy. The front door clicked shut; they were standing in darkness.

They couldn't find the light switch. Samir tripped on a step and hit his left eyebrow on a hat stand. Özcan stumbled over Samir's feet and grabbed his back for support as he fell. Samir groaned under his weight. Manólis was still standing, but he had forgotten the flashlights.

Their eyes adjusted to the darkness. Samir wiped the blood off his face. Finally, Manólis found the light switch. The interior of the house was Japanese—Samir and Özcan just didn't see how anyone could live this way. It took them only a few minutes to locate the safe—the description they'd been given was a good one.

They used crowbars to pry it out of the wall, then dragged it to the car. Manólis wanted to go back into the house—he'd discovered the kitchen and he was hungry. They argued about it for a long time, until Samir decided it was too dangerous. They could easily stop at a café on the way back. Manólis grumbled.

They tried to open the safe in a cellar in Neukölln. They had some familiarity with heavily armoured safes, but this one resisted them. Özcan had to borrow his brother-in-law's high-powered drill. Four hours later, when the safe opened, they knew it had been worth it. They found 120,000 euros in cash and six watches in a box. And there was also a small casket made of black lacquered wood. Samir opened it. It was lined with red silk and inside was an old bowl. Özcan thought it was hideous and wanted to throw it away, Samir wanted to give it to his sister, and Manólis didn't care—he was still hungry. Finally, they agreed to sell the bowl to Mike. Mike had a little shop with a big sign outside. He called himself an antiques dealer, but basically all he had was a small truck, and most of his business was clearing out apartments and dealing in junk. He paid them thirty euros for the bowl.

As they left the cellar, Samir clapped Özcan

on the shoulder, said 'Özcan's Eleven' again, and they all laughed. Manólis's sister would get three thousand euros for her friend. Each of them had almost forty thousand euros in his pocket, and Samir would sell the watches to a fence. It had been a simple, clean break-in; there wouldn't be any problems.

They were wrong.

Hiroshi Tanata stood in his bedroom and looked at the hole in the wall. He was seventy-six years old. His family had left its mark on Japan for many hundreds of years; they were in insurance, banking and heavy industry. Tanata didn't cry out; he didn't wave his arms; he simply stared into the hole. But his secretary, who had served him for thirty years, told his wife that night that he had never seen Tanata in such a rage.

The secretary had a great deal to do that day. The police were in the house, asking questions. They suspected the employees—the alarm had certainly been switched off and there was no sign of forced entry—but their suspicions hadn't yet focused on anyone in particular. Tanata was standing up for his employees. The forensic investigation wasn't producing anything much, either.

The technicians found no fingerprints, and there wasn't even a question of DNA evidence—the cleaning lady had done a thorough job before the police were called. The secretary knew his employer very well, and his answers to the officers were evasive and monosyllabic.

It was more important to get word to the press and the leading collectors: should the Tanata tea bowl be offered to anyone, the family who had owned it since the sixteenth century would pay the highest price for its return. In such an instance, all Mr Tanata would ask would be the name of the seller.

The hairdresser's on the Yorckstrasse had the same name as its owner: Pocol. The shop window displayed two faded advertising posters for styling products that dated from the 1980s: a blonde beauty in a striped sweater with too much hair and a man with a long chin and a moustache. Pocol had inherited the shop from his father. In his youth, Pocol had actually cut people's hair himself, having learned to do this at home. Now he ran some legal gambling joints and many more illegal ones. He kept the shop, sat all day in one of the comfortable tilting chairs, drank tea, and conducted his business. Over the years, he'd grown fat—he had a weakness for Turkish pastries. His brother-in-law owned a bakery three doors down and made the best *balli elmali*—honeyed apple fritters—in the city.

Pocol was short-tempered and brutal, and he knew that this was the capital he traded on. Everyone had heard the story at least once about the café owner who'd told Pocol he should pay for what he ate. That was fifteen years ago. Pocol didn't know the café owner and the café owner didn't know Pocol. Pocol threw his food at the wall, went to the trunk of his car, and came back with a baseball bat. The landlord lost the sight in his right eye, his spleen, and his left kidney, and spent the rest of his life in a wheelchair. Pocol was sentenced to eight years for attempted murder. The day the sentence was handed down, the landlord fell down the stairs in the subway in his wheelchair, breaking his neck. After Pocol had served out his sentence, he never had to pay for another meal again.

Pocol read about the robbery in the newspaper. After a dozen phone calls to relatives, friends, fences and other business associates, he knew who'd broken into Tanata's house. He sent off a torpedo, an ambitious boy who did everything for him. The torpedo told Samir and Özcan that Pocol wanted to talk to them. Now.

The two of them showed up at the hairdresser's a short time later—you didn't make Pocol wait. There were pastries and tea; the atmosphere was friendly. Then suddenly Pocol began to scream, grabbed Samir by the hair, dragged him through the shop, threw him in a corner, and started kicking him. Samir didn't fight back, and between kicks he offered a cut of 30 percent. Pocol grunted, nodded, turned away from Samir, picked up a flat piece of wood he kept in the shop for things like this, and slammed Özcan in the forehead with it. After that, he calmed down, sat back in the tilting chair, and summoned his girlfriend from the room next door.

Pocol's girlfriend had still been working as a model a few months ago and had managed to be selected as *Playboy*'s September Playmate of the Month. She was dreaming of becoming a catwalk model or making it big with a music producer when Pocol discovered her, beat up her boyfriend, and became her manager. He called it 'plucking'. He arranged for her to have her breasts enlarged and her lips plumped. In the beginning, she believed in his plans, and Pocol really did try to get her taken on by an agency.

When it became too much of an effort, there were appearances at discos, then strip clubs, and finally in the kind of extreme porno movies that were illegal in Germany. At some point, Pocol gave her her first shot of heroin, and now she was dependent on him and loved him. Pocol didn't have sex with her anymore, not since his friends had used her as a urinal in one of the movies. She was still around only because he wanted to sell her to Beirut—human trafficking also went on in that direction—and finally he needed to get back the money that had gone to the cosmetic surgeon.

The girlfriend bandaged Özcan's laceration, and Pocol made jokes about how he now looked like an Indian, 'Y'know, a redskin.' More tea and pastries appeared, the girlfriend was banished, and negotiations could proceed. The split was agreed at 50 percent, and Pocol would get the watches and the bowl. Samir and Özcan acknowledged their mistake, Pocol stressed that it was nothing personal, and as they said goodbye he hugged Samir and gave him a big kiss.

Shortly after the two of them had left the shop, Pocol called Wagner. Wagner was a liar and a con man. He was five feet two inches tall, his skin had turned yellow from years in tanning salons, and his hair was dyed brown, with a quarter of an inch of grey regrowth at the roots. Wagner's apartment was a 1980s cliché. It was a duplex; the bedroom, with its mirrored closets, flokati rugs and a gigantic bed, was on the upper floor. The living room downstairs was a landscape of white leather sofas, white marble floors, lacquered white walls and diamond-shaped side tables. Wagner loved everything shiny; even his mobile phone was encrusted with little pieces of glass.

Some years previously, he had declared personal bankruptcy, dividing his property among his relatives, and because justice in these matters is slow, he continued to accumulate debts. In fact, Wagner owned nothing anymore; the apartment belonged to his ex-wife, he hadn't been able to pay his medical insurance for months, and he still owed the beauty salon for his girlfriend's total makeover. The money he had earned so easily in earlier years had all been spent on cars and champagne and coke parties on Ibiza. Now the investment bankers he used to party with had all disappeared and he could no longer afford new tyres for his ten-year-old Ferrari. Wagner had spent a long time waiting for the big opportunity, the one that would make everything good again. In cafés, he told waitresses he needed a big one, and then roared with laughter every time over the hoary joke. Wagner had spent his whole life struggling with his own insignificance.

While the average con man just cons, Wagner was more skilled. He presented himself as the 'tough Berlin kid from the bottom' who'd 'made it'. Middle-class people put their trust in him. They thought he was rough, noisy and unpleasant but, for those very reasons, genuine and honourable. Wagner was neither hard nor honourable. He hadn't 'made it'—not even by his own standards. He was sly rather than intelligent, and because he was weak himself, he recognised the weaknesses in other people. He exploited these, even when it gained him no advantage.

Sometimes Pocol made use of Wagner. He beat him up when he got cheeky, when it was too long since the last time, or simply when he felt so inclined. Otherwise, he considered him to be garbage. But Wagner struck him as the right man for this job. Pocol had learned from experience that because of his origins and the way he spoke, nobody outside his own circle would take him seriously.

Wagner was given the task of getting in touch with Tanata to tell him he could buy back both bowl and watches, details to be sorted out later. Wagner agreed. He got hold of

Tanata's phone number and talked for twenty minutes to the secretary. Wagner was assured that the police would not be brought into it. After he'd hung up, he felt terrific, stroked the two chihuahuas he'd named Dolce and Gabbana, and pondered how he could screw Pocol just a little in the bargain.

A garrotte is a thin length of wire with little wooden handles at either end. It was developed from a medieval instrument of torture and execution—until 1974, it was the official instrument of execution in Spain—and even today it is a favoured murder weapon. Its constituent parts can be bought at any hardware store; it's cheap, easy to transport, and effective: the wire is passed around the neck from behind and pulled tight into a noose; the victim cannot cry out, and death is swift.

Four hours after the phone call to Tanata, the doorbell rang at Wagner's apartment. Wagner opened the door a crack. The gun he'd stuck into the belt of his pants didn't save him. The first blow to his larynx cut off his breath, and when the garrotte ended his life fifteen minutes later, he welcomed his death.

Wagner's cleaning lady put down the groceries in the kitchen next morning and saw two severed fingers stuck in the sink. She called the police. Wagner was lying in bed, his thighs clamped together in a vise, two carpenter's nails in the left kneecap and three in the right. There was a garrotte around his neck and his tongue hung out of his mouth. Wagner had wet himself before he died, and the investigating officers racked their brains trying to figure out what information he had divulged to the perpetrator.

In the living room, where the marble floor met the wall, lay the two dogs; their yapping must have disturbed the visitor, who had stomped on them both. The trace analysts tried to get a print of the soles from the bodies, but it took the pathology people to locate a little fragment of plastic inside one of the dogs. The perpetrator had obviously worn plastic bags over his shoes.

During the same night that Wagner died, at around five o'clock in the morning Pocol carried the takings from his gambling dens into the hair-dresser's in two plastic buckets. He was tired, and as he bent forward to unlock the door, he heard a high-pitched hum. He recognised it. His brain couldn't process it fast enough, but a fraction of a second before the ball at the end of the telescoping steel rod smashed against his head, he knew what it was.

His girlfriend found him in the shop when she came begging for heroin. He was lying face down on one of the two tilting chairs, his arms around it as if to embrace it. His hands were bound underneath it with zip ties; the massive body was jammed between the armrests. Pocol was naked, and the broken shaft of a broom was protruding out of his anus. The medical examiner testified at the autopsy that the force with which the stick had been inserted had also perforated the bladder. Pocol's body showed 117 lacerations on the back and head; the killer's steel ball had broken fourteen bones. Which one of the blows finally killed him could not be ascertained with any certainty. Pocol's safe had not been broken into, and the two buckets of coins from the slot machines stood almost undisturbed in the doorway. There was a coin in Pocol's mouth when he died, and another was found in his oesophagus.

The investigations went nowhere. The fingerprints in Pocol's shop could be attributed to any number of criminals in Neukölln and Kreuzberg. The torture with the broom handle pointed to Arab involvement, since they ranked it as a particular form of humiliation. There were a few arrests and interrogations of people who might be associated with it; the police thought it was a turf war, but they had nothing definite. Pocol and Wagner had never surfaced together in any police investigation and the homicide division could build no connection between the two cases. When it came down to it, there was only a pile of theories.

Pocol's shop and the footpath outside it were closed off with red-and-white security tape, and searchlights illuminated the area. Every single person in Neukölln who wanted to know found out during the on-site police investigation just how Pocol had died. And now Samir, Özcan and Manólis were truly frightened. At 11:00 a.m. they were standing in front of Pocol's shop with the money, the watches and the bowl. Mike, the antiques dealer they had sold the bowl to, was putting ice on his right eye four streets away. He had had to give back the bowl and pay a so-called 'expense allowance'. His black eye was part of it; those were the rules.

Manólis said what everyone was thinking: Pocol had been tortured, and if they had been part of the discussion, he would, of course, have given them up. If someone had felt confident enough to kill Pocol, their own lives were not going to be worth much. Samir said the thing with the bowl had to be settled, and quick. The others agreed, and finally Özcan thought maybe they should get a lawyer.

The three young men told me their story; that is to say, Manólis did the talking, but he kept wandering off into the philosophical and had trouble concentrating. The whole thing took quite some time. Then they said they weren't sure if Tanata knew who had done the break-in. They laid the money, the watches and the little lacquered casket with the tea bowl on the conference table and asked me to return the objects to the owner. I recorded everything as accurately as I could, and I refused to take the cash, as that would have been money laundering. I telephoned Tanata's secretary and arranged an appointment for that afternoon.

Tanata's house was on a quiet street in Dahlem. There was no doorbell; an invisible electric eye triggered a signal, a dark gong sound, like something in a Zen monastery. The secretary gave me his card with both hands, fingers outstretched, which seemed a little pointless, since I was already there. Then I remembered that the exchange of cards is a ritual in Japan, and I reciprocated. The secretary was affable and serious. He led me to a room with earth-coloured walls and a floor of black wood. We seated ourselves at a table on hard stools; otherwise, the room was bare, except for a dark green ikebana arrangement in a niche in the wall. The indirect lighting was warm and subdued.

I opened my attaché case and laid out the objects. The secretary placed the watches on a leather tray that was standing ready, but he didn't touch the closed casket with the tea bowl. I asked him to sign the receipt I had prepared. He excused himself and disappeared behind a sliding door.

It was absolutely silent.

Then he came back, signed the receipt for the watches and the tea bowl, took the tray with him, and left me alone again. The casket remained unopened.

Tanata was a small man and looked desiccated somehow. He greeted me in the Western fashion, seemed in a good mood, and told me about his family in Japan.

After a time, he went to the table, opened the casket, and lifted out the bowl. He held it at the base with one hand and turned it slowly before his eyes with the other. It was a matcha bowl, in which gleaming green tea powder is beaten with a bamboo whisk. The bowl was black, with a glaze over its dark body. Such bowls were not turned on a wheel, but shaped by hand, and none of them resembled any other. The most ancient school of pottery signed its ceramics with the character raku. A friend had once told me that ancient Japan lived on in these bowls.

Tanata placed it carefully back in the casket and said, 'The bowl was made for our family by Chojiro in 1581.' Chojiro was the founder of the raku tradition. The bowl stared out of its red silk like a black eye. 'You know, there has already been a war over this bowl. It was a long time ago, and the war lasted almost five years. I'm glad things went quicker this time.' He let the lid of the casket snap shut. It echoed.

I said the money would also be repaid. He shook his head.

'What money?' he asked.

'The money in your safe.'

'There wasn't any money in there.'

I didn't understand him at first.

'My clients said—'

'If there had been any money in there,' he interrupted me, 'it might have been untaxed.'

'Yes?'

'And since a receipt would have to be presented to the police, questions would be asked. When the charges were presented, I never admitted that the money had been stolen.'

We finally agreed that I would inform the police of the return of the bowl and the watches. Naturally, Tanata did not ask me who the criminals were, and I didn't ask about Pocol and Wagner. Only the police asked questions; I was able to invoke the lawyer-client privilege to protect my clients.

Samir, Özcan and Manólis survived.

Samir received a call inviting him and his friends to a café on the Kurfürstendamm. The man who met them was polite. He showed them Pocol's and Wagner's dying minutes on his mobile-phone display, apologised for the quality of the images, and invited the three of them to share some cake with him. They didn't touch the cake, but next day they returned the 120,000 euros. They knew what was proper, and paid an additional 28,000 euros 'for expenses'; it was all they could raise. The friendly gentleman said it really wasn't necessary, and took the money.

Manólis retired, took over one of his family's restaurants, got married, and settled down. They say there are pictures of fjords and fishing boats in his restaurants, and Finnish vodka, and that he's planning to take his family and move to Finland.

Özcan and Samir turned to drug dealing; they never stole anything again that they couldn't classify.

Tanata's cleaning lady, who'd provided the tip that triggered the robbery, took a holiday in Anatolia two years later; she'd forgotten the whole thing long ago. She went swimming. Although the sea was calm that day, she hit her head on a rock and drowned.

I once saw Tanata again at the Philharmonic Hall in Berlin; he was sitting four rows behind me. When I turned around, he saluted me amicably but silently. Six months later, he was dead. His body was taken back to Japan, the house in Dahlem was sold, and his secretary also returned to his homeland.

The bowl is now the centrepiece of the Tanata Foundation Museum in Tokyo.

Postscript

When Manólis met Samir and Özcan, he was under suspicion for drug dealing. The suspicion was unfounded, and the court-ordered wire tap was disconnected shortly thereafter. But the first contact between Manólis and Samir was recorded. Özcan listened to it on the mobile phone's loud-speaker and joined in.

Samir: 'Are you Greek?'

Manólis: 'I'm a Finn.'

Samir: 'You don't sound like a Finn.'

Manólis: 'I'm a Finn.'

Samir: 'You sound like a Greek.'

Manólis: 'So what. Just because my mother and my father and my grandmothers and my grand-fathers and everyone in my family are Greeks doesn't mean I have to run around my whole life being a Greek. I hate olive trees and tzatziki and that idiotic dance. I'm Finnish. Every particle of me is Finnish. I'm an inner Finn.'

Özcan to Samir: 'He also looks like a Greek.'

Samir to Özcan: 'Let him be a Finn if he wants to be a Finn.'

Özcan to Samir: 'He doesn't even look Swedish.' (Özcan knew a Swede from school.)

Samir: 'Why are you a Finn?'

Manólis: 'Because of the thing with the Greeks.'

Samir: 'Huh?'

Özcan: 'Huh?'

Manólis: 'It's been going on for hundreds of years with the Greeks. Imagine there's a ship going down.'

Özcan: 'Why?'

Manólis: 'Because it's sprung a leak or the captain's drunk.'

Özcan: 'But why has the ship sprung a leak?'

Manólis: 'Shit, it's only an example.'

Özcan: 'Hmm.'

Manólis: 'The ship's just sinking, okay?'

Özcan: 'Hmm.'

Manólis: 'Everyone drowns. Everyone. Got it? Only one Greek survives. He swims and swims and swims and eventually makes it to shore. He pukes all the salt water out of his throat. He pukes out of his mouth. Out of his nose. Out of every pore. He spits it all out, until he eventually falls asleep, half-dead. The guy is the only survivor. All the rest of them are dead. He lies on the beach and sleeps. When he wakes up, he realises he's the only one who's survived. So he stands up and slays the next person he meets who's out for a walk. Just like that. Only when the other guy is dead is everything evened out.'

Samir: 'Huh?'

Özcan: 'Huh?'

Manólis: 'D'you understand? He has to kill someone else, so that the one who didn't drown is dead, too. The other guy has to stand in for him. Minus one, plus one. Get it?'

Samir: 'No.'

Özcan: 'Where was the leak?'

Samir: 'When are we going to meet?'

The Cello

Tackler's dinner jacket was light blue, his shirt pink. His double chin overflowed both collar and bow tie; his jacket strained over his stomach and made folds across his chest. He stood between his daughter Theresa and his fourth wife, both of whom towered over him. The black-haired fingers of his left hand clutched his daughter's hip. They lay there like a dark animal.

The reception had cost him a lot of money, but he felt it had been worth it, because they had all come: the first minister of the state, the bankers, the powerful and the beautiful and, most important of all, the famous music critic. That was all he wanted to think about right now. It was Theresa's party.

Theresa was twenty at the time, a classical slender beauty with an almost perfectly symmetrical face. She seemed calm and composed, and only a little vein in her neck betrayed how fast her heart was beating.

After a short speech by her father, she took her seat on the red-carpeted stage and tuned her cello. Her brother Leonhard sat next to her on a stool to turn the pages of the sheet music. The contrast between the two of them could not have been greater. Leonhard was a head shorter than Theresa; he had inherited his father's features and physique but not his toughness. Sweat ran down his red face into his shirt; the edge of his collar had darkened with it. He smiled out at the audience, friendly and softhearted.

The guests sat on tiny chairs. They gradually fell silent, and the lights were dimmed. And while I was still deciding whether I was in fact going to leave the garden and go back into the salon, she began to play. She played the first three of Bach's six cello suites, and after a few bars I realised I would never be able to forget Theresa. On that warm summer evening in the grand salon of the nineteenth-century villa, with its tall mullioned glass doors opened wide onto the park that was all lit up, I experienced one of those rare moments of absolute happiness that only music can give us.

★　★　★

Tackler was a second-generation building contractor. He and his father were self-assertive, intelligent men who'd made their money in Frankfurt with real estate. All his life, his father had carried a revolver in his right trouser pocket and a roll of cash in the left. Tackler no longer needed a weapon.

Three years after Leonhard was born, his mother visited one of her husband's new high-rise buildings. The topping-out ceremony was taking place on the eighteenth floor. Someone had forgotten to secure a parapet. The last Tackler saw of his wife was her handbag and a champagne glass, which she had set down next to her on a table.

In the years that followed, a whole cavalcade of 'mothers' paraded past the children. None of them stayed longer than three years. Tackler ran a prosperous home; there was a driver, a cook, a whole series of cleaning women, and two gardeners for the park. He didn't have time to occupy himself with his children's upbringing, so the one constant in their lives was an elderly nurse. She had already brought up Tackler, smelled of lavender, and was known to one and all simply as Etta. Her main interest was ducks. In her two-room attic apartment in Tackler's house, she had hung five stuffed specimens on the walls, and even the brown felt hat she always wore when she went out had two blue drake's feathers tucked into the band. Children didn't especially appeal to her.

Etta had always stayed; she'd long ago become one of the family. Tackler considered childhood a waste of time and barely remembered his own. He trusted Etta, because she agreed with him about the fundamentals of child rearing. They should grow up with discipline and without what Tackler called 'conceit'. Sometimes severity was required.

Theresa and Leonhard had to earn their own pocket money. In summer, they weeded dandelions in the garden and received a ha'penny for each plant—'but only with its roots; otherwise you get nothing,' said Etta. She counted the individual plants as meanly as she counted the pennies. In winter, they had to shovel snow. Etta paid by the yard.

When Leonhard was nine, he ran away from the house. He climbed a pine tree in the park and waited for them to come searching for him. He imagined first Etta and then his father despairing and lamenting his flight. Nobody despaired. Before supper, Etta called that if he didn't come right now, there would be nothing more to eat and he'd get his bottom smacked. Leonhard gave up. His clothes were full of resin, and he was given a slap on the ears.

At Christmas, Tackler gave the children soap and pullovers. There was only one time when a business friend, who'd made a lot of money with Tackler in the course of the year, gave Leonhard a toy gun and Theresa a doll's kitchen. Etta took the toys down to the cellar. 'They don't need that sort of thing,' she said, and Tackler, who hadn't been listening, agreed.

Etta considered their upbringing complete when brother and sister could behave themselves at the table, speak proper German, and otherwise keep quiet. She told Tackler she thought they'd come to a bad end. They were too soft, not real Tacklers like him and his father. It was a sentence he remembered.

Etta got Alzheimer's, slowly regressed, and became gentler. She left her birds to a museum of local history, which had no use for them and ordered the stuffed creatures destroyed. Tackler and the two children were the only ones at her funeral. On the way back, he said, 'So, now that's out of the way.'

Leonhard worked for Tackler during the holidays. He would rather have gone off with friends, but he had no money. That was how Tackler wanted it. He took his son to one of the building sites, handed him over to the foreman, and told him to 'really let him have it'. The foreman did what he could, and when Leonhard threw up at the end of the second day from exhaustion, Tackler said he'd get used to it. He himself had sometimes slept on building sites with his father when he was Leonhard's age and shat in the open air like the other bar benders. Leonhard shouldn't get any ideas he was 'better' than the others.

Theresa had holiday jobs, too; she worked in the company bookkeeping department. Like Leonhard, she received only 30 percent of the average salary. 'You're no help; you actually create work. Your pay is a gift, not something you've earned,' said Tackler. If they wanted to go to the movies, Tackler gave the two of them a total of ten euros, and since they had to take the bus, it was only enough for one ticket. They didn't dare tell him that. Sometimes Tackler's driver took them into town secretly and gave them a little money—he had children himself and knew his boss.

Other than Tackler's sister, who was employed in the company and had always given up every one of her secrets to her brother since her own childhood, there were no relatives. The children began by fearing their father, then hated him, until finally his world became so alien to them that they had nothing more to say to him.

Tackler didn't despise Leonhard, but he loathed his softness. He thought he had to harden him; 'forge' him was the way he put it. When Leonhard was fifteen, he put up a picture in his room of a ballet production he had gone to with his class. Tackler tore it off the wall and roared at him that he'd better be careful or he'd be turning gay. He was too fat, Tackler said to Leonhard; he'd never get a girlfriend like that.

Theresa spent every minute with her cello and her music teacher in Frankfurt. Tackler didn't understand her, so he left her in peace—with one exception. It was summertime, shortly after Theresa's sixteenth birthday. She went skinny-dipping in the pool. When she came out of the water, Tackler was standing at the edge. He'd been drinking. He looked at her as if she were a stranger, picked up the towel, and began to dry her. As he touched her breasts, he smelled of whiskey. She ran into the house. She never used the pool again.

On the rare occasions they all had dinner together, conversation revolved around his themes of watches, food and cars. Theresa and Leonhard knew the price of every car and every famous make of watch. It was an abstract game.

Sometimes their father showed them financial statements, stock market and business reports. 'This will all belong to you someday,' he said, and Theresa whispered to Leonhard that he was quoting from a movie. 'The inner self,' he said, 'is nonsense.' It gained no one anything.

All the children had was each other. When Theresa was accepted at the conservatory, they decided they would both leave their father together. They wanted to tell him at dinner and had rehearsed it, working out how he would react and what their responses should be. When they began, Tackler said he didn't have time today, and disappeared. They had to wait for three weeks; then Theresa took the lead. The two of them thought that if she were the one, Tackler would at least be unable to hit her. She said they were both going to leave Bad Homburg now. 'Leave Bad Homburg' sounded better, they thought, than saying it directly. Theresa said she was going to take Leonhard with her, that they would make their way somehow.

Tackler didn't understand, and kept eating. When he asked Theresa to pass him the bread, Leonhard screamed, 'You've tortured us enough,' and Theresa, more quietly, said, 'We don't ever want to become like you.' Tackler let his knife drop onto his plate. It echoed. Then he stood up without a word, went to his car, and drove to his girlfriend's. It was almost 3:00 a.m. when he returned.

Later that same night, Tackler sat alone in the library. A silent home movie was running on the screen he'd had built into the bookshelves. It had been transferred to video from a Super-8 camera. The footage was overexposed.

His first wife is holding the two children by the hand; Theresa is probably three years old and Leonhard two. His wife says something; her mouth moves soundlessly. She lets go of Theresa's hand and points into the distance. The camera follows her arm; there is the ruin of a castle in the blurry background. Pan back to Leonhard, who hides himself behind his mother's leg and cries. Stones and grass blur in the foreground; the camera is passed to someone else while it's still running. It pans upward again, showing Tackler in jeans and an open shirt, his chest hair exposed. He roars with soundless laughter, he holds Theresa up to the sun, he kisses her, he waves to the camera. The image flares and the film breaks off.

That night, Tackler decided to arrange a farewell concert for Theresa. His contacts should suffice; he would 'put her right on top'. Tackler didn't want to be a bad person. He wrote each of his children a cheque for 250,000 euros and put them on the breakfast table. He felt that was enough.

The day after the concert, there was an article in the regional newspaper that bordered on the euphoric. The great music critic certified that Theresa had a 'brilliant future' as a musician.

She didn't register at the conservatory. Theresa believed her gift to be so great that she could still take her time. For now, it was something else that mattered. The two of them spent most of the next three years travelling through Europe and the United States. She gave a few private concerts and otherwise played only for her brother. Tackler's money made them independent, at least for a while. They remained inseparable. They took none of their love affairs seriously, and there was scarcely a day in those years that either of them spent away from the other. They seemed to be free.

Almost two years to the day after her concert in Bad Homburg, I encountered the two of them again at a party near Florence, in the Castello di Tornano, a ruined castle from the eleventh century, surrounded by olive trees and cypresses amid the vineyards. The host described them both as 'gilded youth' when they arrived in a 1960s convertible sports car. Theresa kissed him and Leonhard doffed his idiotic Borsalino straw hat with studied elegance.

When I told Theresa later that I had never heard the cello suites performed with more intensity than in her father's house, she said, 'It's the prelude to the first suite. Not the sixth, which everyone thinks is the most important and is the most difficult. No, it's the first.' She took a mouthful of wine, leaned forward, and whispered in my ear, 'D'you understand, the prelude to the first. It's all of life packed into three minutes.' Then she laughed.

At the end of the following summer, the two of them were in Sicily. They spent a few days with a commodities trader who had rented a house there for the summer and was somewhat infatuated with Theresa.

Leonhard woke up with a light fever. He thought it was due to the alcohol of the previous night. He didn't want to be ill, not on a glorious day like this, not when they were having the time of their lives. The *E. coli* bacteria colonised his body at great speed. They had been in the water he'd drunk at a petrol station two days before.

They found an old Vespa in the garage and were headed toward the sea. The apple was lying in the middle of the asphalt; it had fallen off one of the harvest trucks. It was almost round and glinted in the noonday light. Theresa said something, and Leonhard turned his head to hear her properly. The front wheel went over the apple and slid sideways. Leonhard lost control. Theresa was lucky; she only sprained her shoulder and had a couple of abrasions. Leonhard's head got wedged between the back wheel and a boulder and burst open.

During the first night in the hospital, his condition deteriorated. Nobody tested his blood; there were other things to do. Theresa called her father and he used the corporate Learjet to send a doctor from Frankfurt; the man arrived too late. Leonhard's kidneys had released their poison into his bloodstream. Theresa sat in the waiting area outside the operating theatre. The doctor held her hand as he spoke to her. The air conditioning was loud, and the pane of glass Theresa had been staring at for hours was clouded with dust. The doctor said it was a sepsis of the urinary tract, engendering multiple organ failures. Theresa didn't understand what he was telling her. Urine had spread through Leonhard's body, and he had a 20 percent chance of survival. The doctor kept talking, and his words gave her some distance. Theresa had not slept for almost forty hours. When he went back into the operating room, she closed her eyes. He had said 'decease,' and she saw the word in front of her in black letters. They had nothing to do with her brother. She said, 'No.' Just 'No.' Nothing else.

On the sixth day after Leonhard's admission to hospital, his condition stabilised. He could be flown to Berlin. When he was admitted to the Charité Hospital, his body was covered with black, leathery, necrotic patches that indicated the death of cellular tissue. The doctors operated fourteen times. The thumb, forefinger and fourth finger of the left hand were amputated. The left toes were cut off at the joint, as was the front half of the right foot and parts of the back. All that remained was a deformed lump that could barely support any weight, with bones and cartilage pressing visibly against the skin.

Leonhard lay in an artificially induced coma. He had survived, but the effects of the injury to his head could not yet be measured.

The hippocampus is Poseidon's pack animal, a Greek sea monster, half horse, half worm. It gives its name to a very ancient part of the brain within the temporal lobe. It's where the work is done that transforms short-term memories into long-term ones. Leonhard's hippocampus had been damaged. When he was revived from the coma after nine weeks, he asked Theresa who she was and then who he was. He had lost all power of recall and couldn't hold on to any perception for longer than three or four minutes. After endless tests, the doctors tried to explain to him that it was amnesia, both anterograde and retrograde. Leonhard understood their explanations, but after three minutes and forty seconds he had forgotten them again. He also forgot the fact that he forgot.

And when Theresa was tending him, all he saw was a beautiful woman.

After two months, they were able to move together into their father's Berlin apartment. Every day a nurse came for three hours and otherwise Theresa took care of everything. At first, she still invited friends to come for dinner; then she ceased to be able to bear the way they looked at Leonhard. Tackler came to see them once a month.

They were lonely months. Gradually, Theresa

deteriorated; her hair turned to straw and her skin lost its colour. One evening, she took the cello out of its case; she hadn't touched it for months. She played in the half darkness of the room. Leonhard was lying on the bed, dozing. At a certain point, he pushed off the bedclothes and began to masturbate. She stopped playing and turned away to the window. He asked her to come to him. Theresa looked at him. He sat up, asked to kiss her. She shook her head. He let himself fall back and said at least she could unbutton her blouse. The scarred stump of his right foot lay on the white sheet like a lump of flesh. She went to him and stroked his cheek. Then she took off her clothes, sat down on the chair, and played with her eyes closed. She waited until he fell asleep, stood up, used a towel to wipe the sperm off his stomach, covered him up, and kissed his forehead.

She went into the bathroom and vomited.

Although the doctors had ruled out any possibility that Leonhard could recover his memory, the cello seemed to move him. When she was playing, she seemed to feel a pale, almost imperceptible connection to her former life, a weak reflection of the intensity she missed so much.

Sometimes Leonhard actually remembered the cello the next day. He talked about it, and even if he couldn't make any connections, something did seem to remain captured in his memory. Theresa now played for him every evening, he almost always masturbated, and she almost always collapsed in the bathroom afterward and wept.

Six months after the last operation, Leonhard's scars began to hurt. The doctors said further amputations would be required. After doing a PET scan, they told her he would also soon lose the power of speech. Theresa knew that she wouldn't be able to bear it.

The twenty-sixth of November was a cold, grey autumn day; darkness came early. Theresa had put candles on the table and pushed Leonhard to his place in his wheelchair. She had bought the ingredients for the fish soup in Berlin's best market; he had always liked it. The soup, the peas, the venison roast, the chocolate mousse, even the wine were all laced with Luminal, a barbiturate she had no problem obtaining to treat Leonhard's pain. She gave it to him in small amounts so that he wouldn't vomit it up again. She herself ate nothing and waited.

Leonhard grew sleepy. She pushed him into

the bathroom and ran water in the big tub. She undressed him. He barely had the strength anymore to haul himself into the tub by using the new handles. Then she took off her own clothes and got into the warm water with him. He sat in front of her, his head leaning back on her breasts, breathing calmly and steadily. As children, they had often sat in the bath this way, because Etta didn't want to waste water. Theresa held him in a tight embrace, her head on his shoulder. When he had fallen asleep, she kissed his neck and let him slide under the surface. Leonhard breathed in deeply. There was no death struggle; the Luminal had disabled his capacity to control his muscles. His lungs filled with water and he drowned. His head lay between her legs, his eyes were closed, and his long hair floated on the surface. After two hours, she climbed out of the cold bath, covered her dead brother with a towel, and called me.

She confessed, but it was no mere confession. She sat for more than seven hours in front of the two investigators and dictated her life onto the record. She rendered an account of herself. She began with her childhood and ended with the death of her brother. She left nothing out. She didn't cry; she didn't break down. She sat as straight as a die and spoke steadily, calmly, and in polished sentences. There was no need for intervening questions. While her statement was being typed up, we smoked a cigarette in an adjoining room. She said she wasn't going to talk about it anymore; she had said all there was to say. 'I don't have anything else,' she said.

Naturally, she was ordered to be detained because of the murder charge. I visited her almost every day in prison. She arranged for books to be sent in, and didn't leave her cell even when the prisoners had their yard exercise. Reading was her anaesthetic. When we met, she didn't want to talk about her brother. Nor did the imminent trial interest her. She preferred to read to me from her books, things she'd sought out in her cell. It was like a series of lectures in a prison. I liked her warm voice, but at the time I didn't understand: it was the only way she had left to express herself.

On the twenty-fourth of December, I was with her until the end of visiting time. Then they locked the bulletproof glass doors behind me. Outside, it had been snowing. Everything was peaceful; it was Christmas. Theresa was taken back to her cell; she sat down at the little table and wrote a letter to her father. Then she tore the bedsheet, wound it into a rope, and hanged herself from the window handle.

On the twenty-fifth of December, Tackler received a call from the lawyer on duty. After he'd put down the phone he opened the safe, took out his father's revolver, put the barrel in his mouth, and pulled the trigger.

The prison administration placed Theresa's belongings in the house vault for safekeeping. Under our powers of criminal procedure, we lawyers have the right to receive objects on behalf of our clients. At some point, the authorities sent a package of her clothes and her books. We forwarded it to her aunt in Frankfurt.

I kept one of her books; she had written my name on the flyleaf. It was F. Scott Fitzgerald's *The Great Gatsby*. The book lay untouched in my desk for two years before I could pick it up again. She had marked the passages she wanted to read to me in blue, and drawn tiny little staves of music notes next to them. Only one place was marked in red, the last sentence, and when I read it, I can still hear her voice:

So we beat on, boats against the current, borne back ceaselessly into the past.

The Hedgehog

The judges put on their robes in the conference room, one of the jury arrived a few minutes too late, and the constable was replaced after he complained of a toothache. The accused was a heavily built Lebanese man, Walid Abu Fataris, and he was silent from the very beginning. The witnesses testified, the victim exaggerated a little, and the evidence was analysed. The case being heard was that of a perfectly normal robbery, which normally carries a sentence of five to fifteen years. The judges were in agreement: given the previous record of the accused, they would give him eight years; there was no question about his guilt or his criminal responsibility. The trial babbled on all day. Nothing special, then, but there had been no expectation of that anyhow.

It turned three o'clock and the time for the

main hearing would soon be over. There wasn't much left to do for today. The judge looked at the witness list; only Karim, a brother of the accused, was still to be heard. Hmmm, thought the presiding judge, we all know what to expect from alibis provided by relatives, and he eyed the witness over his reading glasses. He had only one question for this witness—namely, if he actually did mean to assert that his brother Walid had been at home when the pawnshop on the Wartenstrasse was looted. The judge put the question to Karim as simply as possible; he even asked twice if Karim had understood it.

No one had expected that Karim would even open his mouth. The presiding judge had explained to him at length that, as the brother of the accused, he had the right to remain silent. Now they were all waiting to see what he would do; his brother's future might hang on it. The judge was impatient, the lawyer bored, and one of the jury kept staring at the clock because he wanted to make the 5:00 p.m. train to Dresden. Karim was the last witness in this main hearing, the minor ones would get heard by the court at the end. Karim knew what he was doing. He'd always known.

★ ★ ★

Karim grew up in a family of criminals. It was a much-told tale about his uncle that he'd shot six men in Lebanon over a crate of tomatoes. Each of Karim's eight brothers had a record that took up to half an hour to read out in court at any trial. They had stolen, robbed, pulled con tricks, black-mailed and committed perjury. The only things for which they hadn't yet been found guilty were murder and manslaughter.

For generations in this family, cousins had married cousins and nephews had married nieces. When Karim started school, the teachers groaned—'Yet another Abu Fataris'—and then treated him like an idiot. He was made to sit in the back row, and his first-grade teacher told him, at age six, that he wasn't to draw atten-tion to himself, get into fights, or talk at all. So Karim didn't say a word. It quickly became clear to him that he must not show he was different. His brothers smacked him on the back of the head because they didn't understand what he said. That is, if he was lucky. His classmates—thanks to a municipal integration plan, the first grade consisted of 80 percent foreigners—made fun of him when he tried to explain things to them. And just like his brothers, they, too, usually hit him whenever he seemed too different. So Karim deliberately set out to get bad grades. It was the only thing he could do.

By the time he was ten years old, he had taught himself stochastic theory, integral calculus and analytical geometry from a textbook. He had stolen the book from the teachers' library. As for class work, he had figured out how many of the ridiculous exercises he had to get wrong in order to be awarded an inconspicuous C2. Sometimes he had the feeling that his brain buzzed when he came upon a mathematical problem in the book that was reputed to be insoluble. Those were the moments that defined his personal happiness.

He lived, as did all his brothers, even the eldest of them, who was twenty-six, with his mother; his father had died shortly after he was born. The family apartment in Neukölln had six rooms. Six rooms for ten people. He was the youngest, so he got the box room. The skylight was made of milky glass and there was a set of pine shelves. This space was where things found a home after no one wanted them anymore: broomheads without broomsticks, buckets without handles, cables for appliances now lost and forgotten. He sat there all day in front of a computer, and while his mother assumed he'd be busying himself with video games like his big strong brothers, he was reading the classics on Gutenberg.org.

When he was twelve, he made his last attempt to be like his brothers. He wrote a program that could override the electronic firewalls in the post office savings bank and unobtrusively debit a matter of hundredths of a cent from millions of accounts. His brothers didn't understand what 'the moron', as they called him, had given them. They smacked him on the back of the head again and threw away the CD with the program on it. Walid was the only one to sense that Karim outclassed them, and he protected him against his cruder brothers.

When Karim turned eighteen, he finished school. He had made sure that he would barely pass his final exams. No one in his family had ever gotten that far. He borrowed eight thousand euros from Walid. Walid thought Karim needed the money for a drug deal and gave it to him gladly. Karim, in the meantime, had learned so much about the stock market that he was trading on the foreign-exchange market. Within a year, he had earned almost 700,000 euros. He rented a little apartment in a nice part of the city, left his family's place every morning, and took endless roundabout routes to be sure no one was following him. He furnished his refuge, bought books on mathematics and a faster computer, and spent his time trading on the stock exchange and reading.

His family, assuming 'the moron' was now dealing dope, was content. Of course he was far too slight to be a true Abu Fataris. Karim never went to the kickboxing and extreme-sports club, but he always wore gold chains like the others, and satin shirts in garish colours, and black nappa leather jackets. He talked Neukölln slang and even earned a little respect for never having been arrested. His brothers didn't take him seriously. If they'd been asked about him, the answer would have been simply that he was part of the family. Beyond that, nobody thought about him twice.

Karim's double life went unnoticed. No one was aware either that he owned a completely different set of clothes or that he'd used night school for fun to sail through his school-graduation certificate and attended lectures in mathematics twice a week at the Technical University. He had a small but significant fortune, he paid his taxes, and had a nice girlfriend, who was studying comparative literature and knew nothing about Neukölln.

★ ★ ★

Karim had read the charges against Walid. Everyone in the family had seen them, but he was the only one who understood their significance. Walid had raided a pawnbroker, robbed him of 14,490 euros, and raced home to establish an alibi. The victim had called the police and given them an exact description of the perpetrator; it was immediately clear to the two investigators that it had to be one of the Abu Fataris family. The brothers looked almost unbelievably alike, a circumstance that had already saved them more than once. No eyewitness could tell them apart at a lineup, and even tapes from security cameras didn't pick up much difference.

This time, the policemen moved fast. Walid had hidden the loot on his way back and thrown his weapon into the River Spree. When the police stormed the apartment, he was sitting on the sofa, drinking tea. He was wearing an apple green T-shirt with the luminous yellow slogan FORCED TO WORK on it in English. He didn't know what it meant, but he liked it. The police arrested him. On the grounds of 'imminent danger', they made a mess of a search warrant, slicing open the sofas, emptying drawers onto the floor, overturning cupboards, and even ripping the skirting boards off the walls on the suspicion that these might conceal hiding places. They found nothing.

But Walid remained under arrest—the pawnbroker had described his T-shirt exactly. The two policemen were pleased to finally have picked up an Abu Fataris who could be put away for at least five years.

Karim sat in the witness chair and looked up at the judges' bench. He knew that nobody in the courtroom would believe a word he said if he merely gave Walid an alibi; when it came down to it, he was an Abu Fataris, one of the family pursued by the prosecutor's office as major repeat criminals. Everyone here expected him to lie. That wouldn't work. Walid would be swallowed up in the prison system for years.

Karim recited to himself the saying of Archilochus, the slave's son, which was his guiding motto: 'The fox knows many things, the hedgehog only one thing.' The judges and the prosecutors might be foxes, but he was the hedgehog and he'd learned his skills.

'Your Honour…' he said with a catch in his voice. He knew this wouldn't move anyone, but it would raise the general level of attention a little.

He was making an enormous effort to sound stupid but sincere. 'Your Honour, Walid was at home all evening.' He let the pause linger as he saw out of the corner of his eye that the prosecutor was writing a provision that would be the basis of a legal proceeding against him for perjury.

'So, indeed, at home all evening…' said the presiding judge, and leaned forward. 'But the victim identified Walid unequivocally.'

The prosecutor shook his head, and the defence lawyer buried himself in his papers.

Karim knew the photos of the scene of the arrest from the files. Four policemen who looked exactly like policemen: little blond moustaches, pouches, bum bags, sneakers. And then there was Walid: a head taller and twice as broad in the shoulders, dark-skinned, green T-shirt with yellow writing. A ninety-year-old half-blind lady, who hadn't been there, could have 'identified him unequivocally'.

Karim's voice caught again, and he wiped his sleeve across his nose. It came away with little things stuck to it. He looked at it and said, 'No, Your Honour, it wasn't Walid. Please believe me.'

'I remind you once again that when you testify here, you are under an oath to tell the truth.'

'But I am.'

'You are risking severe punishment. You could go to jail,' said the judge, wanting to issue a caution that would be on Karim's level. Then he said rather superciliously, 'And who would it have been if it wasn't Walid?' He looked around and the prosecutor smiled.

'Indeed, who was it?' the prosecutor echoed, which earned him a punishing look from the presiding judge, because this was *his* turn to examine the witness.

Karim hesitated for as long as he could, counting silently to five. Then he said, 'Imad.'

'What? What do you mean, Imad?'

'That it was Imad, not Walid,' said Karim.

'And who is this Imad?'

'Imad is my other brother,' said Karim.

The presiding judge looked at him in amazement, and even the defence lawyer suddenly woke up again. An Abu Fataris breaks all the rules and incriminates someone else in his own family? they were all asking themselves.

'But Imad left before the police got there,' Karim added.

'Oh yes?' The presiding judge was beginning to get angry. Idiotic babble, he was thinking.

'He gave me this thing here,' said Karim. Knowing his testimony wasn't going to change anything, he had begun months before the trial to withdraw varying amounts of money from his accounts. Now that money, in the exact same denominations that Walid had stolen, was in a brown envelope, and he passed it to the judge.

'What's in it?' the judge asked.

'I don't know,' said Karim.

The judge tore open the envelope and pulled out the money. He wasn't thinking about finger-prints, but there wouldn't have been any anyway. He counted slowly out loud: 'Fourteen thousand four hundred and ninety euros. And Imad gave you this on the night of the seventeenth of April?'

'Yes, Your Honour, he did.'

The presiding judge paused for thought. Then he posed the question that he hoped would entrap this Karim person. With a certain undertone of contempt, he asked, 'You, the witness, can you remember what Imad was wearing when he gave you the envelope?'

'Ahhh . . . Just a moment.'

General relief on the judges' bench. The presiding judge leaned back.

Go slow, work a pause in there, and make yourself hesitate, thought Karim; then he said, 'Jeans, black leather jacket, T-shirt.'

'What kind of T-shirt?'

'Oh, I really don't remember,' said Karim.

The presiding judge looked smugly at the court reporter, who would have to write up the judgment later. The two judges nodded at each other.

'Ahhh…' Karim scratched his head. 'Oh, hold on, yes I do. We all got these T-shirts from our uncle. He got a great deal on them from somewhere and gave them to us. There's something on them in English, that we're supposed to work and so on. Really funny.'

'Do you mean this T-shirt that your brother Walid is wearing in the photograph?' The presiding judge showed Karim a picture from the folder of photographs.

'Yes, yes, Your Honour. Exactly. That's the one. We've got a whole ton of them. I'm wearing one, too. But that's Walid, not Imad, in the photo.'

'Yes, I know that,' said the judge.

'Show us,' said the prosecutor.

Finally, thought Karim, and said, 'Show how? They're in the apartment.'

'No, I mean the one you're wearing now.'

'Right now?' asked Karim.

When the prosecutor nodded solemnly, Karim shrugged and opened the zipper on his leather jacket as indifferently as he could. He was wearing the same T-shirt as Walid in the picture in the files. Karim had ordered twenty of them the previous week from one of the countless copy shops in Kreuzberg, handed them out to all his brothers, and left ten more in his family's apartment, just in case there would be a further search.

Court was recessed and Karim sent outside. But before that, he heard the judge say to the prosecutor that all they had left was a direct confrontation; they had no other proof. The first round went well, he thought.

When Karim was called back in again, he was asked if he had ever had a previous conviction, and he said no. The prosecutor's office had secured an extract from the criminal register to confirm this.

'Mr Abu Fataris,' said the prosecutor, 'you must be aware of the fact that your statement incriminates Imad.'

Karim nodded. Shamefaced, he looked at his shoes.

'Why are you doing this?'

'Well'—he was even stuttering a little by this point—'Walid is my brother, too. I'm the youngest; they all keep saying I'm the moron and so on. But Walid and Imad are both my brothers. Do you see? And if it was another brother, Walid can't end up in the can because of Imad. It would be better if it was someone quite different—I mean not one of the family—but it's one of my brothers. Imad, and so on.'

And now Karim went for the coup de grâce.

'Your Honour,' he said. 'It wasn't Walid, honest. But it's true, Walid and Imad look exactly alike. See…' And he pulled a creased photo out of his greasy wallet with all nine brothers on it and held it out uncomfortably close to the presiding judge's nose. The judge reached for it irritably and laid it on his table.

'There, the first one right there, that's me. The second, that's Walid, Your Honour. The third one's Farouk, the fourth one's Imad, the fifth one's—'

'May we keep the photograph?' asked the court-appointed defence counsel, interrupting; he was a friendly, older lawyer and suddenly the case didn't look anything like so hopeless.

'Only if I can get it back; it's the only one I have. We had it taken for Auntie Halima in Lebanon. Six months ago, sort of all nine of us brothers together, you get it?' Karim looked at the members of the court to be sure that they got it. 'So Auntie could see all of us. But then we didn't send it, because Farouk said he looked stupid in it.' Karim looked at the picture again. 'He does look stupid in it, Farouk, I mean. He's not even—'

The presiding judge waved him off. 'Witness, go back to your chair.'

Karim sat down in the witness's chair and started over again. 'But see, Your Honour, the first one there, that's me, the second one's Walid, the third one's Farouk, the fourth—'

'Thank you,' said the judge, exasperated. 'We understood you.'

'Well, everyone gets them mixed up; even in school the teachers couldn't tell them apart. Once they were doing this exam in biology class, and Walid was really bad in biology, so they...' Karim ploughed on, undeterred.

'Thank you,' said the judge loudly.

'Nah, I need to tell you about the biology thing, the way it went was—'

'No,' said the judge.

Karim was dismissed as a witness and left the courtroom.

The pawnbroker was sitting on the spectators' bench. The court had already heard him, but he wanted to be there for the verdict. He was, after all, the victim. Now he was called to the front again and shown the family photo. He had understood it was all about number two, that he had to recognise him. He said—rather too quickly, as he himself acknowledged later—that the perpetrator was 'the second man in the picture, naturally'. He had no doubt that man was the perpetrator; yes, it was completely clear. 'Number two.' The court settled down a little.

Outside the door, Karim was wondering meantime how long it would take for the judges to get a handle on the situation. The presiding judge wouldn't need that much time; he would decide to question the pawnbroker again. Karim waited exactly four minutes and then went back, unsummoned, into the courtroom. He saw the pawnbroker at the judges' table, standing over the photograph. Everything was going the way he'd planned. Then he burst out that there was something he'd forgotten. They had to hear him again, please, just quickly; it was really important. The presiding judge, who had an aversion to interruptions like this, snapped, 'So now what?'

'Excuse me, I made a mistake, a really dumb mistake, Your Honour, just stupid.'

Karim was immediately the centre of attention of the entire courtroom again. They were all expecting him to withdraw his accusation against Imad. It happened all the time.

'*Imad*, Your Honour, it's *Imad* that's the second one in the picture. Walid isn't number two, he's number four. I'm so sorry; I'm just all muddled up. The questions and everything. Please excuse me.'

The presiding judge shook his head, the pawnbroker turned red, and the defence counsel grinned. 'The second, yes?' said the judge in a fury. 'So the second—'

'Yes, yes, the second. You see, Your Honour,' said Karim, 'we wrote on the back who everyone was, for Auntie, so that she'd know, because she—Auntie, I mean—doesn't know all of us. She wanted to see us together, just once, but she can't come to Germany, because of Immigration and stuff, you know. But there are so many of us brothers. Your Honour, turn the picture over. You see? All the names are right there in a row, in the same order they are on the front, in the picture. And when can I get it back?'

After they'd pulled slides of Imad out of the files and examined them, the court had to let Walid go.

Imad was arrested. But, as Karim knew perfectly well, he had stamps in his passport for both arrival and exit, proving that he'd been in Lebanon at the time of the crime. He was released again after two days.

The prosecutor's office finally brought charges against Karim for perjury and casting false suspicion on Imad. Karim told me the story, and we decided that from now on he wasn't going to talk about it. And his brothers, as close relatives, could invoke their right to remain silent. The prosecutor's office ran out of means of proof. In the end, all that remained was a strong suspicion concerning Karim. But he had gamed it all out in advance and couldn't be charged. There were too many other possibilities; for example, Walid could have given Imad the money, or one of the other brothers could have travelled on Imad's passport—they really did all look that alike.

Naturally, they still kept smacking Karim on the back of the head, not understanding that he'd saved Walid and defeated justice.

Karim said nothing. He just thought about the hedgehog and the foxes.

Bliss

Her customer had been in politics for twenty-five years. As he undressed, he recounted how he'd worked his way up. He had put up posters, given speeches in the back rooms of little taverns, built his constituency, and won three successive rounds of voting to become a minor member of parliament. He said he had many friends and was even the head of a committee of inquiry. Naturally, it wasn't one of the major committees, but he was the head of it. He was standing in front of her in his underwear. Irina didn't know what a committee of inquiry was.

The fat man found the room too small. He was sweating. Today he had to do it in the early morning, he had a meeting at 10:00 a.m. The girl had said it was no problem. The bed looked clean, and she was pretty. She couldn't have been older than twenty, beautiful breasts, full mouth, at least five foot ten. Like most girls from Eastern Europe, she wore too much makeup. The fat man liked that. He took seventy euros from his brief-case and sat on the bed. He had laid his things carefully over the chair; it mattered to him that the creases not be messed up. The girl took off his undershorts. She pushed up the folds of fat in his stomach; all he could now see of her was her hair, and he knew she was going to need quite some time. But that's her job, he thought, and leaned back. The last thing the fat man felt was a stabbing pain in his chest; he wanted to raise his hands and tell the girl to stop, but all he could do was grunt.

Irina took the grunt to be a sign of assent, and she went on for several minutes before noticing that the man was silent. She looked up. He had turned his head to the side, saliva had run onto the pillow, and his eyes were rolled up toward the ceiling. She screamed at him, but he still didn't move. She fetched a glass of water from the kitchen and poured it on his face. The man didn't stir. He was still wearing his socks, and he was dead.

Irina had been living in Berlin for eighteen months. She would rather have stayed in her own country, where she'd gone first to kindergarten and then to school, where her family and friends lived, and where the language they spoke was her own. Irina had been a dressmaker there. She had had a pretty apartment, filled with all kinds of things: furniture, books, CDs, plants, photo albums, and a black-and-white cat that had adopted her. Her life had stretched out before her and the prospect gave her joy. She designed women's fashions; she'd already made several dresses, and even sold two of them. Her sketches were light and transparent. She dreamed of opening a little shop on the main street.

But her country was at war.

One weekend, she drove to see her brother in the country. He had taken over their parents' farm, which excused him from military service. She persuaded him to walk to the little lake that bordered the farm. They sat on the small dock in the afternoon sun while Irina told him about her plans and showed him the pad with her new designs. He was delighted and put an arm around her shoulder.

When they came back, the soldiers were standing in the farmyard. They shot her brother and raped Irina, in that order. The soldiers were in fours. One spat in her face as he lay on top of her. He called her a whore, punched her in the eyes. After that, she ceased to defend herself. When they all left, she remained lying on the kitchen table. She wrapped herself in the red-and-white tablecloth and closed her eyes, hoping it would be forever.

The next morning, she went to the lake again. She thought it would be easy to drown herself, but she couldn't do it. When she rose back up to the surface, she jerked open her mouth and her lungs filled with oxygen. She stood in the water naked; there was nothing but the trees on the bank, the reeds and the sky. She screamed. She screamed until her strength left her; she screamed against death and loneliness and pain. She knew she would survive, but she also knew that this was no longer her homeland.

A week later, they buried her brother. It was a simple grave with a wooden cross. The priest said something about guilt and forgiveness, while the mayor stared at the ground and clenched his fists. She gave the key to the farm to her next-door neighbour, along with the few remaining live-stock, plus all the contents of the house. Then she picked up her little suitcase and her purse and took the bus into the capital. She did not turn around. She left the sketchbook behind.

She checked on the streets and in bars to find the names of smugglers who could get her into Germany. The agent was practised, and he took all the money she had. He knew that what she wanted was security and that she would pay for it—there were lots like Irina, and they made for good business.

Irina and the others were taken in a minibus toward the West. After two days, they stopped in a clearing, got out, and ran through the night. The man, who led them over streams and through a swamp, didn't say much, and when they had reached the end of their strength, he told them they were in Germany. Another bus brought them to Berlin. It stopped somewhere on the edge of the city. The weather was cold and foggy. Irina was exhausted, but she believed she'd reached safety.

Over the next months, she got to know other men and women from her homeland. They explained Berlin to her, its authorities and its laws. Irina needed money. She couldn't work legally; she wasn't even allowed to be in Germany. The women helped her in the first few weeks. She stood on the Kurfürstenstrasse, and she learned the price for oral and vaginal sex. Her body had become a stranger to her; she used it like a tool. She wanted to survive, even if she didn't know for what. She didn't feel herself anymore.

★ ★ ★

He sat on the footpath every day. She saw him as she got into men's cars, and she saw him in the early mornings when she went home. He had placed a plastic bowl in front of him, into which people sometimes threw money. She got used to the sight of him; he was always there. He smiled at her, and after a few weeks, she smiled back.

When winter set in, Irina took him a blanket from a secondhand shop. He was delighted. 'I'm Kalle,' he said, and let his dog sit on the blanket, wrapping him up and scratching behind his ears, while he himself stayed squatting on some newspapers. Kalle wore thin trousers; he froze even as he kept the dog warm. Irina's legs were trembling and she hurried on. She sat down on a bench around the corner, pulled up her knees, and buried her head. She was nineteen years old, and for a whole year no one had hugged her. She cried for the first time since that afternoon back home.

When his dog was run over, she was standing on the opposite footpath. She saw Kalle running across the street in slow motion and dropping to his knees in front of the car. He lifted up the dog. The driver yelled after him, but Kalle walked down the middle of the street with the dog in his arms, and he did not turn around. Irina ran after him. She understood his pain, and suddenly she knew that they were soul mates. They buried the dog together in the city park, and Irina held Kalle's hand.

That's how it all began. At some point, they decided to try to make a go of it together. Irina moved out of her filthy boardinghouse and they found a one-room apartment. They bought a washing machine and a TV, and then gradually everything else. It was Kalle's first apartment. He had run away from home at sixteen, and since then he'd been living on the street. Irina cut his hair, bought him pants, T-shirts, pullovers and two pairs of shoes. He found a job distributing brochures and helped out in the evenings at a bar.

Now men came to the house and Irina didn't have to walk the streets anymore. When they were alone again in the mornings, they got their bedding out of the cupboard, lay down, and held each other tight, lying together, naked, silent, motionless, listening only to each other's breathing, and shutting out the world. They never spoke about the past.

Irina was afraid of the dead fat man, and she was afraid of being arrested on illegal immigration charges and then deported. She decided to go to her girlfriend's and wait for Kalle there. She grabbed her purse and ran down the stairs, leaving her mobile phone forgotten on the kitchen table.

Kalle had ridden his bike with its little trailer to the industrial zone, as he did every day, but today the man who parcelled out the work said he had nothing for him. It took Kalle half an hour to get home. As he took the elevator up, he thought he heard the sound of Irina's shoes clacking on the stairs. When he unlocked the door to the apartment, she was going out the front door downstairs, on her way to the bus stop.

Kalle sat on one of the two wooden chairs and stared at the dead fat man and his blindingly white undershirt. The breakfast rolls he had brought with him were lying on the floor. It was summer, and the room was warm.

Kalle tried to concentrate. Irina would be put in prison and then she'd have to go back to where she'd come from. Maybe the fat man had hit her—she never did things without a reason. Kalle thought about the day they had taken the train out to the country. They had lain down in a meadow in the summer heat, and Irina had looked like a child. He had been happy. Now he thought he was going to have to pay. And Kalle thought about his dog. Sometimes he went to the place in the park to see if anything had changed.

Half an hour later, Kalle knew he'd made a mistake. He had stripped down to his undershorts and now his sweat was mingling with the blood in the bathtub. He had pulled a plastic bag over the man's head because he didn't want to see his face while he was working. At first, he'd gone at it the wrong way and tried to sever the bones. Then he remembered how you dismember a chicken, and he twisted the fat man's arm out of his shoulder. Now it was going better, all he had to do was cut through the muscles and the fibrous tissue. At some point, the arm lay on the yellow tiled floor, the watch still on the wrist. Kalle turned around to the toilet bowl and threw up again. Then he ran water in the washbasin, dunked his face into it, and rinsed out his mouth. The water was cold and made his teeth ache. He stared into the mirror and didn't know whether he was standing in front of it or behind it. The man facing him had to move in order for him to do likewise. When the water overflowed the edge of the basin and splashed down onto his feet, Kalle pulled himself together. He knelt back down on the floor and picked up the saw.

Three hours later, he had detached the various limbs. He bought black garbage bags in a grocery store, attracting odd looks from the girl at the checkout counter. Kalle tried not to think about what he was going to do with the head, but he was unsuccessful. If it stays attached to the neck, I won't be able to get him into the trailer, he thought. There's no way. He left the store. Two housewives were having a conversation on the footpath, the suburban train went by, and a boy kicked an apple across the street. Kalle felt himself getting angry. 'I'm not a murderer,' he said out loud as he was passing a pram. The mother turned around and stared after him.

Back at home, he pulled himself together. One of the handles of the handsaw had come loose and Kalle cut his fingers. He burst out crying like a child; bubbles formed below his nostrils. He cried and sawed and sawed and cried, holding the fat man's head tightly under his arm. The plastic bag had become slippery and kept sliding out of his grip. When he had finally detached the head from the trunk, he was astonished to find how heavy it was. Like a sack of charcoal for a barbecue, he thought, and wondered how charcoal had popped into his mind. He'd never cooked anything on a barbecue.

He dragged the biggest bags into the elevator and used them to block the automatic door. Then he fetched the rest. The garbage bags didn't tear—he'd doubled them for the torso. He pulled the bicycle trailer into the lobby, where there was no one to see him. There were four garbage bags. The only things he'd had to put in his backpack were the arms; the trailer was full, and they would have fallen out.

Kalle had put on a clean shirt. He needed twenty minutes to reach the park. He thought about the head, about its sparse hair, and about the arms. He felt the fat man's fingers against his back. They were wet. He fell off the bike and tore off his backpack, then just dropped to the grass. He waited for people to come running and start screaming, but they didn't. Nothing happened.

Kalle lay there, looking up into the sky, and waited.

He buried the fat man in the city park in his entirety. The handle of the spade broke, so he knelt down and used the blade in his hands. He crammed everything into the hole, not a metre from the dead dog. It wasn't deep enough, so he trampled the garbage bags together. His clean shirt was filthy, his fingers black and bloody, and his skin itched. He threw the remains of the spade into a garbage container. Then he sat on a park bench for almost an hour, watching students play frisbee.

★ ★ ★

When Irina got back from her girlfriend's, the bed was empty. The fat man's jacket and folded trousers were still hanging over the chair. She clapped her hand over her mouth so as not to cry out. She understood immediately: Kalle had tried to save her. The police would find him. They would believe he'd killed the fat man. The Germans solve every murder; you keep seeing it on television, she thought. Kalle would go to prison. A mobile phone was ringing endlessly in the fat man's jacket. She had to do something.

She went into the kitchen and called the police. The men on duty could hardly understand a word she said. When they came, they looked into the bathroom and took her into custody. They asked where the body was, Irina didn't know what to reply. She kept saying the fat man had died 'normally', that it had been a 'dead heart'. The police, naturally, didn't believe her. As she was being taken out of the building, Kalle came riding up. She looked at him and shook her head. Kalle misunderstood, leapt off his bike, and ran to her. He stumbled. The police apprehended him, too. Later, he said it was fine, that he wouldn't have known what to do without Irina anyway.

★　★　★

Kalle remained silent. He had learned silence, and prison didn't frighten him. He had been there more than once already—break-ins, thefts. He'd heard my name inside, and asked me to take on his defence. He wanted to know what was going on with Irina; he didn't care about himself. He said he had no money but that I had to take care of his girlfriend.

I knew if Kalle would testify, he'd be saved, but he was hard to convince. All he kept asking was if that wouldn't damage Irina. He clutched at my forearms, trembled, said he didn't want to make any mistakes. I calmed him down and promised I would find a lawyer for Irina. Finally, he agreed.

He led the detectives to the hole in the city park and stood by as they dug up the fat man and sorted out the body parts. He also showed the police the place where he'd buried his dog. It was a misunderstanding. They also dug up the dog's skeleton and looked at him questioningly.

The forensic pathologist established that all the wounds had occurred after death. The fat man's heart was examined. He had died of a heart attack; there was absolutely no question about it. The suspicion of murder had been eliminated.

In the end, the only thing actionable was the dismemberment. The prosecutor considered a charge of disturbing the dead. The law states that it is forbidden to commit a 'public nuisance' with a corpse. There was no doubt, said the prosecutor, that sawing up and burying a dead body constituted a public nuisance.

The prosecutor was right. But that was not the issue. The only issue was the intention of the accused. Kalle's goal was to save Irina, not to desecrate the body. 'A public nuisance caused by love,' I said. I cited a decision of the federal court that justified Kalle's actions. The prosecutor raised his eyebrows, but he closed the file.

The arrests were nullified, and both were let go. With the help of a lawyer, Irina filed a claim for asylum and was allowed to remain in Berlin for the moment. She was not placed in a detention centre pending deportation.

They sat next to each other on the bed. The hinge on one of the cupboard doors had been broken and pulled loose during the search, and the door hung at an angle. Otherwise, nothing had changed. Irina held Kalle's hand as they looked out of the window.

'Now we have to do something new,' said Kalle. Irina nodded and thought how blissfully lucky they were.

Summertime

Consuela was thinking about her grandson's birthday: today was the day she'd have to buy the PlayStation. Her shift had started at 7:00 a.m. Working as a maid was demanding, but it was a secure job, better than most she'd had before this. The hotel paid somewhat over the going rate; it was the best in town.

All she had left to do was to clean room number 239. She entered the time on the work sheet. She was paid by the room, but the hotel management insisted that the work sheet be adhered to. And Consuela did whatever the management wanted. She couldn't lose the job. She wrote 3:26 p.m. on the work sheet.

She rang the bell. When no one opened the door, she knocked and waited some more. Then she inserted a key card into the electronic lock and pushed the door open a hand's breadth. Following the way she'd been taught, she called out, 'Maid service.' When there was no answer, she went in.

The suite occupied about thirty-five square metres and was decorated in tones of warm brown. The walls were padded with beige cloth, and there was a bright carpet on the parquet floor. The bed was rumpled and a bottle of water stood open on the nightstand. Between the two orange chaises longues was the naked body of a young woman. Consuela saw her breasts, but the head was hidden. Blood had soaked into the woollen fibres along the edge of the carpet, leaving a jagged pattern of red. Consuela held her breath. Her heart racing, she took two cautious steps forward. She had to see the woman's face. That was when she screamed. In front of her was a mushy mass of bone, hair and eyes, a portion of the whitish brain matter had sprayed out of the ruptured skull onto the dark parquet, and the heavy iron lamp that Consuela dusted every day was sticking up out of the face, covered in blood.

Abbas was relieved. He had now confessed it all. Stefanie sat next to him in her little apartment and wept.

He was a child of Palestinian refugees and had grown up in the settlement of Shatila in Beirut. His playgrounds lay between barracks with corrugated iron doors, five-storey houses pockmarked with bullet holes, and ancient cars from Europe. The children wore tracksuits and T-shirts with Western slogans on them, five-year-old girls covered their heads despite the heat, and there was warm bread wrapped in thin paper. Abbas had been born four years after the great massacre. Back then, the Christian Lebanese militia had mutilated and killed hundreds of people, women had been raped, and even children were shot. No one could arrive at an accurate count afterward, and the fear never went away again. Sometimes Abbas lay down on the clay of his unpaved street and tried to count the hopeless tangle of power lines and phone lines that were slung between the houses and carved up the sky.

His parents had paid the smugglers a great deal of money; he was supposed to have a future in Germany. He was seventeen then. Naturally, he wasn't granted asylum and the authorities gave him no permission to hold a job. He lived on state benefits; everything else was forbidden him. Abbas couldn't go to the movies or to McDonald's; he owned neither a PlayStation nor a mobile phone. He learned the language on the street. He was a pretty boy, but he had no girlfriend. And if he'd had one, he couldn't have invited her to a meal even once. All Abbas had was himself. He sat around, he spent twelve months throwing stones at pigeons, watching TV in the hostel for asylum seekers, and dawdled along the Kurfürstendamm, looking in shop windows. He was bored to death.

At some point, he began with minor break-ins. He got caught, and after the third caution by the judge in juvenile court, he underwent his first prolonged detention. It was a wonderful time. He met lots of new friends in jail, and by the time he was released, some things had become clear to him. He'd been told that for people like him—and inside there were a lot of people like him—the only way to go was drug dealing.

It was really easy. One of the bigger dealers, who didn't work the streets anymore himself, took him on. Abbas's turf was one of the subway stations, and he shared it with two other people. At first, he was only the 'bunker', a human safe-deposit box for narcotics. He kept the bags in his mouth. The other guy conducted the negotiations and the third handled the money. They called it 'work'.

The junkies asked for 'browns' or 'whites'; they paid with ten- and twenty-euro bills that they had stolen or begged or earned from prostitution.

Transactions went swiftly. Sometimes women offered themselves to the dealers. If one of them was pretty enough, Abbas would take her along. To begin with, it interested him, because the girls would do anything he asked. But then he began to be disturbed by the craving in their eyes. It wasn't him they wanted; it was the drugs in his jacket.

When the police came, he had to run. He learned quickly how to recognise them; even their civilian clothes were a kind of uniform: sneakers, bum bags and hip-length jackets. And they all seemed to go to the same barber. While Abbas ran, he swallowed. If he managed to choke down the cellophane packages before they caught up with him, the proof would be hard to come by. Sometimes they administered purgatives. Then they sat next to him and waited till he threw up the little packages into a sieve. From time to time, one of his new friends would die when his stomach acids dissolved the cellophane too quickly.

As a business it was dangerous, fast and lucrative. Abbas had money now, and he sent substantial amounts home regularly. He wasn't bored anymore. The girl he was in love with was named Stefanie. He had watched her for a long time dancing in a disco. And when she turned around to him he— the big drug dealer, the king of the street—blushed.

Of course she knew nothing about his drug business. In the mornings, Abbas left love letters for her attached to the refrigerator. He told his friends that when she drank, he could see the water running down inside her throat. She became his homeland; he had nothing else. He missed his mother, his brothers and sisters, and the stars over Beirut. He thought about his father, who had slapped him merely because he had stolen an apple from the fruit stand. He'd been seven years old at the time. 'There are no criminals in our family,' his father had said. He had gone with him to the fruit seller and paid for the apple. Abbas would have liked to become an auto mechanic, or a painter, or a carpenter—or anything. But he became a drug dealer. And now he was no longer even that.

A year earlier, Abbas had gone to an arcade for the first time. At the beginning, he only went there with his friends. They pretended and acted out being James Bond and fooled around with the pretty girls who worked there. But then he went there on his own, though everyone had warned him. The poker machines were what drew him. At some point, he had started to talk to them. Each one of them had its own character, and, like gods, they determined his fate. He knew he was a compulsive gambler. He'd been losing every day for four months. He could hear the melody of the slot machines in his sleep, announcing that somebody had won. He couldn't help himself; he had to play.

His friends no longer took him along when they were dealing; he was nothing but an addict himself now, no different from their customers, the junkies. He would end up stealing money from them, they knew what his future would be, and Abbas knew they were right. But that was nowhere near the worst of it.

The worst of it was Danninger. Abbas had borrowed money from him, five thousand euros, and he had to pay back seven thousand. Danninger was a friendly man; he'd said that anyone could have a problem sometimes. Abbas hadn't felt alarmed, either. He would certainly win back the money again; the poker machines couldn't go on making him lose forever. He was wrong. On the day payment was due, Danninger had come and held out his hand. After that, things happened fast. Danninger had pulled a pair of pliers out of his pocket. Abbas saw the handles; they were covered with yellow plastic and glinted in the sun. Then the little finger of Abbas's right hand was lying on the curb. As he was screaming in pain, Danninger had handed him a handkerchief and told him the quickest way to the hospital. Danninger was still friendly, but he also said that the interest on the debt had now increased. If Abbas failed to repay ten thousand in three months' time, he'd have to cut off his thumb, then his hand, and so on until he reached his head. Danninger said he was really sorry. He liked Abbas, he was a nice guy, but there were rules, and no one could bend those rules. Abbas didn't doubt for one moment that Danninger meant it.

Stefanie cried more over the finger than over the lost money. They didn't know what to do next, but at least they were facing it together. And they would find some solution—they had found solutions for everything in the past two years. Stefanie said that Abbas needed to go into therapy immediately. But that didn't address the financial problem. Stefanie wanted to go back to work as a waitress. With tips, that would be eighteen hundred euros a month. Abbas didn't like the idea of her working in a beer garden; he was jealous about the customers. But that was the only way they could do anything. He couldn't go back to drug dealing; they would just beat him up and throw him out.

A month later, it was clear that they wouldn't be able to pull the money together this way. Stefanie was in despair. She had to find a solution; she was afraid for Abbas. Danninger was a cipher to her, but she had rebandaged Abbas's hand every day for two weeks.

Stefanie loved Abbas. He was different from the boys she'd known before, more serious, less familiar. Abbas did her good, even if her girlfriends made stupid remarks about him. Now she was going to do something for him: she was going to save him. She even found the idea a tiny bit romantic.

Stefanie had nothing she could sell. But she knew how pretty she was. And like all her girlfriends she had read the personal ads in the newspaper and laughed over them. Now she was going to answer one of them, for Abbas and for their love.

At the first meeting with the man in the luxury hotel, she was so nervous, she shook. She was stand-offish to him, but the man was friendly and not at all the way she'd imagined him. He was even nice-looking, and well groomed. Admittedly, she'd felt sick when he took hold of her and she had to service him, but she'd managed somehow. He was no different from men she'd known before Abbas, just older. Afterward, she showered for thirty minutes and brushed her teeth till her gums bled. Now there were five hundred euros in her hiding place in the coffee can.

She lay on the sofa in her apartment, bundled up in her bathrobe. She would only have to do it a few times and she'd have the money she needed. She thought about the man from the hotel, who lived in another world. The man wanted to meet her once or twice a week and pay her five hundred euros per session. She would get through it. And she was confident she would come away from it all unscathed. It was just that Abbas must know nothing about it. She would surprise him and give him the money, telling him she'd gotten it from her aunt.

Percy Boheim was tired. He looked out of the hotel window. Autumn had arrived, the wind was tearing the leaves from the trees, the days with their glowing light were over, and Berlin would soon sink back into its winter grey for at least five months. The student had gone. She was a nice girl, a little shy, but so were they all at the beginning. There was nothing ambiguous about it; it was a business transaction. He paid and got the sex he needed. No love, no phone calls in the night, no other nonsense like that. If she got too close to him, he would end it.

Boheim didn't like prostitutes. He'd tried it once years ago and it repelled him. He thought of Melanie, his wife. She was widely known as a dressage rider, and like many riders, she lived, finally, for her horses. Melanie was cold; it was a long time since they'd had anything to say to each other, but they were polite in their dealings and had reached a mutual understanding. They didn't see each other very often. He knew she would never be able to tolerate his girls. And he couldn't cope with a divorce right now, because of their son Benedict. He would have to wait another few years for the boy to grow up. Benedict loved his mother.

Percy Boheim was one of the leading industrialists in the country; he had inherited the majority shareholding in an auto-parts manufacturing company from his father, sat on the boards of many companies, and was an economic adviser to the government.

He thought about the imminent takeover of a bolt factory in Alsace. His auditors had advised against it, but they were never good judges of anything. He had long had the feeling that lawyers and auditors were good for creating problems, never solving them. Maybe he should just sell everything and go fishing. One day, thought Boheim, one day, when Benedict is old enough. Then he went to sleep.

★ ★ ★

Abbas was uneasy. Stefanie had been asking odd questions recently: did he ever think of other women? Did she still please him? Did he still love her? She had never asked things like that before. Until now she had been a little unsure of herself when they were making love, but she behaved as if she had the upper hand in their relationship; now that all seemed to have been overturned. After they'd had sex, she would nestle against him for the longest time, and even when she was asleep, she held tight to him. That was new, too.

When she had dropped off to sleep, he got up and checked her mobile phone. It wasn't the first time he'd done it. Now there was a new entry: 'P.B.' He ran through all their acquaintances in his head; not one of them that he could think of had those initials. Then he read her stored messages. 'Wednesday 12 noon, Park Hotel. Room 239 as usual.' The text message was from P.B. Abbas went into the kitchen and sat on one of the wooden chairs. He was so enraged, he could hardly breathe. 'As usual,' so it hadn't been the first time. How could she? Now, during the biggest crisis of his life. He loved her; she was everything to him. He had thought they would get through this together. Abbas couldn't get his mind around it.

The next Wednesday at twelve noon, he was standing in front of the Park Hotel. It was the best hotel in Berlin. And that was his problem. The concierge at the front door hadn't let him in. Abbas didn't take it personally; he didn't exactly look like their regular hotel guests. He knew people's reactions to someone who looked like an Arab. So he sat down on a bench and waited. He waited for more than two hours. Finally, Stefanie came out of the hotel. He went to meet her and watched her reaction. She was shocked, and turned red.

'What are you doing here?' she asked.

'I was waiting for you.'

'How did you know I was here?' She was asking herself how much he actually knew.

'I followed you.'

'You followed me? Are you nuts? Why did you do that?'

'You have somebody else. I know it.' Abbas had tears in his eyes and was clutching her arm.

'Don't be ridiculous.' She pulled free and ran across the square, feeling like she was in a movie.

He ran two steps behind her and seized hold of her again.

'Stefanie, what did you do in the hotel?'

She had to pull herself together. Think clearly, she told herself. 'I applied for a job; they pay better than the beer garden.' It was the best she could think of.

Abbas, naturally, did not believe her. They had a loud fight on the square. She was embarrassed. Abbas yelled; she pulled him away. At some point, he calmed down. They drove back to the apartment. Abbas sat at the kitchen table, drinking tea, saying nothing.

Boheim had been meeting Stefanie for two months now. She had set aside her shyness. They got on well together, too well perhaps. Stefanie had told him that her boyfriend had followed her two weeks before. Boheim was uneasy; he knew he would have to end the arrangement. That was the dumb thing in such relationships. A jealous boyfriend spelled problems.

He arrived late today; the meeting had gone on forever. He switched on the car phone and dialled her number. It was good to hear her voice. He said he would be there in a moment. She was pleased and told him she was already naked.

He hung up as he drove into the hotel garage. He would tell her it was over. Best that it be right away, today. Boheim was not a man to procrastinate.

The file lay open on the desk. For now, there were only two folders in the customary red cardboard binders for criminal files, but this number would increase. The file displeased Assistant Prosecutor Schmied. He closed his eyes and leaned back. Only eight months till I retire, he thought. For the last twelve years, Schmied had been the head of the Capital Crimes Section in the prosecutor's office in Berlin. And now he'd had enough. His father came from Breslau; Schmied considered himself to be a Prussian through and through. He didn't hate the criminals he pursued; it was simply his duty. He didn't want another big case; he would have preferred a few straightforward murders, dramas that played themselves out within families, cases that resolved themselves speedily. But he prayed there would not be anything requiring a lot of reports he'd have to take to the prosecutor.

Schmied was looking at the request for a warrant against Boheim. He still hadn't signed it. It'll set off the whole frenzy with the press, he thought. The tabloids were already full of the naked student in the ritziest hotel. He could

pretty much imagine what would happen if
Percy Boheim, chairman and principal share-
holder of Boheim Industries, was arrested.
All hell would break loose and the spokesman
for the prosecutor's office would be getting new
orders by the day for what he had to say.

Schmied sighed and thought back to the note
his new colleague had briefed him with. The new
colleague was a good man, still a little overzealous,
but that would temper itself with time. The note
summarised the files in an orderly fashion.

Stefanie Becker had been found dead at 3:26 p.m.
Her head had been beaten in with numerous
blows of extreme force. The murder weapon
was a cast-iron lamp stand, part of the standard
furnishings of the room. 'Blunt-force trauma,' in
the language of medical examiners.

Percy Boheim had been the last caller to the
victim's mobile phone. The day after the body
was discovered, two officers of the Homicide
Division had visited him in his Berlin office.
'Only a couple of routine questions,' they'd said.
Boheim had asked a company lawyer to join him
at the meeting. The police report indicated that
aside from this, he had evinced no reaction. They
had shown him a photo of the deceased and he
had denied knowing the girl. The phone call he

explained by saying he had misdialled, and the location of his mobile phone by the fact that he'd driven past the hotel. The policemen wrote up his statement right there in the office; he read it through and signed it.

At this point, it was already clear that the conversation had lasted almost a minute, far too long to be a wrong number. Nonetheless, the police had not pointed this out to Boheim. Not yet. They had also not yet revealed that his number was stored in the deceased's phone memory. Boheim had made himself suspicious.

The next day, the analysis of the trace evidence came in: sperm had been found in the hair and on the breasts of the deceased. The DNA had not been on file in the data bank. Boheim had been asked to give a sample of his saliva voluntarily. His DNA was analysed immediately—it matched the sperm. That, in a nutshell, was the report.

The yellow folder with the autopsy photographs was, as always, distasteful to Schmied. He went through it only briefly: pitiless images against a blue background, the sight of them bearable only if deliberately contemplated for a very long time.

Schmied thought of the many hours he'd

spent in autopsy. Everything happened quietly there, just the sound of scalpels and saws, the voices of the doctors murmuring their short-hand into dictating machines as they handled the bodies with respect. Jokes around the autopsy table happened only in thrillers. The only thing he would never get used to was the smell, that typical odour of decay—almost every patholo-gist felt the same way. Nor was it possible to smear some Vicks under your nose, as certain trace evidence could only be deduced from the smell of the corpse. As a young prosecutor, Schmied had been sickened when the blood was ladled out of the bodies and weighed or when the organs were placed back in the body after the postmortem. Later he had come to understand that there was a specific art in sewing the corpse back up after autopsy firmly enough to prevent it from leaking, and he had realised that medical examiners had serious conversations about it. It was a parallel universe, just as his was. Schmied and the chief medical examiner were friends, they were almost the same age, and they never discussed their professional lives in private.

Assistant Prosecutor Schmied sighed a second time, then signed the order of arrest and took it to the examining magistrate. Only two hours later, the judge issued the warrant, and six hours later, Boheim was arrested in his apartment. Simultaneously, searches were initiated in the couple's various apartments, offices and houses in Düsseldorf, Munich, Berlin, and Sylt. The police had organised it well.

Three lawyers appeared for the arraignment, looking like alien beings in the examining magistrate's little office. They were civil lawyers, highly paid specialists in corporate takeovers and international arbitration. None of them had appeared before a judge; the last time they'd been engaged with criminal law was when they were studying for their law degrees. They didn't know what motions they should file, and one of them said threateningly that he might have to bring politics into this. The judge remained calm nonetheless.

Melanie Boheim sat on the wooden bench outside the door to the hearing room. No one had told her she couldn't see her husband—the arraignment was not open to the public. On the advice of his lawyers, Boheim said nothing when the warrant was read. The lawyers had come with a blank cheque and certification from the bank that he was good for up to fifty million euros. The examining magistrate was angered by the figure; it reeked of the class system. He refused bail—'We're not in America here'—and asked the lawyers if they wished to apply for a formal review of the remand in custody.

Assistant Prosecutor Schmied had said almost nothing during the hearing. This was going to be a fight, and he thought he could hear the starting bell.

Percy Boheim was impressive. The day after his arrest, I went to find him in the house of detention where he was being held, after having been asked by the chief counsel of his firm to take over the defence. Boheim sat behind the table in the visitor's cell as if it were his office, and greeted me warmly. We talked about the government's failed tax policies and the future of the car industry. He behaved as though we were at a stand-up reception and not preparing for a jury trial. When we got around to the actual matter at hand, he said immediately that he had lied to the police when they had questioned him, in the hopes of protecting his wife and saving his marriage. To all my other questions, his answers were precise, focused, and devoid of hesitation.

Of course he had known Stefanie Becker. She had been his lover; he had got to know her via an ad in one of the Berlin papers. He had paid her for sex. She was a nice girl, a student. He had thought about offering her a place as a trainee in one of his companies once she'd graduated. He had never asked her why she was working as a prostitute, but he was certain he had been her only customer; she was shy and it was only over time that she thawed out. 'It all sounds ugly now, but it was what it was,' he said. He'd liked her.

On the day it happened, he'd had a meeting that ran until 1:20 and had reached the hotel somewhere around 1:45. Stefanie was waiting; they'd had sex. After that, he'd showered and then left immediately, because he wanted to have some time alone to prepare for his next appointment. Stefanie had stayed in the room in order to take a bath before she set off, and she had told him she didn't want to be out of there until 3:30. He had tucked five hundred euros in her purse, which was their standard arrangement.

He had used the elevator next to the suite to go down directly to the underground garage; it would have taken him a minute, two at most, to get to his car. He had left the hotel at around 2:30 and driven to the zoological garden, Berlin's biggest park, and taken a walk for the better part of an hour, thinking in part about his relationship with Stefanie and deciding that he had to end it. He'd left his mobile phone switched off; he hadn't wanted to be disturbed.

At four o'clock, he'd been at a meeting on the Kurfürstendamm with four other men. Between 2:30 and 4:00, he had met no one, nor had he had any phone conversations. And no one had passed him when he left the hotel.

Defendants and defence lawyers have a curious relationship. A lawyer doesn't always want to know what actually happened. This also has its roots in our code of criminal procedure: if the defence counsel knows that his client has killed someone in Berlin, he may not ask for 'defence witnesses' to take the stand who would say that the man had been in Munich that day. It's a tightrope walk. In other cases, the lawyer absolutely has to know the truth. Knowledge of the actual circumstances may be the tiny advantage that can protect his client from a guilty verdict. Whether the lawyer thinks his client is innocent is irrelevant. His task is to defend the accused, no more, no less.

If Boheim's explanation was correct—that is, that he'd left the room at 2:30 and the cleaning lady had found the girl's body at 3:26, then there was a little under an hour to deal with. It was enough. In the space of sixty minutes, the real perpetrator could have entered the room, killed the girl, and disappeared before the cleaning lady entered. There was no proof of what Boheim had told me. If he had kept silent during his first interview, it would have been easier. His lies had made the situation worse, and there was absolutely no trace of another attacker. Admittedly, I did think it unlikely that a jury would end up convicting him in a major trial. But I doubted that any judge would withdraw his arrest warrant right now—a suspicion clung.

Forty-eight hours later, the examining magistrate called me to arrange a time for the formal review of Boheim's remand in custody. We settled on the next day. I could have the file picked up by a courier; the prosecutor's office had approved its release.

The file contained new inquiries. Everyone in the victim's mobile-phone address book had been questioned. A girlfriend, in whom Stefanie Becker had confided, explained to the police why she had turned to prostitution.

But what was much more interesting was that the police had located Abbas in the meantime. He had a record—break-ins and drug dealing and, two years previously, an offence involving grievous bodily harm, a fight outside a discotheque. The police had questioned Abbas. He said he had followed Stefanie to the hotel once, out of jealousy, but she'd been able to explain what she was doing there. The interrogation went on for many pages, and the detectives' suspicions were clear in every line. But finally when it came down to it, they had a motive but no proof.

Late in the afternoon, I paid a visit to Assistant Prosecutor Schmied in his office. As always, he welcomed me in both a friendly and a professional way. He didn't feel good about Abbas, either. Jealousy was always a powerful motive. Abbas could not be excluded as the alternative killer. He knew the hotel, she was his girlfriend, and she had slept with another man. If he had been there, he could also have killed her. I explained to Schmied why Boheim had lied, then said, 'Sleeping with a student isn't, finally, a crime.'

'Yes, but it's not very attractive, either.'

'Thank god that's not the issue,' I said. 'Infidelity is no longer punishable under the law.' Schmied himself had had an affair with a female prosecutor some years ago, as everyone knew around the Moabit courthouse. 'I can't see a single reason why Boheim would have wanted to kill his lover,' I said.

'Nor do I, yet. But you know motives don't

count that much with me,' said Schmied. 'He really did lie his head off under questioning.'

'That makes him suspicious, I grant you, but it doesn't prove anything. Besides which, his first statement at the hearing is probably unusable.'

'Oh?'

'The police had already analysed the phone records by then. They knew he'd had long conversations with the victim. They knew from the nearest mobile-phone tower that his car was in the neighbourhood of the hotel. They knew he had reserved the room in which the girl was killed. The police should therefore have interrogated him formally as the accused, but they only questioned him under the guise of a witness and only cautioned him as such.'

Schmied thumbed through the transcript of the interrogation. 'You're right,' he said finally, and pushed the files away. He disliked such little games by the police; they never really got anybody anywhere.

'Besides which, the weapon involved, the lamp the student was killed with, showed no fingerprints,' I said. The trace evidence had revealed only *her* DNA.

'That is correct. But the sperm in the girl's hair came from your client.'

'Oh come on, Mr Schmied, that's just crazy. He ejaculates on the girl and then pulls on his gloves to bash her head in? Boheim's not a moron.'

Schmied's eyebrows shot up.

'And all the other traces, the ones that were lifted off water glasses, door handles, window handles, and so on, are perfectly explicable by the fact that he stayed in the hotel—they imply no guilt.'

We argued for almost an hour. At the end, Schmied said, 'On condition that your client lays out his relationship to the deceased in detail at the hearing, I will agree that the arrest warrant may be withdrawn tomorrow morning.'

He stood up and held out his hand to say goodbye. As I was standing in the doorway, he said, 'But Boheim will surrender his passport, pay a high amount in bail, and check in with the police twice a week. Agreed?'

Of course I agreed.

When I left the room, Schmied was pleased that the affair would now die down. He had never really believed Boheim to be the perpetrator. Percy Boheim gave no appearance of being a raving madman who would crush the head of a student with a rain of blows. But, Schmied was also thinking, who knows his fellow human being? Which was why, for him, motive was very seldom the deciding factor.

Two hours later, just as he was locking the door to his office on his way home, his phone rang. Schmied cursed, went back, picked up the receiver, and let himself down into his chair again. It was the Homicide Division's leading investigator on the case. When Schmied hung up six minutes later, he looked at the clock. Then he pulled his old fountain pen out of his jacket, wrote a brief summary of the conversation, and inserted it as the first page on top of the file, switched off the light, and remained sitting for some time in the darkness. He now knew that Percy Boheim was the killer.

The next day, Schmied asked me to come to his office again. He looked almost sad as he pushed the pictures at me across his desk. The photos clearly showed Boheim behind his car window. 'There's a high-resolution camera positioned at the exit from the hotel garage,' he said. 'Your client was filmed leaving that garage. I received the pictures this morning—the Homicide Division called me last night after you and I had spoken. I wasn't able to reach you again.'

I looked at him, puzzled.

'The pictures show Mr Boheim leaving the hotel garage. Please look at the time on the first photograph; the video camera always stamps them in the bottom left-hand corner. The time is shown as 3:26:55. We checked the clock setting on the camera; it's correct. The cleaning lady discovered the dead girl at 3:26. That time is also correct; it's confirmed by the first call to the police, which came in at 3:29. I'm sorry, but there can't be any other perpetrator.'

I had no alternative but to withdraw from the remand hearing. Boheim would remain in detention as a suspect until the trial.

The next months were taken up with preparations for the trial. All the lawyers in my chambers were working on it; every tiny detail from the file was checked and rechecked—the mobile-phone tower, the DNA analysis, the camera in the garage. The Homicide Division had done good work; there were almost no mistakes we could find. Boheim Industries commissioned a private detective agency, but it came up with nothing new. Boheim himself stuck to his story, despite all proof to the contrary. And despite his miserable prospects, he remained good-humoured and relaxed.

Police work proceeds on the assumption that there is no such thing as chance. Investigations consist 95 percent of office work, checking out factual details, writing summaries, getting statements from witnesses. In detective novels, the person who did it confesses when he or she is screamed at; in real life, it's not that simple. And when a man with a bloody knife in his hand is bent over a corpse, that means he's the murderer. No reasonable policeman would believe he had only walked past by chance and tried to help by pulling the knife out of the body. The detective superintendent's observation that a particular solution is too simple is a screenwriter's conceit. The opposite is true. What is obvious is what is plausible. And most often, it's also what's right.

Lawyers, by contrast, try to find holes in the structures of proof built by prosecutors. Their ally is chance; their task is to disrupt an overhasty reliance on what appears to be the truth. A police officer once said to a federal judge that defence lawyers are no more than brakes on the vehicle of justice. The judge replied that a vehicle without brakes isn't much use, either. Any criminal case can function only within these parameters. So we were hunting for the chance that would save our client.

Boheim had to spend Christmas and New Year's in detention. Assistant Prosecutor Schmied had given him wide-ranging permission for conversations with his operating officers, accountants and civil lawyers. He saw them every second day and ran his companies out of his detention cell. His board members and his staff declared openly that he had their support. His wife also visited him regularly. The only person he refused to be visited by was his son; he didn't want Benedict to see his father in prison.

But still there was no ray of hope that broke through for the trial, due to start in four days. Aside from a few procedural motions, no one had a basic concept for a successful defence. A deal, otherwise a regular occurrence in criminal cases, was out of the question. Murder carries a life sentence, manslaughter a sentence of five to fifteen years. I had nothing that would allow me to negotiate with the judge.

The printouts of the video pictures were on the library table in my chambers. Boheim had been captured on them in piercing detail. It was like a pocket camera strip with six images.

Boheim activates the exit button with his left hand. The barrier opens. The car drives past the camera. And then suddenly it was all completely clear. The solution had been in the file for four months, so simple that it made me laugh. And we'd all overlooked it.

The trial took place in Room 500 in the courthouse in Moabit. The state's case was for manslaughter. Assistant Prosecutor Schmied represented the prosecutor's office himself, and as he read out the charges, the courtroom fell silent. Boheim took the stand as the accused. He was well prepared; he spoke for more than an hour without notes. His voice was sympathetic; people liked listening to him. He spoke with great focus about his relationship with Stefanie Becker. He left nothing out; there were no dark, shadowy areas. He described the course of their meeting on the day of the crime and how he had left the hotel at 2:30. He answered the relevant questions from the judges and the prosecutors both fully and precisely. He explained both that he had paid Stefanie Becker for sex and why, adding that it would be absurd to assume that he would have killed a young girl with whom he had had no deeper relationship.

Boheim was masterful. The discomfort of everyone involved in the trial was evident. It was a strange situation. No one wanted to suspect him of murder—it was just that it couldn't have been anyone else. Witnesses were not due to be called until the next day.

The tabloids the following morning led with such headlines as MILLIONAIRE NOT KILLER OF BEAUTIFUL STUDENT? That was one way of summing it up.

On the second day of the trial, they called Consuela, the hotel maid. Finding the body had taken its toll on her. Her statements about the time were credible. Neither the prosecution nor the defence had any questions for her.

After her, it was Abbas's turn. He was in mourning. The court asked about his relationship to the deceased, in particular whether Stefanie had ever spoken about the accused and, if so, what she had said. Abbas had nothing he could report.

Then the presiding judge asked Abbas about his meeting with Stefanie in front of the hotel, his jealousy, and his spying on her. The judge was fair; he did everything to ascertain if Abbas had been in the hotel on the day of the murder. Abbas responded no to every question in this vein. He described his gambling obsession and his debts, said he had recovered now and had a limited work permit, which enabled him to wash dishes in a pizzeria to clear those debts. No one in the court believed Abbas was lying: anyone willing to lay bare his private circumstances in such a way would be telling the truth.

Assistant Prosecutor Schmied also tried everything. But Abbas stuck to his story. He was on the witness stand for almost four hours.

I didn't have any questions for Abbas. The presiding judge looked at me in surprise; after all, Abbas was the only potential alternative killer. I had something else in mind.

Famously, the most important rule for a defence counsel when examining a witness is never to ask a question to which you do not already know the answer. Surprises are not always happy ones, and you do not play with the fate of your client.

The trial produced almost nothing new; the contents of the files were laid out step by step. Stefanie's girlfriend, to whom she had admitted why she had turned to prostitution, merely cast a shadow on Boheim, who had taken advantage of the girl's plight. One of the female jurors, who seemed to me to be on our side, shifted uneasily on her chair.

On the fourth day of the trial, the policeman we'd been waiting for was called as the twelfth witness. He hadn't been part of the Homicide Division for very long. It had been his job to secure the video from the surveillance camera in the garage. The presiding judge asked how the policemen had handled the video's transfer from the security team at the hotel. Yes, he had immediately checked the time coded on the video on the monitors in the hotel's security office. He had been able to establish that there was a mere thirty-second deviation from the actual time. And he had written this up in his report.

When the defence was invited to cross-examine, I first asked him to confirm that the date he had secured the video was October 29. Yes, that was correct. It was a Monday, around 5:00 p.m.

'Sir, did you ask the watchman at the hotel whether he moved the clocks back to winter time on October twenty-eighth?' I asked.

'Excuse me? No. The time stamp was correct, I checked it...'

'The video was taken on October twenty-sixth, which still falls within summer time. The changeover to winter time only occurred two days later, on October twenty-eighth.'

'I don't understand,' said the policeman.

'It's quite simple. It could be that the clock setting inside the surveillance camera was showing winter time. If this clock registered three o'clock in summer, it would actually be two o'clock, but if it were winter, three o'clock would be the correct time.'

'Right.'

'On the day of the murder, October twenty-sixth, it was still summer time. The clock showed three-twenty-six. If the clock hadn't been reset, it would actually have been two-twenty-six. Do you understand?'

'Yes,' said the policeman, 'but that's all very theoretical.'

'The theory is the point. The question is whether the clock was correctly set. If not, then the accused left the room an hour before the maid discovered the body. This hour would have allowed any other person to kill the victim. That, sir, is why it would have been critical to ask the hotel's security staff this question. Why did you not ask it?'

'I can't remember if I asked or not. Probably the security people told me…'

'I have here a statement from the head of the

security team that we obtained some days ago. He said the clock had never been reset. Ever since the camera was installed, it has run on the same time, which is winter time. Could you now try to better recall whether you asked him this question or not?' I handed the presiding judge and the prosecutor's staff a copy of the statement.

'I…I think I didn't pose that question,' the policeman now said.

'Your Honour, would you please show the witness sheets twelve to fifteen from picture folder B? It concerns the pictures that show the accused leaving the garage.'

The presiding judge found the yellow picture folder and spread out the prints from the video camera in front of him. The witness stepped over to the judges' table and looked at them.

'There it is: three twenty-six fifty-five—that's the time,' said the policeman.

'Yes, the wrong time. May I direct your attention to the accused's arm as it appears in image number four? Please look carefully. His left hand is clearly visible because he's pressing the buzzer. Mr Boheim was wearing a Patek Philippe that day. Can you make out the numerals in the picture?'

'Yes, they're perfectly legible.'

'Sir, what time are they telling?'

'Two twenty-six,' said the policeman.

Unrest broke out on the jammed press bench. Assistant Prosecutor Schmied now approached the judges' table himself to look at the original pictures. He took his time, picked up the photos one by one, and inspected them closely. Finally, he nodded. That gave us the sixty minutes needed to present the theory of an alternative killer and free Boheim. The rest of the trial would be over quickly now; there were no other pieces of evidence against Boheim. The presiding judge declared a recess.

Half an hour later, the prosecutor's office lifted the order of detention on Boheim, and at the next day's proceedings, he was formally exonerated without any further evidence being heard.

Assistant Prosecutor Schmied congratulated Boheim on the verdict. Then he went back down the long hall to his office, finished a summary report on the outcome of the trial, and opened the next file that was lying on his desk. Three months later, he retired.

Abbas was arrested that same evening. The police interrogator was skilful. He explained to Abbas that Stefanie had only prostituted herself to save him, and read him the statement from the girlfriend to whom Stefanie had told the whole story. When Abbas understood the sacrifice she'd made, he broke down. But he had had experience with the police, and he didn't confess—the crime remains unsolved to this day. Abbas could not be accused of it; the evidence was insufficient.

Melanie Boheim instituted divorce proceedings four weeks after the end of the trial.

Schmied didn't cotton onto the whole time business until some months later, after he'd retired. It was a mild autumn day and he just shook his head. It wouldn't justify a retrial, nor would it explain the time as shown on Boheim's watch. He kicked a chestnut out of the way and walked slowly down the allée, thinking how strange life was.

Self-Defence

Lenzberger and Beck were ambling along the platform. Shaved heads, military pants, Doc Martens,
big strides. Beck's jacket said THOR STEINAR; Lenzberger's T-shirt said PITBULL GERMANY.

Beck was somewhat shorter than Lenzberger.
Eleven convictions for assault, his first when he
was fourteen and went along with the big guys,
joining in when they kicked a Vietnamese to a
pulp. It only got worse from there. He was fifteen
when he did his first stretch in juvie; at sixteen,
he got himself tattooed. Above the knuckle on
each finger of his right hand was a letter of the
alphabet; taken together they read H-A-T-E; on
his left thumb he had a swastika.

Lenzberger had only four convictions on his
sheet, but he had a new metal baseball bat. In

Berlin, they sell fifteen times more baseball bats than balls.

Beck started by picking on an old lady, who became frightened. He laughed and took two big strides toward her with his arms held high. The lady's little steps grew quicker; she clutched her purse against her chest and vanished.

Lenzberger swung the bat against a rubbish bin. The reverberation rang through the station; he didn't need much strength to put a dent in the metal. The platform was almost empty, the next train, an intercity express to Hamburg, would not be leaving for forty-eight minutes. They sat down on a bench. Beck put his feet up; Lenzberger squatted on the armrest. Bored, they threw the last beer bottle down onto the tracks. It broke, and the label peeled off slowly.

That was when they discovered him. The man was sitting two benches away. Mid-forties, bald on top, the rest of his head surrounded by a fringe of hair, glasses with standard-issue black frames, grey suit. A bookkeeper or a clerk, they thought, some bore with a wife and children waiting for him back home. Beck and Lenzberger grinned at each other: a perfect victim, easily frightened. It hadn't been a good night so far, no women, not enough money for really good stuff.

Beck's girlfriend had split up with him on Friday; she'd had enough of the brawling and the booze. Life this Monday morning was shit—until they came across the man. Their fantasies running to violence, they clapped each other on the shoulder, linked arms, and went up to him. Beck sat down with a thump on the bench next to him and burped in his ear, releasing a stench of alcohol and undigested food. 'Hey, old man, had a fuck today?'

The man pulled an apple out of his pocket and polished it on his sleeve.

'Hey, arsehole, I'm talking to you,' said Beck. He hit the apple out of the man's hand and crushed it underfoot so that flesh spurted over his Doc Martens.

The man didn't look at Beck. He stayed sitting, motionless, looking down. Beck and Lenzberger took this as a provocation. Beck jabbed his fore-finger into the man's shirt. 'Oh, someone doesn't want to talk,' he said, and hit the man over the ear. The glasses slipped down, but the man didn't push them back into place. He still hadn't moved, so Beck pulled a knife out of his boot. It was a long knife, the tip sharpened on both sides and the back serrated. He brandished it in front of the man's face, but the man's eyes didn't move. Beck

137

stabbed it a little into the man's hand, nothing deep, a pinprick. He looked at the man expectantly as a drop of blood welled up on the back of his hand. Lenzberger was enjoying the idea of what would come next and swung the baseball bat against the bench in his excitement. Beck stuck a finger into the blood and smeared it around. 'Well, arsehole, feeling better?'

The man still didn't react. Beck lost his temper. The knife sliced through the air twice from right to left, a mere fraction of an inch from the man's chest. The third time, it made contact, slashing his shirt and making an eight-inch gash in his skin, almost horizontally, which bled into the material and left a thickening red streak.

A doctor who was intending to take the early train to Hannover to a conference of urologists was standing on the platform opposite. He would testify later that the man barely moved; it all happened so fast. The CCTV camera on the platform recorded the incident, showing only individual images in black and white.

Beck swung again and Lenzberger whooped. The man gripped the hand holding the knife and simultaneously struck the crook of Beck's arm. The blow altered the direction of the knife without interrupting the swing itself. The blade described an arc as the man aimed the tip between Beck's third and fourth ribs. Beck stabbed himself in the chest. As the steel penetrated the skin, the man struck Beck's fist hard. It was all one single motion, fluid, almost a dance. The blade disappeared completely into Beck's body and pierced his heart. Beck lived for another forty seconds. He stood there, looking down at himself, clutching the knife handle, and seemed to be reading the tattoos on his fingers. He felt no pain; the nerve synapses were no longer transmitting any signals. Beck didn't realise he was in the process of dying.

The man rose, turned toward Lenzberger, and looked at him. His body language didn't convey any message; he just stood there and waited. Lenzberger didn't know whether to fight or flee, and because the man still looked like a bookkeeper, he made the wrong decision. He swung the baseball bat high in the air. The man hit him only once, a brief chop to Lenzberger's neck that happened so fast the CCTV camera couldn't capture it on the individual frames. Then he sat down again without casting another glance at his opponent.

The blow was precise, hitting the carotid sinus, which is a brief surface dilation of the internal carotid artery. This tiny location contains a whole bundle of nerve endings, which registered the blow as an extreme increase in blood pressure and sent signals to Lenzberger's cerebrum to reduce his heartbeat. His heart slowed and slowed, and his circulation did likewise. Lenzberger sank to his knees; the baseball bat landed on the ground behind him, bounced a couple of times, rolled across the platform, and fell onto the train tracks. The blow had been so hard that it had torn the delicate wall of the carotid sinus. Blood rushed in and overstimulated the nerves. They were now transmitting a constant signal to inhibit the heartbeat. Lenzberger collapsed facedown on the platform; a little blood trickled into the ridged tiles and pooled against a cigarette pack. Lenzberger died: his heart had simply stopped beating.

Beck remained standing for another two seconds. Then he, too, fell; his head banged against the bench and left a smear of red. He lay there, eyes open, seeming to be looking at the man's shoes. The man straightened his glasses, crossed his legs, lit a cigarette, and waited to be arrested.

A policewoman was the first to arrive. She and a colleague had been dispatched when the two skinheads went onto the platform. She saw the bodies, the knife in Beck's chest, the man's slashed shirt, and she registered that he was smoking. All information being processed in her brain with equal importance, she pulled out her gun, aimed it at the man, and yelled, 'Smoking is forbidden everywhere in the station.'

'A key client has asked for our help. Please take the case and we will be responsible for the costs,' said the lawyer when he called. He said he was calling from New York, but it sounded as if he was there right next to me. He was making it urgent. He was the senior partner in one of those corporate law firms that have at least one branch in every industrialised country. A 'key client' is one who produces a large stream of business for the law firm, hence a client with very special rights. I asked him what it was about, but he didn't know anything. His secretary had received a phone call from the police; all she'd been told was that someone had been arrested at the station. She didn't get a name. It definitely involved 'manslaughter or something', but that was all she knew. It had to be a 'key client', because they were the only ones who were ever given that number.

I drove to the Homicide Division in the Keithstrasse. It makes no difference whether police stations are in modern high rises built of glass and steel or in two-hundred-year-old guardhouses—they're all alike. There is grey-green linoleum in the corridors, the air smells of detergents, and there are oversize posters of cats in all the interrogation rooms, along with postcards that colleagues have sent from their holidays. Clippings with jokes are stuck to computer screens and cupboard doors. There is lukewarm filtered coffee from orange-yellow coffee machines with scorched warming plates. On the desks there are heavy I LOVE HERTHA mugs, green plastic pencil holders, and some-times there are photos of sunsets on the walls in glass holders without frames, taken by some clerk. The décor is practical and light grey, the rooms are too cramped, the chairs are too ergonomic, and on the windowsills are plastic-looking plants in self-irrigating pebble trays.

Head of Homicide Dalger had conducted hundreds of interrogations. When he had arrived at Homicide sixteen years earlier, it was the leading division in the whole police structure. He was proud to have made it, and he knew that he owed his successful rise to one quality above all others: patience. When necessary, he listened for hours on end; nothing was too much for him, and even after all the long years in the police, he still found everything interesting. Dalger avoided interrogations right after an arrest, when everything was still fresh and he didn't know very much. He was the man for confessions. He didn't use tricks, he didn't use blackmail, and he didn't use humiliation. Dalger was glad to leave the first interrogation to his juniors; he didn't want to start asking questions until he felt he knew everything there was to know about the case. He had a brilliant memory for details. He didn't rely on instinct, even when that instinct had never let him down in the past. Dalger knew that the most absurd stories can be true and the most believable stories false. 'Interrogations,' he told his juniors, 'are hard work.' And he never forgot to finish by saying, 'Follow the money or follow the sperm. Every murder comes down to one or the other.'

Although we almost always had conflicting interests, we respected each other. And when I had finally talked my way through to him and entered the interrogation room, he seemed almost delighted to see me. 'We're not getting anywhere here,' was the first thing he said. Dalger wanted to know who had retained me. I gave him the name of the law firm. Dalger shrugged his shoulders. I asked everyone to leave the room so that I could speak to my client undisturbed. Dalger grinned. 'Good luck.'

The man didn't look up until we were alone. I introduced myself; he nodded politely but didn't say anything. I tried it in German, English, and rather bad French. He just looked at me and didn't utter a word. When I set out a pen for him, he pushed it back toward me. He didn't *want* to talk. I put a power of attorney form in front of him; somehow, I had to be able to document that I had the authority to represent him. He seemed to be thinking, and then suddenly he did something strange: He opened an ink pad that was on the table and pressed his right thumb first into the blue colour and then onto the space for the signature on the power of attorney. 'That's another possibility,' I said, and collected the form. I went into Dalger's office, and he asked me who the man was. This time, I was the one to shrug my shoulders. Then he gave me a thorough rundown of what had happened.

Dalger had taken custody of the man the day before from the federal police, who were responsible for the station. The man hadn't uttered a single syllable either when arrested or while he was being transported, or during the first attempted interrogation in the Keithstrasse. They had tried with different interpreters; they had read him his rights before the interrogation in sixteen languages—nothing.

Dalger had ordered the man to be searched, but they found nothing. He had no briefcase, no passport, and no keys. He showed me the so-called Search Protocol, Part B, which listed the objects that had been found. There were seven:

1. Tempo brand tissues with a price tag from the station pharmacy.
2. Cigarette packet with six cigarettes, German customs sticker.
3. Plastic lighter, yellow.
4. Second-class ticket to the central station in Hamburg (no seat reservation).
5. 16,540 euros in notes.
6. 3.62 euros in coins.
7. A card from the legal firm of Loruis, Metcalf and Partners, Berlin, with a direct-dial phone number on it.

The most striking thing, however, was that his clothes had no labels—the trousers, jacket and shirt could have come from a tailor, but there aren't many people who have their own socks and undershorts custom-made. Only his shoes gave evidence of origin; they came from Heschung, a shoemaker in Alsace—and it was possible to buy them in good shops outside France, as well.

The man was processed by the police Records Department. He was photographed and finger-printed. Dalger also ran this information through all the databases. There was no match; the man was unknown to the investigating authorities. Not even the origin of the ticket gave them anything; it had come from an automatic dispenser in the station.

In the meantime, the videotape from the station had been viewed, and the doctor on the opposite platform and the frightened old lady interviewed. The police had worked with utter thoroughness and utter lack of success.

The man had been arrested and spent the night at the police station. The next day, Dalger had dialled the number on the card. He had waited as long as he could before doing this. Lawyers never make things simple, he thought.

We sat in Dalger's room, drinking lukewarm filtered coffee. I watched the videotape twice and said to Dalger that it was self-evidently a virtual textbook case of self-defence. Dalger didn't want to release the man: 'Something about him doesn't add up.'

'Yes, of course that's obvious. But apart from this instinct of yours, you know you have no grounds to hold him,' I replied.

'We still don't know anything, not even his identity.'

'No, Herr Dalger, that's not anything; it's the *one* thing you don't know.'

Dalger made a call to prosecutor Kesting. It was a so-called Cap-One, which is to say a legal proceeding that fell within the Capital Crimes parameters of the prosecutor's office. Kesting was already familiar with the case from Dalger's first report. He was at a loss, but resolute: a quality that is sometimes effective in the prosecutor's office. Which is why he decided to have the man appear before the examining magistrate. A few telephone calls later, we were given instructions to be there at five that afternoon.

The examining magistrate's name was Lambrecht, and he was wearing a Norwegian sweater, although it was springtime. He suffered from low blood pressure, had felt cold his whole life, which was also why he was in an almost permanent bad temper. He was fifty-two years old, and he wanted clarity; things had to be orderly and he didn't want to take any demons home with him from the office.

Lambrecht was a guest lecturer in trial law at the high school, and because of the real-life examples he used, his lectures had become legendary. He told the students it was a mistake to believe that judges enjoyed convicting people. 'They do it when it is their duty, but they don't do it when they have doubts.' The real meaning of judicial independence was that judges, too, wanted to be able to sleep at night. That was the point at which the students always laughed. Nonetheless, it was the truth; he had come across almost no exceptions.

The job of examining magistrate is perhaps the most interesting in the criminal justice system. You get a brief look into everything, you don't have to put up with boring, long trials, and you aren't obliged to listen to anyone else. But that is only one side of it. The other is the loneliness. The examining magistrate reaches his decisions alone. Everything depends on him: he sends a man to prison or sets him free. There are simpler ways of earning a living.

Lambrecht wasn't exactly thrilled by defence lawyers. But then he wasn't exactly thrilled by prosecutors, either. What interested him was the case, and he reached decisions that were hard to predict in advance. Most people complained about him; his massively oversized glasses and his pale lips gave him a strange look, but he commanded universal respect. At the celebration for his twentieth year on the job, he received a certificate from the president of the district court. The president asked him if he still enjoyed what he did after so many years. Lambrecht's response was that he'd never enjoyed it. He was an independent man.

Lambrecht read the witnesses' statements, and after he, too, failed to get the man to speak, he said he wanted to see the video. We had to watch it with him around a hundred times in succession. I could draw each frame by then; it went on for an eternity.

'Switch the thing off,' he finally said to the sergeant, and turned to face us. 'Now, gentlemen, I'm listening.'

Kesting, naturally, had already provided the request for an arrest warrant, without which there would have been no meeting. He was applying for the man's arrest for two instances of manslaughter, and stating that the man was a flight risk, as he had no provable identity. Kesting said, 'It is certainly plausible that this was a situation involving self-defence. But excessive force was used.'

The prosecutor's office was therefore going for a charge of so-called excessive self-defence. When you are attacked, you have the right to defend yourself, and there is no limit to your choice of means. You may respond to a fist with a cudgel, and to a knife with a gun; you are under no obligation to choose the mildest form of counterattack. But equally, you may not overreact: if you've already rendered your attacker helpless with a pistol shot, you may not cut off his head for good measure. The law does not tolerate such excesses.

'The excess was constituted by the man striking the knife that was already embedded in the victim's chest,' said Kesting.

'Aha,' said Lambrecht. He sounded astonished. 'And now defence counsel, please.'

'We all know this is madness,' I said. 'Nobody is obliged to tolerate an assault with a knife, and of course he was allowed to defend himself in his fashion. And the prosecutor's office is certainly not occupied with these questions. Prosecutor Kesting is far too experienced to believe he could bring any such charge before a jury. He simply wants to establish the man's identity, and needs the time to do so.'

'Is this so, Mr Prosecutor?' asked Lambrecht.

'No,' said Kesting. 'The prosecutor's office does not file frivolous requests for arrest warrants.'

'Aha,' said the judge again. This time, it sounded ironic. He turned toward me. 'And can you tell us who the man is?'

'Herr Lambrecht, you know I may do no such thing, even if I were able. But I can provide a viable address.' I had had another telephone conversation in the meantime with the lawyer who had engaged me. 'The man can be summoned via a lawyer's office, and I can verbally guarantee the lawyer's agreement.' I handed over the address.

'You see!' exclaimed Kesting. 'He declines to speak out. He knows much more, but he declines to speak out.'

'These legal proceedings are not against me,' I said. 'But this is how we find ourselves: we do not know why the accused declines to speak. It's possible he doesn't understand our language. But it's also possible that he's declining to speak for some other—'

'He's contravening paragraph one eleven of the law,' Kesting interrupted. 'It is absolutely clear he's contravening it.'

'Gentlemen, I would be grateful if you would take turns speaking,' said Lambrecht. 'Paragraph one eleven states that every defendant must provide his or her particulars. In this, I agree with the prosecutor's office.' Lambrecht was taking off his glasses, putting them on again, taking them off again. 'But this, of course, in no way constitutes a rule that justifies an order of arrest. Twelve hours are the limit during which a person may be detained simply for purposes of establishing the particulars of an identity. And these twelve hours, Mr Prosecutor, have already long expired.'

'Besides which,' I said, 'the accused is not always invariably obliged to provide all his particulars. If his truthful statements might expose him to the risk of criminal prosecution, he is allowed to remain silent. If the man were to say who he is, and if this were to lead to his arrest, then of course he has the right to remain silent.'

'There you have it,' said Kesting to the examining magistrate. 'He will not tell us who he is, and there's nothing we can do.'

'That's how it is,' I said. 'There's nothing you can do.'

The man sat on the bench, radiating indifference. He was wearing a shirt with my initials on it; I'd had it sent over to him. It fitted him, but it looked odd.

'Mr Prosecutor,' said Lambrecht, 'is there any prior relationship between the accused and the victims?'

'No, we have no such information,' said Kesting.

'Were the victims drunk?' Lambrecht was correct in this line of thought, too; in any situation involving self-defence, a drunk is to be avoided.

'Point zero four and point zero five blood-alcohol levels respectively.'

'That's insufficient,' said Lambrecht. 'Have you found out anything about the perpetrator that is not yet in the files? Is there any evidence of another crime or another arrest warrant?' Lambrecht seemed to be ticking off a list.

'No,' said Kesting, knowing that every 'no' was putting him further and further from his goal.

'Are there any ongoing inquiries?'

'Yes. The complete autopsy report has not yet been delivered.' Kesting was happy he had turned up something he could cite.

'Yes, well, the two of them are unlikely to have died of heatstroke, Herr Kesting.' Lambrecht's voice now softened, a bad sign for the prosecutor's office. 'If the prosecutor has nothing more to produce than what I have here on my table, I will now render my decision.'

Kesting shook his head.

'Gentlemen,' said Lambrecht, 'I have heard enough.' He leaned back. 'The issue of self-defence is more than clear. If someone is threatened with a knife and a baseball bat, if he's stabbed and swung at, he is allowed to defend himself. He is allowed to defend himself in such a way that the attack is definitively ended, and the accused did no more than that.'

Lambrecht paused for a moment, then went on: 'I agree with the prosecutor that the case seems unusual. I can only say that I find the calm with which the accused faced the victims frightening. But I cannot recognise where the claim of excessive force resides. The correctness of this conclusion is also demonstrated by the fact that I would certainly have granted an order of arrest against the two attackers if they were in front of me now instead of lying on the pathologist's table.'

Kesting clapped his files shut. The noise was too loud.

Lambrecht dictated into the records, 'The prosecutor's request for an arrest warrant is hereby denied. The accused is to be released forthwith.' Then he turned to Kesting and me. 'That's all. Have a good evening.'

While the court recorder was preparing the release form, I went outside. Dalger was sitting on the visitor's bench, waiting.

'Good evening. What are you doing here?' I asked. It's unusual for a policeman to show such interest in the outcome of a legal proceeding.

'Is he out?'

'Yes. It was a clear case of self-defence.'

Dalger shook his head. 'Thought so,' he said. He was a good policeman who hadn't had any sleep for the last twenty-six hours. The business was obviously annoying him, and this was, obviously, equally unusual for him.

'What's up?'

'Well, you don't know about the other thing.'

'What other thing?'

'The same morning your client was taken into custody, we found a dead body in Wilmersdorf. Stabbed in the heart. No fingerprints, no traces of DNA, no fibres, nothing. Everyone associated with the dead man has an alibi, and the seventy-two hours are running out.'

The seventy-two-hour rule states that the chances of solving a murder or manslaughter start to decline rapidly after seventy-two hours.

'What are you trying to say?'

'It was a professional job.'

'Stab wounds to the heart are not infrequent,' I said.

'Yes and no. At least they're not this precise. Most people need to stab more than once, or the knife gets stuck in the ribs. It usually goes wrong.'

'And?'

'I have this feeling . . . your client . . .'

Naturally, it was more than a feeling. Every year, around 2,400 fatal crimes are recorded in Germany, approximately 140 of them in Berlin. That's more than in Frankfurt, Hamburg and Cologne combined, but even with an annual success rate of 95 percent, that leaves seven cases a year in which the perpetrator is never caught. And here a man had just been released who fitted perfectly into Dalger's theory.

'Herr Dalger, your feeling—' I began, but he didn't let me finish.

'Yes, yes, I know,' he said, and turned away. I called after him that he should phone me if there were any new developments. Dalger muttered something incomprehensible, along the lines of 'no cause . . . lawyers . . . always the same . . .' and went home.

* * *

SELF-DEFENCE

The man was released straight from the hearing room, he collected his money and the other objects, and I signed for him. We walked to my car and I drove him to the same station where he had killed two men thirty-five hours earlier. He got out without saying a word and disappeared into the crowd. I never saw him again.

A week later, I had a lunch date with the head of the corporate law firm. 'So who is your key client who wanted an unknown man looked after?' I asked.

'I'm not permitted to tell you; you would know him. And I myself don't know who the unknown man is. But I have something for you,' he said, and pulled out a bag. It held the shirt I'd given the man. It had been cleaned and ironed.

On the way to the parking lot I threw it in the garbage.

Green

They had brought a sheep again. The four men stood around the animal in their rubber boots and stared at it. They had driven it into the court-yard of the manor house in the bed of a pickup truck, and now it was lying there in the drizzle on a sheet of blue plastic. The sheep's throat had been cut and its mud-stained fleece was dotted with stab wounds. The crusted blood was gradually dissolving again in the rain, running across the plastic in thin red threads until it seeped away among the paving stones.

Death was no stranger to any of the men; they were livestock farmers, and every one of them had slaughtered animals before. But this dead body was giving them the shivers: the sheep was a Bleu-du-Maine, a vigorous breed with a bluish head and prominent eyes. The animal's eyeballs had been gouged out and the rims of the dark eye sockets showed the frayed remains of the optic nerves and cords of muscle.

Count Nordeck greeted the men with a nod; nobody was in the mood to talk. He glanced briefly at the animal, shaking his head, then pulled a wallet out of his jacket pocket, counted out four hundred euros, and gave the money to one of the men. It was more than double what the sheep was worth. One of the farmers, capturing what every one of them was thinking, said, 'This can't go on.' As the men drove away from the yard, Nordeck turned up his coat collar. The farmers are right, he thought. I have to speak to him.

Angelika Petersson was a fat, contented woman. She had been the policewoman in Nordeck for twenty-two years, there had never been a killing in her district in all that time, and she had never needed to draw her gun in the course of duty. Work was over for the day, and she'd completed the report on the drunk driver. She rocked her chair back and forth, enjoying the prospect of the weekend, despite the rain. She would finally get around to sticking the photos from her last holiday into the album.

When the bell rang, Petersson groaned. She pressed the buzzer; no one came through the door, so she got to her feet with a sigh and a curse and went out onto the street. She wanted to give an earful to the village boys who still thought this idiotic game of ringing bells was funny.

Petersson almost didn't recognise Philipp von Nordeck standing on the footpath outside the guardhouse. It was pouring. Thick strands of wet hair hung down into his face, and his jacket was dripping mud and blood. He was holding the kitchen knife so tightly that his knucklebones stood out white. Water was running over the blade.

Philipp was nineteen, and Petersson had known him since he was a child. She walked up to him slowly, speaking to him soothingly and quietly, the way she had once talked to the horses on her father's farm. She took the knife out of his hand and stroked his head; he made no protest. Then she put an arm around his shoulders, led him up the two shallow stone steps into the little building, and took him to the washroom.

'Just get yourself cleaned up; you look awful,' she said. She was no forensic detective, and she just felt sorry for Philipp.

He let the hot water run and run over his

hands until they turned red and the mirror fogged up. Then he bent over and washed his face; blood and dirt sluiced into the washbasin and clogged the drain. He stared into the basin and whispered, 'Eighteen.' Petersson didn't understand him. She took him into the little guardroom where she had her desk. The air smelled of tea and floor polish.

'Now please tell me what happened,' said Petersson as she sat him down in the visitor's chair. Philipp laid his forehead against the edge of her desk, closed his eyes, and said nothing.

'You know what, we're going to call your father.'

Nordeck came at once, but the only thing Philipp said was 'Eighteen. It was an eighteen.'

Petersson explained to the father that she would have to notify the local prosecutor's office, as she didn't know if something bad had happened, and Philipp wasn't saying anything that made sense.

Nordeck nodded. 'Of course,' he said, and thought, Here we go.

The prosecutor mobilised two detectives from the nearest town. When they arrived, Petersson and Nordeck were drinking tea in the office. Philipp was sitting by the window, looking out, totally cut off.

The detectives gave him the usual formal notice that he was being taken into custody, then left him under Petersson's charge. They wanted to go to the manor house with Nordeck to search Philipp's room. Nordeck showed them the two rooms on the second floor that the boy occupied. While one of the policemen was taking a look around, Nordeck stood with the other in the entrance hall. The walls were hung with hundreds of antlers of native animals, and trophies from Africa. It was cold.

The policeman stood before the enormous stuffed head of a black buffalo from East Africa. Nordeck was trying to explain the thing with the sheep. 'This is how it is,' he said, searching for the right words. 'In the last few months, Philipp has killed some sheep. Well, he slit their throats. The farmers caught him at it once and told me about it.'

'Ah, slit their throats,' said the policeman. 'These buffalo weigh more than one tonne, don't they?'

'Yes, they're pretty dangerous. A lion doesn't stand a chance against a full-grown specimen.'

'So, the boy slaughtered sheep, yes?' The detective could hardly tear himself away from the buffalo.

Nordeck took this to be a good sign. 'Of course I paid compensation for the sheep, and we also wanted to have Philipp begin ... But somehow we were hoping it would all blow over. We were wrong.' Better leave out the details about the stab wounds and the eyes, thought Nordeck.

'Why does he do it?'

'I don't know. I have no idea.'

'Sounds odd, no?'

'Yes, it's odd. We have to do something with him,' Nordeck said again.

'Looks that way. Do you know what happened today?'

'What do you mean?'

'Well, was it another sheep?' asked the detective. He simply couldn't leave the buffalo alone, and had put his hands on the horns.

'Yes, one of the farmers called my mobile phone a little while ago. He's found another.'

The policeman nodded absentmindedly. He was annoyed at having to spend his Friday evening with a sheep killer, but the buffalo wasn't bad at all. He asked Nordeck if he could go to police headquarters in town on Monday to give a brief statement. He'd had enough of paperwork and wanted to get home.

'Of course,' said Nordeck.

The second detective came down the stairs holding an old cigar box with VILLIGER KIEL on it in brownish-yellow lettering.

'We have to impound this box,' he said.

Nordeck realised that the policeman's voice had suddenly taken on an official tone. Even the latex gloves he was wearing somehow conveyed a new formality. 'If you think so,' said Nordeck. 'What's in there? Philipp doesn't even smoke.'

'I found this box behind a loose tile in the bathroom,' said the policeman. Nordeck was angered by the very idea that there were loose tiles in the house at all. The policeman cautiously opened the box. His colleague and Nordeck leaned forward, then immediately recoiled.

The box was lined with plastic and divided into two compartments. An eyeball, somewhat compressed and still a little wet, stared out of each compartment. A photograph of a girl was glued to the inside of the lid—Nordeck recognised her immediately: it was Sabine, the daughter of Gerike, the primary school teacher. She had celebrated her sixteenth birthday the previous day. Philipp had been there, and he had often talked about her before. Nordeck had assumed his son had fallen in love with her. But now he blanched: the girl in the picture had no eyes—they'd been cut out.

Nordeck, hands trembling, hunted for the teacher's phone number in his address book. He held the receiver so that the policemen could listen in. Gerike was surprised by the phone call. No, Sabine was not at home. She had gone on directly after the birthday party to visit a friend in Munich. No, she hadn't yet checked in, but that was nothing unusual.

Gerike tried to calm Nordeck: 'Everything's okay. Philipp took her to the night train.'

The police questioned two employees at the train station, they turned Nordeck's house upside down, and they interviewed everyone who'd been at the birthday party. It all produced nothing about where Sabine might actually be.

The pathologist examined the eyes in the cigar box. They were sheep's eyes. And the blood on Philipp's clothing was animal blood.

A few hours after Philipp's arrest, a farmer found another sheep behind his farmyard. He loaded it onto his shoulders and carried it down the village street in the rain all the way to the police station. The animal's fleece was saturated; it was heavy. Blood and water streamed down over the farmer's waxed jacket. He threw the carcass down onto the steps of the station house; the wet fleece smacked against the door and left a dark stain on the wood.

Halfway between the manor house and the village, which consisted of roughly two hundred low houses, a narrow path branched off and led to the abandoned reed-thatched Friesian house on the dike. By day, it was the focal point of children's games; by night, couples met under the pergola. You could hear the sea from here, and the crying of the gulls.

The detectives found Sabine's mobile phone in the wet beach grass, and, not far from it, a hair band. Sabine had been wearing it the evening of her birthday, her father said. The area was sealed off and a hundred policemen combed the marshland with their bloodhounds. Forensic investigators in their white overalls were summoned and did a search for further evidence, but they found nothing more.

The army of policemen also attracted the press to Nordeck, and anyone who set foot on the street was interviewed. Almost no one left the house, curtains stayed closed, and even the village tavern remained empty. Only the journalists with their garish computer bags filled the tables in the bar, laptops open, cursing the slow internet connection and stringing one another along with invented pieces of news.

It had been raining uninterrupted for days, at night the mist pressed down heavily on the roofs of the low houses, and even the cattle seemed to be morose. The villagers talked about it all, and they no longer greeted Nordeck when they saw him.

On the fifth day after Philipp's arrest, the media liaison in the prosecutor's office issued a photograph of Sabine to the newspapers, along with an appeal for information as to her whereabouts. The next day, someone smeared the word *murderer* in red on the wooden gate to the manor house.

Philipp was in jail. For the first three days, he said almost nothing, and the few words he did utter were incomprehensible. On the fourth day, he pulled himself together. The police took his statement; he was open and answered their questions. It was only when they tried to talk about the sheep that he hung his head and fell silent. Naturally, the detectives were more interested in Sabine, but Philipp kept repeating his explanation that he'd taken her to the train station. Before that, they'd gone to the house on the dike and talked. 'Like friends,' he said. Maybe that was when she'd mislaid her mobile phone and the hair band. He had done nothing to her. There was nothing more to be pried out of him. And he didn't want to speak to the psychiatrist.

Prosecutor Krauther led the interrogations. He slept so badly in the course of those days that his wife told him at breakfast he was grinding his teeth at night. His problem was that nothing had apparently gone on prior to this. Philipp von Nordeck had killed some sheep, but that was no more than property damage, technically speaking, and an offence against animal-protection laws. There had been no claim for financial damages, the sheep had been paid for by his father, and none of the farmers had filed charges. Sabine had not, indeed, arrived at her friend's in Munich. 'But she's a young girl, and the fact that she hasn't been heard from could be for any number of innocent reasons,' Krauther said to his wife. The cigar box was no proof, in and of itself, that Philipp had murdered the girl, even if the examining magistrate had accepted the premise of the prosecutor's application for an arrest warrant thus far. Krauther felt uneasy.

Because there weren't many cases out here in the country that raised these sorts of questions, Philipp's medical examination at least had gone quickly. No results indicating brain malfunction, no disease of the central nervous system, and no anomalies of the chromosomes. But, thought Krauther, he is, of course, absolutely insane.

When I had my first meeting with the prosecutor, it was six days after the arrest, and the review of his remand in custody was due the next day. Krauther looked tired, but he seemed pleased to be able to share his thoughts with somebody. 'Aberrant behaviour,' he said, 'has a tendency to escalate rather rapidly. If his victims have thus far been limited to sheep, couldn't they now be people?'

Wilfred Rasch established a reputation unchallenged in his lifetime as the doyen of forensic psychiatry. The view that aberrant behaviour intensifies over time is one of his scientific theories. But from everything we knew thus far about Philipp's acts, it struck me as unlikely that we were dealing with such an aberration.

Before my conversation with Krauther, I had talked to the veterinarian who, on orders from

Nordeck, had destroyed the animals' remains. The police had had better things to do than interview this man, or perhaps quite simply nobody had thought to do so. The vet was a meticulous observer, and the incidents had struck him as so bizarre that he had written a short report on every dead sheep. I gave his notes to the prosecutor, who made a rapid survey. Each sheep gave evidence of eighteen stab wounds. Krauther looked at me. The policemen had also mentioned that Philipp had uttered nothing but the word *eighteen*. So it might have to do with the number itself in some way.

I said I did not think Philipp exhibited deviant sexual behaviour. The pathologist had examined the last sheep, but had found no evidence that Philipp had been sexually aroused by the killing of the animals. There was no sperm and no sign that he had penetrated the sheep.

'I don't believe Philipp suffers from perversities,' I said.

'So then what?'

'He may very well be schizophrenic,' I said.

'Schizophrenic?'

'Yes, there's something that's terrifying him.'

'That may be. But he won't talk to the psychiatrist,' said Krauther.

'Nor is he obliged to,' I replied. 'It's very simple, Herr Krauther. You have nothing. You have no corpse and you have no proof of any crime. You don't even have evidence that might point toward it. You had Philipp von Nordeck locked up because he killed sheep. But the arrest warrant was issued for the killing of Sabine Gerike. Nonsense. The only reason he's in custody is because you sort of have a bad feeling about things.'

Krauther knew I was right. And I knew that he knew. Sometimes it's easier to be a defence lawyer than a prosecutor. My task was to be partisan and to stand in front of my clients. Krauther had to remain neutral. And he couldn't. 'If only the girl would show up again,' he said. Krauther was sitting with his back to the window. The rain hit the glass and slicked down it in broad streams. He turned in his office chair and followed my eyes to the outdoors and the grey sky. We sat there for almost five minutes, looking at the rain, and neither of us said a word.

I spent the night at the Nordecks'; the last time I'd been there was nineteen years ago for Philipp's christening. During dinner, a windowpane was shattered by a flying stone. Nordeck said it was the fifth time this week, so what was the point of calling the police. But he thought maybe I should get my car and drive it into one of the barns on the farm; otherwise, my tyres would be slashed by morning.

As I was lying in bed sometime around midnight, Philipp's sister Victoria came into the room. She was five, and her pyjamas were very jazzy. 'Can you bring Philipp home?' she asked. I got up, lifted her onto my shoulders, and took her back to her bedroom. The lintels were high enough to avoid any risk of her bumping her head, one of the few advantages of an old house. I sat down on her bed and pulled the covers up around her.

'Have you ever had a cold?' I asked her.

'Yes.'

'Well, Philipp's got something like a cold in his head. He's not so well and he needs to get better.'

'How does he sneeze in his head?' she asked. My example obviously was a bit problematic.

'You can't sneeze in your head. Philipp's just all muddled up. Maybe the same way you are when you've had a bad dream.'

'But when I wake up, everything comes right again.'

'Exactly. Philipp needs to wake up properly.'

'Are you going to bring him back here?'

'I don't know,' I said. 'I'm going to try.'

'Nadine said Philipp did something bad.'

'Who's Nadine?'

'Nadine's my best friend.'

'Philipp isn't bad, Victoria. You need to go to sleep now.'

Victoria didn't want to go to sleep. She wasn't happy that I knew so little, and she was worried about her brother. Then she asked me to tell her a story. I invented one that had no sheep in it and nobody who was sick. When she'd gone to sleep, I fetched my files and my laptop and worked in her room until the morning. She woke up twice, sat up for a moment, looked at me, and then went back to sleep again. At about 6:00 a.m., I borrowed one of the pairs of rubber boots standing in the hall and went out into the yard to smoke a cigarette. The air was raw, I was bleary-eyed from lack of sleep, and there were only eight hours until the custody hearing.

The day brought no news of Sabine, either. She'd now been missing for a week. Prosecutor Krauther was filing for an extension.

Most custody hearings are a grim business. The law requires that there be an investigation of whether there is a compelling reason to believe that the person being held in custody has committed a crime. This sounds clear and unambiguous, but is hard to grapple with in reality. At this point, the interviews of witnesses have barely begun, the legal proceedings are just starting, and there is no general overview. The judge may not make things simple for himself; he has to decide about the incarceration of someone who may not be guilty at all. Custody hearings are much less formal than trials, the public is not admitted, judges, prosecutors and defence lawyers don't wear robes, and in practice it's a serious conversation about the questions surrounding the prolonging of detention.

The examining magistrate in the case against Philipp von Nordeck was a young man who had just finished his probationary period. He was nervous and didn't want to make any mistakes. After half an hour, he said he'd heard the arguments and his decision would be issued departmentally— that is, he wanted to use the fourteen-day grace period to await further evidence. It was unsatisfying all round.

When I left the court, the rain was still coming down in buckets.

★ ★ ★

175

Sabine was sitting on a wooden bench on the lower deck of the ferry between Kollund and Flensburg. She had spent a happy, if wet, week with Lars at the seaside resort, which had almost nothing to offer except its beach and a furniture store. Lars was a young construction worker who had the name of his football club tattooed on his back. Sabine had kept the week with him a secret from her parents; her father didn't like Lars. Her parents trusted her, and anyway, she doubted they would call her on their own account.

Lars had accompanied her to the boat, and now Sabine was afraid. From the moment she'd boarded the little ferry, the man with the threadbare jacket had been staring at her. He was still looking right at her face, and now he was coming over to where she was. She was about to stand up and move away when the man said, 'Are you Sabine Gerike?'

'Um, yes.'

'For god's sake, girl, call home at once. They're looking for you everywhere. Take a look at the newspaper.'

Shortly after this, the phone rang in Sabine's parents' house, and half an hour later Prosecutor Krauther called me. He said Sabine had simply run off with her boyfriend and was expected back that afternoon. Philipp would be released, but he must be placed in psychiatric care. I had just agreed on this with Philipp and his father anyway. Krauther made me promise formally that I would take care of this.

I collected Philipp from the detention centre, which looked like a little jail in a children's book. Philipp, of course, was overjoyed to be free and to know that Sabine was fine. On the way back to his parents' house, I asked him if he'd like to go for a walk. We stopped by a path across the fields. The cloudy sky above us was enormous, the rain had stopped, and you could hear the harsh cries of the gulls. We talked about his boarding school, his love of motorbikes, and the music he was listening to right now. Suddenly, out of nowhere, he said what he hadn't wanted to say to the psychiatrist: 'I see people and animals as numbers.'

'How do you mean?'

'When I see an animal, it has a number. For example, the cow over there is a thirty-six. The gull's a twenty-two. The judge was a fifty-one, and the prosecutor a twenty-three.'

'Do you think about this?'

'No, I see it. I see it right away. The same way other people see faces. I don't ever think about it; it's just there.'

'And do I have a number?'

'Yes, five. A good number.' We both had to laugh. It was the first time since he'd been arrested. We walked on silently side by side.

'Philipp, what is it with eighteen?'

He looked at me, startled. 'Why eighteen?'

'You said it to the policewoman, and you killed the sheep with eighteen stab wounds.'

'No, that's not right. I killed them first and then I stabbed them six times in each side and then six times in the back. I had to take the eyes out, too. It was hard, the first few times they came apart.' Philipp began to tremble. Then he blurted out, 'I'm afraid of eighteen. It's the devil. Three times six. Eighteen. Do you get it?'

I glanced at him questioningly.

'The apocalypse. The Antichrist. It's the number of the beast and the number of the devil.' He was almost screaming.

The number 666 is indeed in the Bible; it appears in the Revelation of Saint John: 'Here is wisdom. Let him that hath understanding count the number of the beast: for it is the number of a man; and his number is six hundred threescore and six.' It was a popular belief that with these words the Evangelist was alluding to the devil.

'If I don't kill the sheep, the eyes will consume the land with fire. The apples of the eye are sin itself; they are the apples from the tree of knowledge, and they will destroy everything.' Philipp began to cry with a child's lack of all restraint, shaking from head to foot.

'Philipp, please listen to me. You're afraid of the sheep and their terrible eyes. I can understand that. But the whole thing with the Revelation of Saint John is absolutely cuckoo. John didn't mean the devil when he used the number six sixty-six; it was a hidden play on the name of Nero, the Roman Caesar.'

'What?'

'If you add up the numbers in the Hebrew spelling of Caesar Nero, you get six sixty-six. That's all. Saint John couldn't write that out; he had to say it in numbers. It has nothing to do with the Antichrist.'

Philipp kept crying. There was no point in telling him that there's nowhere in the Bible that talks about an apple tree in paradise. Philipp was living in his own world. At a certain point, he began to calm down, and we walked back to the car. The air had been washed clean and tasted of salt. 'I have one last question,' I said after a while.

'And?'

'What does all this have to do with Sabine? Why did you do that with her eyes?'

'A few days before her birthday, I saw her eyes in my room,' said Philipp. 'They'd become sheep's eyes. And that's when I understood. I told her that evening of her birthday in the house on the dike, but she didn't want to hear it. She got frightened.'

'What was it that you understood?' I asked.

'Her first name and her last name each have six letters.'

'Did you want to kill her?'

Philipp looked at me for a long time. Then he said, 'No, I don't want to kill anyone.'

A week later, I took Philipp to a psychiatric clinic in Switzerland. He didn't want his father to go with us. After we'd unpacked his suitcase, we were welcomed by the head of the hospital, who showed us around the bright and airy modern buildings. Philipp was in a good place, insofar as you can say that about any mental hospital.

I had had lengthy phone conversations with the chief of medicine. He, too, even at long distance, had agreed that everything pointed to a case of paranoid schizophrenia. It is not an infrequent disorder; the evidence suggests that approximately 1 percent of the population will be afflicted with it once in their lives. It often manifests itself in phases that lead to the disruption of thought processes and perceptions, distorting both their form and content. Most patients hear voices; many believe they're being pursued, that they're responsible for catastrophes of nature, or they're tortured, like Philipp, by mad ideas. The treatment involves both drugs and extensive psychotherapy. Patients need to be able to trust, and to open themselves up. The odds of a full recovery are around 30 percent.

At the end of the tour, Philipp came with me to the main door. He was just a lonely, sad, anxious boy. He said, 'You never asked what number I am.'

'That's true. And what number are you?'

'Green,' he said, and he turned on his heel and went back into the clinic.

The Thorn

Feldmayer had already had many jobs in his life. He'd been a mailman, a waiter, a photographer, a pizza maker and, for six months, a blacksmith. When he was thirty-five, he applied for a post as guard in the local museum of antiquities and got it, greatly to his astonishment.

After he'd filled out all the forms, answered the questions, and provided photographs for his building pass, he went to the uniform store, where he was handed out three grey uniforms, six medium-blue shirts, and two pairs of black shoes. A future colleague led him through the building, showed him the canteen and the rest rooms, and explained how to use the time clock. At the end, he was shown the room he would be guarding.

While Feldmayer was going through the museum, Frau Truckau, one of the two employees in HR, organised his documents, sent some of them to Accounts, and started a file. The names of the guards were put on little cards and sorted into a file-card box. Every six weeks, the staff was shuffled in different combinations to another of the town's museums, to make the work more varied.

Frau Truckau thought about her boyfriend. Yesterday, in the café where they'd been meeting for almost eight months after work, he'd asked her to marry him. He'd turned red and stuttered. His hands had been damp; they'd left outlines on the little marble table. She had leapt to her feet with joy, kissed him in front of everyone, and then they'd run to his apartment. Now she was dead tired and bursting with plans; she would be seeing him again very soon; he'd promised to pick her up from work. She spent half an hour on the toilet, sharpened pencils, sorted paper clips, dawdled around in the hall, until finally she'd made it. She threw on her jacket, ran down the stairs to the exit, and fell into his arms. But she'd forgotten to close the window.

When the cleaning lady opened the door to the office later, a gust of wind seized the half-completed file card, which was blown to the floor and then swept up. The next day, Frau

Truckau was thinking about everything imaginable, except for Feldmayer's file card. His name
did not become part of the staff-rotation system,
and when Frau Truckau went on maternity
leave a year later because of her baby, he'd been
forgotten.

Feldmayer never complained.

The hall was almost empty, eight metres high and
roughly one hundred and fifty square metres. The
walls and vaulted ceiling were built of brick, their
red tempered to a warm glow by a coat of lime
wash. The floor was made of grey-blue marble. It
was at the end of a run of twelve interconnecting
rooms in one wing of the museum. A bust stood
in the centre of the hall, mounted on a grey stone
plinth. The chair stood under the middle one of
the three tall windows, and the window seat to the
left held a machine that measured the humidity. It
had a glass cover and ticked gently. Outside the
window was an inner courtyard with a solitary
chestnut tree. The next guard was installed four
rooms farther along; sometimes Feldmayer could
hear the distant squeaking of his rubber-soled
shoes on the stone floor. Otherwise, all was silent.
Feldmayer sat down and waited.

In the first weeks, he was restless, stood up every five minutes, walked around his hall, counted every step he took, and was happy to see each visitor. Feldmayer looked for things to do. He measured his hall, his only assistance a wooden ruler he'd brought from home. First, he measured the length and width of one of the marble floor slabs, then used that to calculate the size of the floor. Then he realised he'd forgotten the cracks, so he measured these as well and added them to the total. The walls and ceiling were harder, but Feldmayer had plenty of time. He kept a school notebook, in which he entered every measurement. He measured the doors and their frames, the size of the keyholes, the length of the handles, the skirting boards, the radiator covers, the window catches, the distance between the double glazing, the circumference of the humidity machine, and the light switches. He knew how many cubic metres of air there were in the hall, and how far and to which marble slab the sun's rays penetrated on every day of the year; he knew the average humidity level and its variations in the morning, at midday, and in the evening. He noted that the fifth crack between the marble slabs, counting from the door, was half a millimetre narrower than the others. The second window catch to the left had a dash of blue on the underside, something he couldn't explain, for there was nothing blue in the hall. The painter had missed a spot on the radiator cover, and there were pin-sized holes in the bricks on the back wall.

Feldmayer counted the visitors and noted how long they spent in his hall, which side they chose to view the statue from, how often they looked out of the window, who gave him a nod. He assembled statistics about male versus female visitors, about children, about classes and their teachers, about the colours of jackets, shirts, coats, pullovers, trousers, skirts and stockings. He counted how often anyone breathed in his hall, and registered how often which marble slabs got stepped on, and how often which words got spoken the most. There was one statistic for hair colour, another for eye colour, another for skin colour, yet another for shawls, for purses, for belts, and one for bald spots, for beards, and for wedding rings. He counted the flies and tried to evolve a system to account for their flight patterns and landing spots.

The museum changed Feldmayer. It began when he found himself unable to tolerate the sound of his TV in the evenings. He let it run on mute for another six months, then stopped turning it on at all, then finally gave it to the young student couple who had moved into the apartment across the hall. The next thing was the pictures. He had a few art prints, *Apples on a Cloth*, *Sunflowers* and *The Alps*. At some point, the colours began to irritate him; he took the pictures off the wall and put them in the trash. He gradually emptied his apartment: illustrated magazines, vases, decorated ashtrays, coasters, a lilac bedspread, and two plates with motifs from Toledo. Feldmayer threw them all away. He stripped the wallpaper, spackled the walls smooth and whitewashed them, got rid of the carpet, and polished the floorboards.

After a few years, Feldmayer's life had an absolutely set rhythm. He got up every morning at 6:00 a.m. Then, regardless of the weather, he walked through the municipal garden in a circle that required precisely 5,400 steps. He moved unhurriedly and knew exactly when the traffic light at the street crossing would switch to green. If ever he failed to keep to this rhythm, the rest of his day felt wrong.

Every evening, he put on a pair of old trousers and got down on his knees to polish the floorboards in his apartment—a demanding job that took almost an hour and calmed him. He did the housework with care and slept a deep, quiet sleep. On Sunday, he always went to the same local restaurant, where he ordered a grilled chicken and had two beers. Mostly, he talked to the owner, with whom he'd been at school.

Before the museum, Feldmayer had always had girlfriends, but then they began to interest him less and less. They were simply 'too much', as he said to the restaurant's owner. 'They're loud and they ask things I don't have answers to, and I can't tell them about my work.'

Feldmayer's only hobby was photography. He owned a beautiful Leica, which he'd bought secondhand at a very good price; in one of his jobs, he'd learned to develop his own films. He'd set up a darkroom in the storage closet of his apartment, but after years in the museum, he couldn't think of any possible subjects.

He phoned his mother regularly and visited her every three weeks. When she died, he had no relatives anymore. He had his phone disconnected.

His life flowed along quietly, and he avoided any form of excitement. He was neither happy nor unhappy—just content with his life.

Until he got involved with the sculpture.

★ ★ ★

It was the thorn puller, one of the motifs of classical art. A naked boy sits on a boulder, leaning forward, his left leg bent and resting on his right thigh. With his left hand, he holds his left instep as his right hand pulls a thorn out of the sole of his foot. The marble figure in Feldmayer's hall was a Roman copy of the Greek original. It wasn't particularly valuable; there were countless such copies.

Feldmayer had measured the figure long ago, had read everything about it he could find, and would even have been able to draw from memory the shadow it cast on the floor. But sometime between his seventh and eighth year at the museum, he couldn't remember exactly anymore. That was when the trouble began. Feldmayer was sitting in his chair looking at the statue without really seeing it, when he suddenly asked himself if the boy had in fact found the thorn in his foot. He didn't know where the question came from; it was just there, and it wouldn't go away.

He went over to the figure and examined it. He couldn't find the thorn in the foot. Feldmayer became nervous, a feeling he hadn't had in years. The longer he looked, the less clear it seemed to him that the naked boy had actually managed to get hold of the thorn. That night Feldmayer slept badly. The next morning, he skipped the circuit of the municipal garden and spilled his coffee. He arrived at the museum too early and had to wait half an hour for the staff entrance to open. There was a magnifying glass in his pocket. He all but ran to his hall, then used the magnifying glass to examine the statue millimetre by millimetre. He found no thorn, either between the boy's thumb and forefinger or in his foot. Feldmayer wondered if maybe the boy had dropped it. He crawled around the statue on his knees, searching the floor. Then he felt sick and he went to the toilet and threw up.

Feldmayer wished he'd never discovered the problem with the thorn.

In the following weeks, things went downhill. He sat in the hall every day with the boy and brooded. He imagined the boy playing, maybe hide-and-seek or football. Then Feldmayer, having read about this, thought, 'No, it must have been a footrace. They were always having those in Greece. And the boy had felt a tiny prickle, which hurt, and he'd no longer been able to put weight on that foot. The others had run way ahead, but he'd had to sit down on the boulder. And the damn invisible thorn had now been sticking in his foot for hundreds and hundreds of years and was refusing to be pulled out'. Feldmayer got more and more upset. After a few months, he was having anxiety attacks as soon as he woke up. In the mornings, he kept wandering around in the staff room and (this was the man his colleagues called 'the monk' behind his back) spent time in the canteen gossiping with anyone around, doing whatever he could to postpone his arrival in his hall until the very last minute. When he was finally there with the boy, he couldn't look at him.

It got worse. Feldmayer had sweating attacks, suffered palpitations, and started biting his fingernails. He could hardly get to sleep; when he nodded off, he had nightmares, from which he awoke soaking wet. His everyday life was no more than a shell. Soon he began to believe that the thorn was inside his head and still growing. It was scraping against the inner surface of his skull; Feldmayer could *hear* it. Everything in his life that had been empty, calm and ordered until now was transformed into a chaos of pointed barbs. And there was no way out. He had lost all sense of smell; and was having trouble breathing. Sometimes he got so little air that he did what was absolutely forbidden and pulled open one of the windows in the hall. He ate only the tiniest amounts, because he believed the food was going to choke him. He convinced himself that the boy's foot had become infected, and when he stole a glance now and then, he was sure the boy was growing bigger by the day. He had to set him free; he had to release him from the pain. Which is how Feldmayer came upon the idea of the drawing pins.

In an office-supply shop, he bought a box of drawing pins with strikingly harsh yellow heads. He bought the smallest ones he could find; he didn't want the pain to be too great. There was a shoe shop three streets farther on. Feldmayer didn't have to wait long: a scrawny man tried on a shoe, cried out in pain, hopped over to a bench on one leg, cursing, and pulled a yellow drawing pin out of the ball of his foot. He held it up against the light between his thumb and forefinger and showed it to the other customers.

Feldmayer's brain released so many endorphins at the sight of the drawing pin being removed that it almost undid him. Pure joy flooded him for hours on end. Every inhibition and every sense of impotence disappeared at a stroke. He longed to embrace the wounded boy and the entire universe. In the wake of this high, he finally, after many months, managed to sleep through the night and had a recurring dream: the boy pulled out the thorn, stood up, laughed, and waved at him.

A mere ten days went by before the boy with the thorn held out his wounded foot to him again in reproach. Feldmayer groaned, but he knew what had to be done; the little box with the drawing pins was still in his pocket.

He had worked for the museum for twenty-three years and now within a few minutes his time there would be over. Feldmayer stood up and gave his legs a shake; recently they had often gone numb from his sitting so long. Another two minutes, and that would be that. He set the chair under the middle window, the way he had found it on his first day, then straightened it and dusted it with his jacket sleeve, then for the last time he went over to the statue.

He had never in twenty-three years touched the boy pulling out the thorn. Nor had he planned any of what happened next. He saw himself grip the statue with both hands; he felt the smooth, cool marble as he lifted it off the plinth. It was heavier than he expected. He held it up to his face—it was very close to him now—then higher and higher above his head, and then he stood on tiptoes so that it was as high as he could manage. He held it this way for almost a minute, until he began to tremble. He breathed as deeply as he could, then hurled the statue to the floor with all his strength and screamed. Feldmayer screamed louder than he had ever screamed in his whole life. His scream rang through the rooms, bouncing from wall to wall, and was so terrible that a waitress in the museum café nine rooms away dropped a loaded tray. The sculpture shattered on the floor with a dull crash and one of the marble slabs cracked.

Then something strange happened. It seemed to Feldmayer that the blood in his veins changed colour, it turned bright red. He felt it surge and pulse from his stomach, spreading throughout his body, all the way to the tips of his fingers and toes, illuminating him from inside. The cracked marble slab, the indentations in the brick walls, the motes of dust all became three-dimensional. Everything swelled toward him. The flying splinters of marble seemed to stand still in midair. Then he saw the thorn. It glinted with a strange light; he saw it from all sides at once before it dissolved and vanished.

Feldmayer sank to his knees, lifted his head slowly, and looked out of the window. The chestnut tree stood veiled in the soft green that only the first days of spring could summon, and the afternoon sun was casting flickering shadows on the floor of the hall. The pain had ceased. Feldmayer sensed the warmth on his face, his nose itched, and then he began to laugh. He laughed and laughed. He was clutching his stomach with laughter and couldn't stop.

The two policemen who took Feldmayer home were surprised by the meagre furnishings in his apartment. They sat him down on one of the two chairs in the kitchen, intending to wait until he'd calmed down and perhaps would be able to explain things.

One of the policemen went in search of the bathroom. He opened the bedroom door by mistake, stepped into the dark room, and groped for a light switch. And this was when he saw it: the walls and ceiling were papered with thousands of photos, stuck one over the other; there wasn't an empty inch of space. They were even lying on the floor and the night table. Every one of them featured the same thing; only the location changed. Men, women and children sat on steps, on chairs, on sofas, and on window seats; they sat in swimming pools, shoe shops, meadows, and on the banks of lakes. And all of them were pulling a yellow drawing pin out of one foot.

The directors of the museum pressed charges against Feldmayer for damaging their property and wanted to sue him for financial restitution. The prosecutor's office investigated hundreds of cases of grievous bodily harm. The head of the relevant department decided to have Feldmayer examined by an expert psychiatrist. It was a remarkable report. The psychiatrist couldn't make up his mind: on the one hand, he thought Feldmayer had been in the grip of a psychosis; on the other hand, it was possible that he had healed himself by the very act of destroying the statue. Perhaps Feldmayer was dangerous, and one day the drawing pins would be knives instead. But then again, perhaps not.

Finally, the prosecutor brought charges that would involve a trial by jury. This signified that he was going for a sentence of two to four years. When such charges are brought, the judge must decide whether they are sufficient to order a trial.

The judge institutes proceedings if he considers that a verdict of guilty is more likely than one of not guilty. At least that's what it says in the textbooks. In reality, quite different questions come into play. No judge likes to have his decision taken up by a higher court, which is why many proceedings are set in motion even though the judge actually thinks he's going to exonerate the accused. If the judge doesn't want to institute proceedings, he sometimes contacts the prosecutor's office to establish that there isn't going to be an appeal.

The judge, the prosecutor and I sat in the judge's office and discussed the case. The prosecution's evidence struck me as sketchy. There were only the photos. No witnesses were cited in the charge. And it was unclear how old the pictures were—the events could have taken place years ago and thus be subject to the statute of limitations. The expert psychiatrist's report didn't provide much support, and Feldmayer had not made any confession. What was left was the damage to the statue. It seemed clear to me that the museum's management bore most of the blame. They had locked Feldmayer in a room for twenty-three years and forgotten him.

The judge agreed with me. He was indignant.

He said he would prefer to see the museum's management sitting where the accused sat; after all, it was the town's administrators who had destroyed a man. The judge wanted the charge revised to reflect a more minor offence. He was extremely explicit. But dropping the graver charges would require the agreement of the prosecution, and our prosecutor wasn't ready to make that agreement.

A few days later, however, I received notification of the reduction in the charges. When I called the judge, he told me our prosecutor's boss had, surprisingly, agreed. The reason was, naturally, never made official, but it was clear nonetheless: if the trial had gone ahead, the museum's management would have been subjected to rather unpleasant questions in open court. And an indignant judge would have given the defence a very free hand. Feldmayer would have come out with a trivial sentence, but the town and the museum would have been made to look very bad.

The museum also eventually gave up on its civil suit. When we had lunch, the director said he was just glad that Feldmayer hadn't been guarding a room with a Salome painting in it.

Feldmayer kept his pension rights. The museum made an almost invisible announcement that a statue had been accidentally damaged; Feldmayer's name was not mentioned, and he never picked up a yellow drawing pin again.

The shards of the statue were collected in a cardboard box and taken to the museum's workshop. A restorer was given the task of putting it back together again. She spread all the pieces out on a table that was covered in black cloth. She photographed every single splinter and entered confirmation on more than two hundred individual pieces in a notebook.

It was silent in the workshop when she began. She had opened a window; the spring warmth suffused the room as she examined the shards and smoked a cigarette. She was happy to be able to work here after finishing her studies. *The Thorn Puller* was her first big job. She knew that putting it back together could last a long time, maybe even years.

A little wooden head of a Buddha from Kyoto stood opposite the table. It was ancient and had a crack in the forehead. The Buddha was smiling.

Love

She had dozed off, her head lying on his thigh. It was a warm summer afternoon, the windows stood open, and she felt good. They had known each other for two years, both of them were studying economics in Bonn, and they attended the same lectures. She knew he was in love with her.

Patrick stroked her back. The book was boring him; he didn't like Hesse, and he was only reading the poems out loud because that's what she wanted. He looked at her naked skin, her spine and shoulder blades, running his fingers over them. The Swiss army knife he'd used to cut the apple they'd eaten was lying on the night table. He laid the book aside and picked up the knife. Her eyes half-closed, she watched as he got an erection. She had to laugh—they'd only just had sex. He opened the blade. She lifted her head toward his penis. Then she felt the cut in her back. She screamed, struck his hand away to one side, and leapt to her feet. The knife flew onto the polished hardwood floor. She felt the blood running down her back. He looked at her, bewildered; she slapped him, seized her clothes from the chair, and ran into the bathroom. His student apartment was on the ground floor of an old building. She dressed hurriedly, climbed out of the window, and ran.

Four weeks later, the police sent the summons to his registered address. And because, like many students, he hadn't given any formal notification of his change of address, the letter didn't land in Bonn, but in his parents' mailbox in Berlin. His mother opened it, thinking it was a ticket of some kind. That evening, the parents first had a long discussion of what they might have done wrong; then the father called Patrick. The next day, his mother made an appointment with my secretary, and a week later the family was sitting in my office.

They were orderly people, the father was a construction foreman, thickset, chinless, short arms and legs, the mother around forty, former secretary, imperious and full of energy. Patrick didn't seem to go with his parents. He was an uncommonly pretty boy, with delicate hands and dark brown eyes. He described the details of the incident. He and Nicole had been together for two years, and they'd never had a fight. His mother interrupted him every second sentence. Then *she* said of course it had been an accident. Patrick said he was sorry. He loved the girl and wanted to apologise to her, but he couldn't reach her anymore.

His mother got a little too loud. 'It's better that way. I don't want you to see her again. Besides which, you're leaving next year anyway to go to the university in St Gallen.'

The father said very little. At the end of the meeting, he asked if things were going to get bad for Patrick.

I thought it was a minor case that would resolve itself quickly. It had already been referred by the police to the prosecutor's office. I called the senior prosecutor, who was preparing the formal examination. She had a wide range of oversight, all so-called DV cases—which is to say domestic violence. There were thousands of such cases every year, caused overwhelmingly by alcohol, jealousy and rows over children. She agreed quickly to let me see the files.

Two days later, I received the contents, barely forty pages, on my computer. The photo of the girl's back showed a six-inch cut with smooth edges to the wound. It would have healed cleanly and left no permanent scar. But I was sure that the cut itself was no accident. A falling knife makes a different kind of wound.

I asked the family to come back for a second discussion, and because the matter wasn't urgent, the appointment was made for three weeks hence.

Five days later, when I locked the office one Thursday evening and switched on the light in the stairwell, Patrick was sitting there on the steps. I asked him to come in, but he shook his head. His eyes were glassy and he was holding an unlit cigarette in his fingers. I went back into the office, collected an ashtray, and offered him a lighter. Then I sat down next to him. The time switch for the light clicked off; we sat in the dark and smoked.

'Patrick, what can I do for you?' I asked after a while.

'It's hard,' he said.

'It's always hard,' I said, and waited.

'I haven't ever told anyone.'

'Take your time; it's quite comfortable here.' In fact, it was cold and it was uncomfortable.

'I love Nicole the way I've never loved anyone, ever. She doesn't call, I've tried everything. I even wrote her a letter, but she never answered. Her mobile phone is switched off. Her best friend hung up when I called.'

'It happens.'

'What do I do?'

'The charge isn't an insoluble problem. You're not going to go to jail. I've read your file…'

'Yes?'

'Honestly, your story doesn't add up. It wasn't an accident.'

Patrick hesitated and lit another cigarette. 'Yes, you're right,' he said; 'it really wasn't an accident. I don't know if I can tell you what really happened.'

'Lawyers are bound by confidentiality,' I said. 'Everything you say to me will remain between us. Only you can decide whether I am allowed to speak, and if so, with whom. Not even your parents will hear anything about this conversation.'

'Is it the same with the police?'

'Most of all with the police and all the other people involved in the prosecution. I have to be silent; if I weren't, I'd make myself legally liable.'

'I still can't talk about it,' he said.

Suddenly, I had an idea. 'There's a lawyer in my

office with a five-year-old daughter. Just the other day she told another child something while the two of them were squatting on the floor. She's a very active child, and she talked and talked and talked while she kept sliding over closer to her friend. She was so excited by her own story that she was soon sitting almost right on top of the other girl. She kept on chattering, until finally she couldn't contain herself any longer. She flung her arms around her friend and was so happy and excited, she bit her on the neck.'

I could feel something at work in Patrick. He was struggling with himself. Finally, he said, 'I wanted to eat her.'

'Your girlfriend?'

'Yes.'

'Why did you want to do that?'

'You don't know her; you'd have to have seen her back. Her shoulder blades come together in points; her skin is firm and clear. My skin is full of pores, almost like holes, but hers is dense and smooth, and it has these tiny little blonde hairs on it.'

I tried to recall the picture of her back that was in the file. 'Was it the first time you wanted to?' I asked.

'Yes. Well, only once before, but it wasn't so strong that time. We were on holiday in Thailand; it was when we were lying on the beach. I bit her a little too hard.'

'How did you want to do it this time?'

'I don't know. I think I just wanted to cut out a little slice.'

'Have you ever wanted to eat anyone else?'

'No, of course not. It's all about her, only her.' He dragged on his cigarette. 'Am I crazy? I'm not some Hannibal Lecter. Or am I?' He was afraid of himself.

'No, you're not. I'm not a doctor, but I think you've become too caught up in your love for her. You know that, too, Patrick; you say so yourself. I think you're quite ill. You need to let people help you. And you need to do it soon.'

There are different kinds of cannibalism. People eat people out of hunger, out of obedience to some ritual, or out of severe personality disorders that often take a sexual form. Patrick thought Hollywood had invented Hannibal Lecter, but he's always existed. In Styria in the eighteenth century, Paul Reisiger ate 'the beating hearts of six virgins'—he believed that if he ate nine, he could become invisible. Peter Kürten drank the blood of his victims; in the 1970s, Joachim Kroll ate at least eight people he'd killed; and in 1948, Bernhard Oehme consumed his own sister.

Legal history abounds with the unimaginable. When Karl Denke was captured in 1924, his kitchen was full of human remains of all kinds: pieces of flesh preserved in vinegar, a tubful of bones, pots of rendered fat, and a sack with hundreds of human teeth. He wore suspenders cut from strips of human skin on which nipples were still identifiable. The number of victims remains unknown to this day.

'Patrick, have you ever heard about the Japanese man Issei Sagawa?'

'No, who is he?'

'Sagawa is a restaurant critic in Tokyo right now.'

'So?'

'In 1981 he ate his girlfriend in Paris. He said he loved her too much.'

'Did he eat all of her?'

'At least several pieces.'

'And'—Patrick's voice shook—'did he say how it was?'

'I don't remember exactly. I think he said she tasted of tuna.'

'Ah ...'

'The doctors back then diagnosed a severe psychotic disturbance.'

'Is that what I have, too?'

'I don't know exactly, but I want you to go
to a doctor.' I switched on the light. 'Please wait
here. I'm going to get you the phone number of
the emergency psychiatric services. If you want,
I'll drive you there now.'

'No,' he said, 'I'd like to think about it first.'

'I can't make you, Patrick. But please come
back here to the office first thing tomorrow. I'll
go with you to a sensible psychiatrist. Okay?'

He hesitated. Then he said he'd come back,
and we got to our feet. 'Can I ask you something
else?' said Patrick, and went very quiet. 'What
happens if I don't go to a psychiatrist?'

'I'm afraid it'll get worse,' I said. I unlocked the
door to my office again to find the phone number
and put back the ashtray. When I came back out
into the stairwell, Patrick had disappeared.

He didn't show up the next day. A week later,
I received a letter and a cheque from his mother.
She no longer wished me to represent them, and
since the letter was also signed by Patrick, it was
valid. I called Patrick, but he didn't want to speak
to me. Finally, I withdrew from his defence.

Two years later, I was giving a lecture in Zürich.
During the break, an elderly criminal lawyer

from St Gallen came over to speak to me. He mentioned Patrick's name and asked if he'd been my client, because Patrick had said some such thing. I asked what had happened. My colleague said, 'Patrick killed a waitress two months ago; until now, nobody's figured out why.'

The Ethiopian

The pale man was sitting right in the middle of the lawn. He had a strangely lopsided face with protruding ears, and his hair was red. His legs stuck out in front of him and his hands were clutching a bundle of banknotes in his lap. The man was staring at a rotting apple lying next to him, watching the ants biting minuscule fragments out of it and carrying them away.

It was shortly after midday on one of those hellishly hot days of high summer in Berlin when no sensible person would willingly set foot out-of-doors at noon. The narrow square had been artificially conjured between the tall buildings by the city planners; their glass and steel construction reflected the sun, and the heat hovered in a trapped layer above the ground. The lawn sprinklers were broken and the grass would be burned by nightfall.

No one paid attention to the man, not even when alarm sirens started to howl at the bank across the street. The three radio patrol cars that arrived very shortly afterward raced past him. Police ran into the bank, others blocked off the square, and reinforcements poured in.

A woman in a suit came out of the bank with several policemen. Putting a hand over her brow to protect herself from the sun, she searched the lawn with her eyes and finally pointed to the pale man. A stream of green-and-blue uniforms formed itself immediately in the direction of her outstretched hand. The policemen screamed at the man; one of them drew his service weapon and roared at him to put his hands in the air.

The man didn't react. A police captain, who'd spent the whole day in the precinct house writing up reports and being bored, ran at him, wanting to be the first. He threw himself at the man and yanked his right arm up behind his back. Banknotes flew through the air, orders were yelled, only to be ignored, and then they were all standing around him in a circle, gathering up the money. The man was lying on his stomach while the policeman drilled his knee into his back and pressed his face into the grass. The earth was warm. Looking between all the boots, the man could see the apple again. The ants, unimpressed, were keeping right on with their work. He breathed in the smell of the grass, the earth, and the rotting apple, closed his eyes, and was in Ethiopia again.

His life began the way lives begin in a terrible fairy tale. He was abandoned. A luminously green plastic tub stood on the steps of a vicarage near Giessen. The newborn was lying on a matted coverlet and was suffering from hypothermia. Whoever had put him down there had left him with nothing—no letter, no picture, no memory. That kind of tub was sold in every supermarket; the coverlet was army issue.

The vicar immediately notified the police, but the mother was never found. The baby was taken to an orphanage, and after three months the authorities put him up for adoption. The Michalkas, who had no children of their own, took him in and baptised him with the name of Frank Xaver. They were taciturn, hard people, hop growers from a quiet region of Upper Franconia; they had no experience with children. His adoptive father would say, 'Life isn't a bowl of cherries,' and then stick out his bluish tongue and lick his lips. He handled human stock, livestock and hop-root stock with equal respect and equal strictness. He got angry with his wife when she was too soft with the child. 'You're spoiling him for me,' he said, thinking of shepherds, who never stroke their dogs.

The boy was teased in kindergarten; he started school when he was six. Nothing went well for him. He was ugly, he was too tall and, above all, he was too rebellious. School was hard for him. His spelling was a catastrophe, and he got the lowest marks in almost every class. The girls were frightened of him, or repelled by the way he looked. He was insecure, which made him a loudmouth. His hair made him an outsider. Most people thought he was stupid; only his German teacher said he had other gifts. She sometimes had him make small repairs around the house, and she gave him his first pocketknife. Michalka carved her a wooden windmill for Christmas. The sails turned when you blew on them. The teacher married a man from Nürnberg and left the village during the summer holiday. She hadn't told the boy, and the next time he went to see her, he found the windmill in front of the house in a skip.

Michalka had to repeat a year of classes twice. When high school was over, he left and became an apprentice to a carpenter in the next-biggest town. No one teased him anymore; he was almost six foot six. He passed his qualifying exam to become an apprentice only because he was outstanding in the practical section. He did his military service in a unit of the signal corps near Nürnberg. He picked a fight with his superiors and spent a day in the brig.

After his discharge, he hitchhiked to Hamburg. He'd seen a film that took place in the city. It had beautiful women, broad streets, a port, and real nightlife. Everything had to be better there. 'Freedom lives in Hamburg,' he'd read somewhere.

The owner of a construction carpentry firm in Fuhlsbüettel took him on and gave him a room at the top of the factory building. The room was clean. Michalka was skilled and they were pleased with him. Although he often didn't know the technical terms, he understood the technical drawings, corrected them, and could implement them. When money was stolen from a locker, the firm dismissed him. He was the last person to have been hired, and there had never been a theft at the company before. The police found the cash box in the apartment of a drug addict two weeks later—Michalka had had nothing to do with it.

On the Reeperbahn, he ran into an old buddy from the army, who got him a job as janitor in a brothel. Michalka became the gofer. He got to know those on the margins of society—pimps, moneylenders, prostitutes, addicts, thugs. He kept himself out of it as best he could. He lived for two years in a dark room in the basement of the brothel, and then he began to drink, unable to bear the misery that surrounded him. The girls in the brothel liked him and told him their stories. He couldn't cope. He got into debt with the wrong people. He couldn't pay them back, and so the interest kept rising. He was beaten up, left lying in a doorway, and then picked up by the police. Michalka knew that any more of this would be the death of him.

He decided to try things abroad; he didn't care which country he landed in. He didn't spend a lot of time thinking it over. He took a stocking from one of the girls in the brothel. Entering the savings bank, he stretched it over his face, the way he'd seen it done in a movie, threatened the cashier with a plastic pistol, and made off with twelve thousand deutschmarks. The police blocked off the streets and checked everyone who was on foot, but Michalka, in a kind of trance, had gotten on a bus headed to the airport. He bought an economy ticket to Addis Ababa because he thought the city was in Asia, or at least far away. Nobody stopped him. Four hours after the holdup he was sitting in the plane, his only luggage a plastic bag. When the plane took off, he was afraid.

After a ten-hour flight, the first plane trip in his life, he landed in the capital of Ethiopia. He bought a visa for six months at the airport.

Five million inhabitants, sixty thousand children on the streets, prostitution, petty crime, poverty, innumerable beggars, cripples by the sides of the roads showing off their deformities to arouse pity—after three weeks, Michalka knew that there was nothing to choose between the misery in Hamburg and the misery in Addis Ababa. He came across a few Germans, a colony of human wrecks. The state of hygiene was catastrophic. Michalka came down with typhus. He ran a fever, his skin broke out in a rash, and he had dysentery, until finally an acquaintance found a doctor, who gave him antibiotics. Once again, he'd reached the end.

Michalka was now convinced that the world was a rubbish dump. He had no friends, no prospects, nothing that could hold him. After six months in Addis Ababa, he decided to end his life, suicide as a form of reckoning. But he didn't want to die in the dirt. There were still about five thousand marks of the money left over. He took the train toward Djibouti. A few kilometres beyond Dire Dawa, he began his wanderings through the pastureland. He slept on the ground or in tiny cheap hostels; he was bitten by a mosquito, which infected him with malaria. He took a bus up into the highlands. The malaria broke out along the way and he started to shake. He got out at some point, sick and confused, and lost his way in the coffee plantations as the world swam in a haze before his eyes. He stumbled and fell to the ground between the rows of coffee bushes. Before he lost consciousness, his last thought was, It was all such shit.

Between two bouts of fever, Michalka woke up. He realised that he was in a bed, and a doctor and a lot of strange people were gathered around him. They were all black. He understood that the people were helping him, and he sank back into his fevered nightmares. The malaria was brutal. Here in the highlands, there were no mosquitoes, but people were familiar with the illness and knew how to treat it. The peculiar stranger they'd found in the plantation would survive.

The fever slowly ebbed, and Michalka slept for almost twenty-four hours. When he awoke, he was lying alone in a whitewashed room. His jacket and trousers had been washed and arranged neatly on the only stool in the room, and his rucksack was standing next to it. When he tried to get up, his legs buckled and everything turned black before his eyes. He sat on the bed and stayed like that for fifteen minutes. Then he tried again. He desperately needed to go to the toilet. He opened the door and stepped out into the hall. A woman came at him, gesticulating wildly and shaking her head: no, no, no. She linked her arm into his and forced him back into the room. He made his need clear to her. She nodded and pointed to a bucket under the bed. He found her beautiful, and went back to sleep.

When he woke up next time, he felt better. He looked in his rucksack; all the money was still there. He could leave the room. He was alone in the tiny house, which consisted of two rooms and a kitchen. Everything was clean and orderly. He went out of the house and into a little village square. The air was fresh and pleasantly cool. Children came storming up to him, laughing and wanting to take hold of his red hair. Once he understood this, he sat down on a stone and let them do it. The children had their fun. Then at some point, the beautiful woman in whose house he was staying arrived. She scolded and pulled at him, got him back inside the house, and gave him corn cakes. He ate them all. She smiled at him.

Slowly, he got to know the coffee farmers' village. They had found him in the plantation, carried him up the hill, and fetched a doctor from the town. They were friendly to him. After he'd regained his strength, he wanted to help. The farmers were astonished; then they accepted.

Six months later, he was still living with the woman, slowly learning her language. First her name: Ayana. He wrote words down phonetically in a notebook. They laughed when he pronounced things wrong. Sometimes she ran her fingers through his red hair. At some point, they kissed. Ayana was twenty-one. Her husband had died two years before in an accident in the provincial capital.

Michalka thought about coffee growing. The harvest was laborious; it was performed by hand between October and March. He quickly grasped the problem: the village was the last link in the chain of trade. The man who collected the dried coffee beans earned more and had less work. But the man owned an old truck, and nobody in the village knew how to drive. For fourteen hundred dollars Michalka bought a better vehicle and drove the crop to the factory himself. He obtained nine times the price and divided the earnings among the farmers. Then he taught Dereje, one of the young men in the village, how to drive. Dereje and he now collected beans from the neighbouring villages as well, and paid the farmers three times what they'd been getting before. Soon they were able to buy a second truck.

Michalka wondered how it might be possible to make the work easier. He drove to the provincial capital, acquired an ancient diesel generator, and used old wheel rims and steel cables to build a cable rail from the plantation to the village. For containers he carpentered together big wooden chests. The rail broke down twice before he worked out the right distance between the wooden supporting beams and reinforced them with steel braces. The village elder observed his experiments with suspicion, but when the cable railway started to run properly, he was the first to clap Michalka on the back. The coffee beans could now be transported faster, and the farmers no longer had to haul them to the village on their backs. They could harvest more quickly and the work was less exhausting. The children loved the cable railway, they painted the wooden chests with faces and animals and a man with red hair.

Michalka wanted to keep improving the yield. The farmers spread the beans out on racks and turned them for five weeks, until they were almost dry. The racks stood outside the huts or on their roofs. The beans spoiled if they got wet and the spread layers had to be thin to prevent rot from setting in. It was demanding work, which each farmer had to do for himself. Michalka bought cement and mixed concrete. He made a flat surface at the edge of the village, which could be used by all the farmers for their crops. He constructed large rakes, and now the farmers could turn the beans together. They stretched clear sheets of plastic above the platform to keep off the rain, and the beans under it dried quicker. The farmers were happy. It was less work and nothing rotted anymore.

Michalka realised the quality of the coffee could be improved if the beans weren't just dried. The village lay close to a small river that ran clear from its source. He washed fresh-picked coffee beans by hand and sorted them into three water tanks. With a little money, he hired a dealer to buy a machine that separated the flesh of the fruit from the beans. The first experiments went wrong; the beans thus stripped of the fruit pulp fermented too long and went bad. He learned it was a matter of keeping the equipment absolutely clean; even a single leftover bean could spoil the whole process. Finally, it worked. He washed the coffee that had been prepared with fresh water and got rid of the remains of the parchment-like skin of the beans. He bordered off a little area on the concrete slab and dried them. When he took a sack of these beans to the dealer, he received three times the usual price. Michalka explained the process to the farmers; using the cable railway, they could bring in the harvest so quickly that the beans would be going through their water bath within twelve hours. After two years, the village was producing the best coffee beans for miles around.

Ayana became pregnant. They rejoiced about the child. When the little girl was born, they named her Tiru. Michalka was proud and happy. He knew he owed his life to Ayana.

The village became prosperous. After three years, there were five trucks, the harvest was perfectly organised, the farmers' plantations were growing larger, and they had installed a watering system and planted trees to form a windbreak. Michalka was respected and known throughout the neighbourhood. The farmers placed a portion of their earnings into a communal cash box. Michalka had brought a young teacher from the town to make sure that the village children learned to read and write.

If someone in the village fell ill, Michalka took care of them. The doctor had put together a kit of emergency supplies and taught him the rudiments of medical knowledge. He learned quickly; he saw how septicaemia was handled, and assisted at births. In the evenings, the doctor often sat with Michalka and Ayana, telling them the long history of the Holy Land. They became friends.

When quarrels broke out, it was the man with the red hair who was asked for advice. Michalka would not allow himself to be bribed, and he judged the way a good judge does, without regard to clan or village. People trusted him.

He had found his life. Ayana and he loved each other; Tiru was growing and was healthy. Michalka couldn't grasp his good fortune. Only sometimes, but less and less often, did the nightmares return. When that happened, Ayana would wake up and stroke him. She said her language had no word for the past. The years with her made Michalka soft-tempered and calm.

At some point, Michalka attracted the attention of the authorities. They wanted to see his passport. His visa had long since expired; he'd been living in Ethiopia for six years now. They were polite but insisted that he go to the capital to clarify matters. Michalka had a bad feeling as he said goodbye. Dereje took him to the airport. His family waved after him; Ayana wept.

In Addis Ababa, he was sent to the German embassy. An official checked the computer and disappeared with his passport. Michalka had to wait for an hour. When the official appeared again, he looked grim, and two guards were accompanying him. Michalka was taken into custody and the official read him the arrest order of a judge in Hamburg. Bank robbery. The damning evidence, the fingerprints he'd left on the counter in the bank. His fingerprints were on file because he'd once been involved in a fight. Michalka tried to pull himself free. He was pushed down onto the floor and handcuffed. After a night in the cell in the basement of the embassy, he was flown to Hamburg in the company of two security guards and led before the examining magistrate. Three months later, he was sentenced to a minimum of five years. The sentence was mild, because it had all happened a long time ago and Michalka had no previous convictions.

He couldn't write to Ayana because there wasn't even an official address. The German embassy in Addis Ababa couldn't, or wouldn't, help him. And of course there was no phone in the village. He had no photo. He barely uttered a word, and became solitary. Day stretched after day, month after month, year after year.

After three years, for the first time he was granted privileges and unaccompanied daytime release. He wanted to go home immediately; he couldn't go back to prison. But he had neither the money for the flight nor a passport. He knew where he could get both. In jail, he'd picked up the address of a forger in Berlin. So that's where he hitch-hiked. In the meantime, they were searching for him. He found the forger, but the forger wanted to see some money. Michalka had almost none.

He was in despair. He wandered the streets for three days without eating or drinking. He struggled with himself. He didn't want to commit a new crime, but he had to get home to his family, to Ayana and Tiru.

Eventually, he used the last of his prison money to buy a toy pistol at the train station and went into the first bank he saw. He looked at the cashier as he held the pistol with the barrel pointed down. His mouth was dry. He said very quietly, 'I need money. Please excuse me. I really need it.' At first, she didn't understand him; then she gave him the money. Later, she said she'd 'sympathised'. She took the money from the pile that had been specially prepared for such attacks and thus triggered the silent alarm. He took it, laid the pistol on the counter, and said, 'I'm so sorry. Please forgive me.' There was a stretch of green grass outside the bank. He couldn't run away anymore. He walked really slowly, then sat down and simply waited. Michalka had come to the end for the third time.

One of Michalka's cell mates asked me to take on the case. He knew Michalka from Hamburg and said he'd pay for the defence. I visited Michalka in the prison in Moabit. He handed me the warrant on the regular red paper used by the court: bank robbery, plus the remaining twenty months from the old sentence in Hamburg. Any defence seemed pointless, Michalka had been captured in the act, and he had already been convicted of the same crime before. So the only question was going to be the length of the sentence, and that, naturally, was going to be dreadfully long. But something about Michalka impressed me; there was something different about him. The man was not a typical bank robber. I took on his defence.

In the weeks that followed, I often visited Michalka. At the beginning, he barely spoke to me. He seemed to have finished with life. Very gradually, he opened up a little and began to tell me his story. He didn't want to divulge anything; he believed he'd be betraying his wife and daughter if he spoke their names in jail.

The defence can demand that a defendant be examined by a psychiatrist or psychologist. The court will accede to such a demand if it is likely to succeed in bringing out facts that suggest the defendant suffers from some form of mental illness, a disorder, or a striking behavioural peculiarity. Of course, the expert's report is not binding on the court—the psychiatrist cannot *decide* if the accused is not criminally responsible or has diminished responsibility. Only the court can decide these matters. But the expert who writes the report helps the court by giving the judges the scientific fundamentals.

It was obvious that Michalka was disturbed at the time of the crime. Nobody apologises in the course of a bank robbery, sits down in a meadow with the stolen cash, and waits to be arrested. The court ordered a psychiatric evaluation, and two months later the written report appeared. The psychiatrist was proceeding from a conclusion of diminished capacity. He would go into all other details at the trial.

The trial opened five months after Michalka's arrest. The court was conducted by a presiding judge, plus her junior, and two female jurors. The presiding judge had set aside a mere day for the proceedings. Michalka admitted he had committed the bank robbery. He spoke hesitatingly and too softly. The police reported how they had arrested Michalka. They described how he had been sitting on the grass. The police captain who'd nailed him said Michalka had put up no resistance.

The cashier said she hadn't felt at all afraid. She had felt sorry for the robber more than anything, as he'd looked so sad. 'Like a dog,' she said. The prosecutor asked if she now experienced anxiety at work, if she'd had to report in sick or had to undergo any course of therapy for the victims of crimes. She said no to all of it. The robber had just been a poor soul, and more polite than most of their customers. The prosecutor was obliged to ask these questions: if the witness really had been afraid, it would have been grounds for a higher sentence.

The toy pistol was introduced into evidence. It was a cheap model from China, weighing only a few grams and looking utterly harmless. When one of the jurors picked it up, it slipped, fell to the floor, and a piece of plastic broke off. It was impossible to take such a weapon seriously.

After the crime itself has been laid out during a trial, it is customary for the accused to be questioned about his 'personal circumstances'.

Michalka was almost entirely withdrawn the whole time; it was hard to move him, at least initially, to tell the story of his life. It was only slowly, piece by piece, that he could try to recount it. He barely succeeded; words failed him. Like many people, he found it hard to express his feelings. It seemed simpler to let the expert psychiatrist present the life of the accused.

The psychiatrist was well prepared and he

laid out Michalka's life in every detail. The judge knew all this already from the written report, but it was new information for the jurors. They were paying attention. The psychiatrist had questioned Michalka over an unusually long series of sessions. When he finished, the presiding judge turned to Michalka to ask if the expert had rendered it all accurately. Michalka nodded and said, 'Yes, he did.'

Then the expert witness was questioned about his professional evaluation of the accused's psychic state during the bank robbery. The psychiatrist explained that the three days Michalka had spent wandering around the city without food or drink had measurably diminished his capacity for rational behaviour. Michalka had hardly known what he was doing anymore, and he had lost almost all control over his actions. The hearing of evidence was concluded.

During a recess in the trial, Michalka said none of it had any point; no matter how much trouble people were going to, he was going to be found guilty anyway.

In a trial, it is the prosecutor who presents his closing argument first. Unlike in the United States or England, the prosecutor takes no position; he or she is neutral. The prosecutor's office is neutral;

it also establishes exonerating circumstances, and thus it neither wins nor loses—the only passion in the prosecutor's office is for the law. The law is all it serves—that, and justice. That at least is the theory. And during preliminary proceedings, it is the rule. But circumstances often change in the heat of a trial, and objectivity begins to suffer in the process. That is only human, because a good prosecutor is always a prosecutor, and it is more than difficult both to prosecute and to remain neutral. Perhaps it is a flaw woven into the very fabric of our criminal justice system; perhaps the law simply demands too much.

The prosecutor demanded nine years for Michalka. He said he didn't believe Michalka's story. It was 'too fantastic and probably a total invention'. Nor did he want to accept an argument of diminished capacity, because the psychiatrist's explanations rested solely on the accused's statements and lacked substantiation. The only fact was that Michalka had committed a bank robbery. 'The minimum sentence for bank robbery in the law is five years,' he said. 'It is the second time the defendant has committed this offence. The only admissible cause for leniency is that the money was secured and he made a full confession. Nine years are thus the appropriate sentence for the crime and the defendant's guilt.'

Of course it cannot all turn on whether a defendant's statements are *believed*. In court, what is at issue is proof. The accused thus has an advantage: he doesn't have to prove anything, neither his innocence nor the accuracy of his statement. But there are different rules for the prosecutor's office and the court: they may not state anything that they cannot prove. This sounds much simpler than it is. No one is so objective as to be able always to distinguish conjecture from proof. We believe we know something for sure, we get carried away, and it's often far from simple to find our way back.

Final arguments are no longer decisive in trials these days. The prosecutor's office and the defence are not speaking to sworn witnesses, but to judges and juries. Every false tone, every bit of hair tearing, and every pretentious turn of phrase is unendurable. The great closing arguments belong to earlier centuries. The Germans no longer tolerate pathos; there's been too much of that already.

But sometimes one can allow oneself a little dramatic production, an unanticipated final request. Michalka himself knew nothing about it.

An acquaintance of mine worked in the

diplomatic service. She was stationed in Kenya, and she helped me. By many roundabout routes, she had located Michalka's friend, the doctor from the local town. The doctor spoke perfect English. I had talked to him on the phone and begged him to testify as a witness. When I told him I would cover the cost of the airfare, he laughed at me and said he was so happy his friend was still alive that he would go anywhere to see him. And now he was waiting outside the door to the courtroom.

From one moment to the next, Michalka woke up. He leapt to his feet as the doctor entered the court, tears poured down his face, and he tried to get to him. The guards held him captive, but the presiding judge waved them away and allowed it. The two men embraced right in the middle of the courtroom, Michalka lifting the small-boned man right off his feet and hugging him. The doctor had brought a video, and a guard was sent off to get a player. We saw the village, the cable railway, the trucks, all the children and grown-ups, who kept laughing into the camera and calling 'Frroank, Frroank.' And then at last we saw Ayana and Tiru. Michalka wept and laughed and wept again, completely beside himself. He sat next to his friend and almost squashed the doctor's fingers in his own enormous hands. The presiding judge and one of the witnesses had tears in their eyes. It was nothing like a normal scene in a courtroom.

Our system of criminal law is based on the requirement of personal guilt. We punish according to someone's guilt; we ask to what extent we can make him responsible for his actions. It's complicated. In the Middle Ages, things were simpler: punishment was only commensurate with the act itself. A thief had his hand chopped off. It was all the same, no matter whether he'd stolen out of greed or because he would otherwise have starved. Punishment in those days was a form of mathematics; every act carried a precisely established weight of retribution. Our contemporary criminal law is more intelligent, it is more just as regards life, but it is also more difficult. A bank robbery really isn't always just a bank robbery. What could we accuse Michalka of? Had he not done what all of us are capable of? Would we have behaved differently if we had found ourselves in his place? Is it not everyone's deepest desire to return to those they love?

Michalka was sentenced to two years. A week after the trial, I ran into the presiding judge in one of the long halls in the court building in Moabit. She said the jurors were getting together to buy him an air ticket.

After Michalka had served half his sentence, he was released on probation. The presiding judge at the parole hearing, a wise old man, had them run through the whole story all over again, and just muttered 'wild'. Then he ordered Michalka set free.

Michalka is back living in Ethiopia today and has acquired full citizenship. Tiru now has a brother and a sister. Sometimes Michalka calls me. He still tells me that he's happy.

Ceci n'est pas une pomme.

GUILT

Things are as they are.
   —*Aristotle*

CONTENTS

Funfair 245

DNA 257

The Illuminati 265

Children 289

Anatomy 299

The Other Man 303

The Briefcase 319

Desire 329

Snow 335

The Key 349

Lonely 377

Justice 385

Comparison 391

Family 409

Secrets 417

Funfair

The first of August was too hot, even for the time of year. The little town was celebrating its six-hundredth anniversary, the air smelled of candied almonds and fairy floss, and greasy smoke rose from the grills to settle in people's hair. There were all the stands you usually find at annual fairs: a carousel had been put up, you could go on the dodgems or shoot an air gun. The older people spoke of 'the Emperor's weather' and the 'dog days' and wore brightly coloured pants and open shirts.

They were respectable men with respectable jobs: insurance salesman, car dealer, master carpenter. You would have no cause to find fault with them. Almost all of them were married, they had children, they paid their taxes, their credit was good and they watched the news on television every evening. They were perfectly normal men, and nobody would have believed that something like this could happen.

They played in a brass band. Nothing exciting, no big events, Queen of the Grape Harvest, annual rifle club outing, firemen's picnic. They had once played for the President of the Republic, out in his garden, with cold beer and sausages afterwards. The photo now hung in their meeting hall, the head of state himself was nowhere to be seen, but someone had stuck the newspaper article up next to it to prove it was all real.

They sat on the stage with their wigs and their fake beards. Their wives were made up with white powder and rouge. The mayor had said that everything was to look dignified today 'in honour of the town'. But things didn't look dignified. They were sweating in front of the black curtain and they'd had too much to drink. Their shirts were sticking to their bodies, the air smelled of sweat and alcohol and there were empty glasses between their feet. They played nonetheless. And if they hit false notes it didn't matter because the audience had drunk too much as well. In the pauses between the pieces they played there was applause, and more beer. When they took a break, a radio announcer acted as DJ.

The wooden floor in front of the curtain was giving off clouds of dust because people were dancing despite the heat, so the musicians went back behind the curtain to drink.

The girl was seventeen and still had to ask permission at home if she wanted to stay the night at her boyfriend's. In a year she would sit her final exams, then she would be off to study medicine in Berlin or Munich. She was looking forward to it. She was pretty, with blue eyes and an open face, and she laughed as she served the drinks. The tips were good; she wanted to travel across Europe with her boyfriend during the summer holiday.

It was so hot that she was only wearing a T-shirt with her jeans, and sunglasses, and a green hairband. One of the musicians came out in front of the curtain, waved at her and pointed to the glass in his hand. She crossed the dance floor and climbed the four steps up to the stage, balancing a tray that was too heavy for her small hands. She thought the man looked funny with his wig and his white cheeks. He smiled, she remembered that; he smiled and his teeth looked yellow against the white of his face. He pushed the curtain aside, letting her in to where the other men were sitting on two benches, all of them thirsty. For a moment her white T-shirt gleamed with an odd, bright flash in the sun; her boyfriend always liked it when she wore it. Then she slipped. She fell backwards, it didn't hurt, but the beer spilled all over her. Her T-shirt became transparent; she wasn't wearing a bra. She felt embarrassed, so she laughed, and then she looked at the men, who had suddenly gone silent and were staring at her. The first man reached out a hand towards her, and it all began. The curtain was closed again, the loudspeakers were blaring a Michael Jackson song, and the rhythm on the dance floor became the rhythm of the men, and later nobody could explain anything.

The police came too late. They didn't believe the man who'd called from the public phone booth. He'd said he was one of the band but didn't give his name. The policeman who took the call told his colleagues, but they thought it was a joke. Only the youngest of them thought he should maybe take a look, and went across the street to the fairground.

It was dark and dank under the stage. She was lying there naked in the mud, wet with semen, wet with urine, wet with blood. She couldn't speak, and she didn't move. She had two broken ribs, a broken left arm and a broken nose; splinters from the glasses and the beer bottles had gashed her back and arms. When the men had finished, they had lifted one of the boards and thrown her under the stage. They had urinated on her as she lay down there. Then they had gone out front again. They were playing a polka as the policemen pulled the girl out of the muck.

'Defence is war, a war for the rights of the accused.' The sentence appeared in the little book with the red plastic cover that I always carried around with me back then. It was the *Defence Lawyer's Pocket Reference*. I had just sat my second set of exams and had been admitted to the bar a few weeks earlier. I believed in that sentence. I thought I knew what it meant.

A friend I had studied with called up to ask me if I'd like to work with him on a pre-trial hearing; they needed two more lawyers. Of course I wanted to; it was a big case, the papers were full of it, and I thought this was going to be my new life.

In a trial, no one has to prove his innocence. No one has to defend himself, only the prosecutor has to provide proof. And that was also our strategy: all of them were simply to keep silent. We didn't have to do anything more than that.

DNA analysis had only recently been admitted at trial. The police had secured the girl's clothing at the hospital and stuffed it into a blue garbage bag. They put it in the boot of their patrol car, to be delivered to the pathologist. They thought they were doing everything right. The car stood in the sun for hour after hour, and the heat caused fungi and bacteria to grow under the plastic wrapping; they altered the traces of DNA so that they could no longer be analysed.

The doctors saved the girl, but destroyed the last of the evidence. As she lay on the operating table, her skin was washed. The traces the perpetrators had left in her vagina, in her rectum and on her body were rinsed away; nobody was thinking of anything except her emergency care. Much later the police and the forensic pathologist from the state capital tried to locate the waste from the operating room. At some point they gave up; at 3 a.m. they sat in the hospital cafeteria in front of pale brown cups of filtered coffee; they were tired, and had no explanations. A nurse told them they ought to go home.

The young woman couldn't name her attackers; she couldn't tell one from another; under the makeup and the wigs they all looked alike. At the line-up she didn't want to look, and when she did manage to overcome her revulsion she couldn't identify any of them. Nobody knew which of the men had called the police, but it was clear that it had been one of them. Which meant that any one of them could have been the caller. Eight of them were guilty, but each of them could also be the one innocent party.

He was gaunt. Angular face, gold-framed glasses, prominent chin. At that time, smoking was still permitted in the visiting rooms in prisons; he smoked one cigarette after the other. As he was talking, spittle built up in the corners of his mouth and he wiped it away with a handkerchief. He had already been detained for ten days when I saw him for the first time. The situation was as new for me as it was for him; I gave him a too-elaborate explanation of his rights and the relationship between lawyer and client, too much textbook knowledge; it was a form of insecurity. He talked about his wife and his two children, about his work, and finally about the fair. He said it had been too hot that day and they'd drunk too much. He didn't know why it had happened. That was all he said—it had been too hot. I never asked him if he'd joined in, I didn't want to know.

The lawyers were staying in the hotel on the town's market square. In the bar we discussed the file. There were photos of the young woman, of her maltreated body, of her swollen face. I had never seen anything like this. Her statements were confused, they gave us no clear picture, and on every page of the file you could read fury, the fury of the police, the fury of the public prosecutor, the fury of the doctors. None of it did any good.

In the middle of the night, the phone rang in my room. All I could hear was the caller's breathing; he didn't say a word. He hadn't dialled a wrong number. I listened to him until he hung up. It took a long time.

The court was on the same square as the hotel, a classical building with a small flight of steps in front, a celebration of the might of the law. The town was famous for its wine presses and merchants, and the winegrowers who lived there; it was a blessed piece of land, sheltered from all wars. Everything radiated dignity and upright behaviour. Someone had planted geraniums on the window ledges of the court.

The judge called us into his room one by one. I wore a robe, because I didn't know you don't wear robes to such meetings. When the review of the remand in custody began, I talked too much, the way you talk when you're young and you think anything's better than saying nothing. The judge only looked at my client; I don't think he even listened to me. But something else was standing between the judge and the man, something much older than our code of legal procedure, an accusation that had nothing to do with the laws as written. And when I had finished, the judge asked once again if the man wished to remain silent. He asked quietly, with no inflection in his voice, while he folded up his reading glasses and waited. The judge knew the answer, but he asked the question. And all of us in the cool air of the courtroom knew that the legal proceedings would end here and that guilt was another matter entirely.

Later we waited out in the hall for the examining magistrate to deliver his decision. We were nine defence lawyers; my friend and I were the youngest. The two of us had bought new suits for this hearing. Like all lawyers we were exchanging jokes, we didn't want the situation to get the better of us, and now I was one of them. At the end of the hall a sergeant was leaning against the wall; he was fat and tired and he despised every one of us.

That afternoon the judge dismissed the case; he

said there was no proof, the accused had remained silent. He read out the decision from a sheet of paper, although it was only two sentences long. After that, everything was still. The defence had been the right one, but now I didn't know if I should stand up until the woman recording the court proceedings gave me the decision and we left the room. The judge could have delivered no other verdict. The hall outside smelled of linoleum and old files.

The men were released. They left by a rear exit and went back to their wives and children and their lives. They paid their taxes and kept their credit good, they sent their children to school, and none of them spoke of the matter again. But the brass band was dissolved. There was never a formal trial.

The young girl's father stood in front of the court; he stood in the middle of the flight of steps as we went past to right and left; nobody touched him. He looked at us, red-eyed from weeping. It was a good face. The town hall opposite still had a poster advertising the anniversary celebration. The older lawyers spoke to the journalists, the microphones glittered like fish in the sun; behind them the father sat down on the courthouse steps and buried his head in his arms.

After the committal hearing, my study partner and I went to the station. We could have talked about the defence victory or about the Rhine right there next to the train tracks, or about anything at all. But we sat on the wooden bench with its peeling paint, and neither of us felt like saying a word. We knew we'd lost our innocence, and that this was irrelevant. We remained silent as we sat in the train in our new suits with our barely used briefcases beside us and as we journeyed home, we thought about the girl and the respectable men, and we didn't look at each other. We had grown up, and when we got out we knew that things would never be simple again.

DNA
For M.R.

Nina was seventeen. She sat outside the subway station at the Zoo, a paper cup with a few coins in it in front of her. It was cold; there was snow on the ground already. She hadn't imagined things would be this way, but it was better than any alternative. The last time she had phoned her mother was two months ago, and her step-father had answered. He had cried and told her she should come home. And it all came back to her: his sweaty old man's smell, his hairy hands. She hung up.

Her new friend Thomas also lived in the station. He was twenty-four, and he looked after her. They drank a lot, the hard stuff that warmed you up and let you forget everything. When the man came towards them, she thought he was a john. She wasn't a prostitute and she got furious if men asked her how much it cost. One time she spat in someone's face.

The old man asked her to come with him, he had a warm apartment, and he didn't want sex. He just didn't want to be alone at Christmas. He looked respectable, he was maybe sixty or sixty-five, thick overcoat, polished shoes. The shoes were always the first thing she checked. She was freezing.

'Only if my friend can come too,' she said.

'Of course,' said the man, in fact he'd like that even better.

Later they sat in the man's kitchen. There was coffee and cake. The man asked if she'd like to take a bath, it would do her good. She felt uneasy, but Thomas was there. Nothing can happen, she thought. The bathroom door had no key.

She lay in the bathtub. It was warm and the bath oil smelled of birch and lavender. She didn't see him at first. He had closed the door behind him and dropped his trousers, and was mastur-bating. It was nothing serious, he said, smiling uncertainly. She could hear the television in the other room. She screamed. Thomas pushed the door open and the handle caught the man in the kidneys. He lost his balance and fell over the edge of the bathtub. He landed next to her in the water, his head on her stomach. She lashed out, pulled her knees up, trying to get out, away from the man. She hit him on the nose, and blood ran into the water. Thomas grabbed him by the hair and held him under the surface. Nina was still screaming. She stood up in the bath, naked, and helped Thomas by pressing on the man's neck. It's taking some time, she thought. Then he stopped moving. She saw the hairs on his arse and punched his back.

'Pig,' said Thomas.

'Pig,' said Nina.

They didn't say anything more after that; they went into the kitchen and tried to think clearly. Nina had wrapped a towel around her. They smoked. They had no idea what to do.

Thomas had to get her things out of the bathroom. The man's body had slid onto the floor and was blocking the door.

'You know they're going to have to lever the door off its hinges with a screwdriver?' he said in the kitchen as he handed her her clothes.

'No, I didn't.'

'Otherwise they won't get him out.'

'Will they manage?'

'It's the only way.'

'Is he dead?'

'I think so,' he said.

'You have to go back in. My wallet and my identity card are still in there.'

He searched the apartment and found 8500 deutschmarks in the desk. It said 'For Aunt Margret' on the envelope. They wiped away their fingerprints, then left the apartment. But they were too slow. The neighbour, an elderly woman with strong glasses, saw them in the arcade.

They took the suburban train back to the station. Later they went to a snack bar.

'It was terrible,' said Nina.

'The idiot,' said Thomas.

'I love you,' she said.

'Yes.'

'What is it? Do you love me too?'

'Was he the only one doing something?' asked Thomas, looking straight at her.

'Yes, what are you thinking?' Suddenly she was afraid.

'Did you do something too?'

'No, I screamed. The old pig,' she said.

'Absolutely nothing?'

'No, absolutely nothing.'

'Things are going to get tough,' he said, after a pause.

A week later they saw the poster on a pillar in the station. The man was dead. A policeman from the squad based at the subway station knew them. He thought the neighbour's description might fit them, and they were taken in for questioning. The old lady wasn't sure. Adhesive tests were done on their clothing and compared to fibres from the dead man's apartment. The results were inconclusive. The man was recognised as a john, he had two previous convictions for sexual assault and intercourse with minors. They were released. The case remained unsolved.

They had done everything right. For nineteen years they had done everything right. Using the dead man's money they had rented an apartment; later they moved into a townhouse. They had stopped drinking. Nina was a checkout girl in a supermarket; Thomas worked as the stores supervisor at a wholesaler. They had got married. Within the year she'd given birth to a boy, and then twelve months later a girl. They made their way; things went well. Once he got into a fist fight at the company. He didn't defend himself; she understood.

When her mother died, she lapsed. She started

smoking marijuana again. Thomas found her at the station, in her old spot. They sat on a bench in the Tiergarten for a couple of hours, then drove home. She laid her head in his lap. She didn't need it anymore. They had friends and were close to his aunt in Hanover. The children were doing well at school.

When the science had advanced sufficiently, the cigarettes in the dead man's ashtray underwent molecular genetic analysis. All those who had been under suspicion back then were summoned for a mass screening. The document looked threatening: a shield, the inscription 'President of Police of Berlin', thin paper in a green envelope. It lay on the kitchen table for two days before they could bring themselves to talk about it. There was no avoiding it, they went, nothing more than a cotton swab in the mouth, it didn't hurt.

A week later they were arrested. The chief commissioner said, 'It's better for you.' He was only doing his job. They admitted everything, they didn't think it mattered anymore. Thomas called me too late. The court could not have ruled out an accident if they had kept quiet.

Six weeks later they were released from custody. The examining magistrate said the case was utterly unusual, the accused had integrated themselves fully into society in the meantime. They were under the gravest suspicion and a conviction was certain, but they were not a flight risk.

No one ever found out where the gun came from. He shot her in the heart and himself in the temple. Both of them died instantly. A dog discovered them next day. They were lying on the shore of the Wannsee, side by side, sheltered in a sand pit. They hadn't wanted to do it in the apartment; they'd painted the walls only two months before.

The Illuminati

The order of the Illuminati was founded on 1 May 1776 by Adam Weishaupt, a teacher in Canon Law at the University of Ingolstadt. Only the students of the Jesuits had access to the libraries, and Weishaupt wanted to change this. The professor had no organisational talent; perhaps at the age of twenty-eight he was simply too young. Adolph von Knigge, a Freemason, took over the leadership of the secret society in 1780. Knigge knew what he was doing; the order grew until it began to pose a threat to the Crown because of its sympathy for the ideas of the Enlightenment, and this led to both him and it being banned as enemies of the state. After that, theories abounded. Because Adam Weishaupt looked a little like George Washington, it was claimed that the Illuminati had murdered the President and replaced him with Weishaupt—for Weishaupt means whitehead and the national symbol of the United States, the white-headed or bald eagle, was proof of this. And because people loved conspiracy theories even back then, suddenly everyone became a member of the Illuminati: Galileo, the Babylonian goddess Lilith, Lucifer, and eventually even the Jesuits themselves.

In reality, Weishaupt died in 1830 in Gotha; the history of the order ended with its ban by the government in 1784, and all that remains is a small memorial tablet in the pedestrian precinct in Ingolstadt.

For some people, that's not enough.

When Henry was six he was sent to school and things began to go wrong. The cornet he was given to celebrate his first day was made of red felt with stars stuck on it and a magician with a pointy beard. It was a heavy cornet, it had a green paper cover, he'd carried it from home all by himself. Then the cornet got caught on the door handle of the classroom and that made a dent in it. He sat on his chair and stared at his cornet and everyone else's cornets, and when the teacher asked his name, he didn't know what he was supposed to say and he began to cry. He was crying because of the dent, because of the strange people, because of the teacher, who was wearing a red dress, and because he'd pictured everything differently. The boy next to him stood up and went in search of a new neighbour. Until that moment Henry thought the world had been created for him; sometimes he had turned around quickly, hoping to catch the objects as they changed places. Now he would never do that again. He remembered nothing about the rest of the lesson, but later he believed his life had been knocked off balance that day in a way that could never be righted again.

Henry's parents were ambitious; his father was the kind of man that no one in their little town ever saw without a tie and polished shoes. Despite all the strains created by his background he had become the deputy director of the power company and a member of the town council. His wife was the daughter of the richest farmer in the area. And because Henry's father had only had ten years of school, he wanted more for his son. He had a false picture of private schools, and he mistrusted state schools, which is why the parents decided to enrol Henry in a boarding school in southern Germany.

★　★　★

An allée lined with chestnut trees led to the former sixteenth-century monastery. The school board had bought the building sixty years before; it had a good reputation. Industrialists, top officials, doctors and lawyers sent their children here. The headmaster was a fat man with a cravat and a green jacket; he greeted the family at the big front door. His parents talked to the unknown man as Henry walked behind them, looking at the leather patches on the man's elbows and the reddish hairs on his neck. His father's voice was softer than usual. Other children came from the opposite direction; one of them nodded to Henry but he didn't want to respond and looked at the wall. The unknown man showed them Henry's room for the next year; he'd be sharing it with eight other boys. The beds were bunk beds, and there was a linen curtain in front of each one. The man told Henry this was now his 'domain'; he could stick posters up with Scotch tape. He said this as if he were being friendly. Then he slapped him on the shoulder. Henry didn't understand him. The unknown man's hands were soft and fleshy. Finally he went away.

His mother packed everything into his cupboard. It was all strange; the sheets and pillow case had nothing to do with home and all the noises sounded different. Henry was still hoping it was all a mistake.

His father was bored. He sat next to Henry on the bed and both of them watched as Henry's mother unpacked the three suitcases. She talked without pause, saying she wished she'd been to a boarding school, and she'd loved holiday camps when she was young. The singsong in her voice made Henry feel tired. He leaned against the head of the bed and closed his eyes. When he was woken, nothing had changed.

A fellow pupil came and said he'd been told to 'show the parents around'. They saw two classrooms, the dining room and the kitchen-ette, everything dated from the seventies, the furniture had rounded corners, the lamps were orange, it was all comfortable and nothing looked as if it belonged in a monastery. His mother was enchanted by everything, and Henry knew how stupid the other pupil thought she was. At the end, his father gave the boy two euros. It was too little, and his mother called him back and gave him more. The boy bowed, holding the money in his hand, and looked at Henry, and Henry knew he'd already lost.

At some point his father said it was late already and they still had the long return journey ahead of them. As his parents drove down the allée, Henry saw his mother turning back towards him one more time and waving. He saw her face through the window and he saw her saying something to his father; her red mouth moved silently, it would move forever, and he suddenly grasped that it wasn't moving for him anymore. He kept his hands in his pockets. The car got smaller and smaller until he could no longer distinguish it from the shadows in the allée.

He was twelve years old now and he knew that all this was premature and much too serious.

The boarding school was a world unto itself, more constricted, more intensive, devoid of compromise. There were the athletes, the intellectuals, the show-offs and the winners. And there were the ones who were ignored, who were mere wallpaper. No one made his own decision as to who he was, it was the others who judged and their judgment was almost always final. Girls could have provided the corrective, but the school didn't admit them, so their voices were missing.

Henry was one of the inconspicuous ones. He said the wrong things, he wore the wrong clothes, he was bad at sports and he couldn't even play computer games. No one expected anything of him, he was one of the ones who went with the flow, people didn't even make fun of him. He was one of the ones no one would recognise in future class reunions. Henry found a friend, a boy in his dorm room, who read fantasy novels and had wet hands. In the dining hall they sat at the table that got served last, and they stuck together on class outings. They got through, but when Henry lay awake at night he wished there were something more for him.

He was an average student. Even when he really tried, it made no difference. When he turned fourteen he developed acne, and everything got worse. The girls he met in his little town during the holidays wanted nothing to do with him. If they cycled to the quarry pond on summer afternoons, he had to pay for the ice cream and the drinks in order to be allowed to sit with them. And so that he would be able to do this, he stole money from his mother's wallet. The girls kissed other boys anyway, and all he had left at night were the drawings he had secretly made of them.

Things went differently only once. She was the prettiest girl in the group; it was during the summer holidays when he had just turned fifteen. She told him he should come with her, just like that. He followed her into the cramped changing cubicle; it was a wooden shed by the lake with a narrow bench and no window, full of junk. She undressed in front of him in the semi-darkness and told him to sit down and unzip his pants. The light coming between the planks divided her body; he saw her mouth, her breasts, her pubic hair, he saw the dust in the air and smelled the old inflatable mattresses under the bench, and he heard the others by the lake. She knelt in front of him and took hold of him; her hands were cold and the light fell on her mouth and her teeth, which were too white. He felt her breath in front of his face, and suddenly he was afraid. He sweated in the dark little room as he stared at her hand, holding his penis, and the veins on the back of her hand. He suddenly thought of an excerpt from their biology textbook: 'the fingers of a hand open and close themselves 22 million times in the course of a life'. He wanted to touch her breasts but he didn't dare. Then he got a cramp in his calf, and as he came, because he had to say something, he said, 'I love you.' She jumped to her feet and turned away; his stomach was sticky with semen. Bending over, she hastily pulled her bikini back on, then opened the door and turned back towards him as she stood in the doorway. He could see her eyes now. They held sympathy and disgust and something else he didn't yet recognise. Then she said 'Sorry' softly and slammed the door, running to join the others out of sight. He sat in the dark for a long time. When they met next day, she was standing among her friends. She said loudly, for everyone to hear, that he shouldn't stare at her so idiotically, she'd lost a bet, that was all, and 'that thing yesterday' had been the stake. Because he was young and vulnerable, the imbalance grew even more severe.

In ninth grade a new teacher arrived at the boarding school; she taught art and suddenly Henry's life changed. Up until then school was a matter of indifference to him; he'd have been happier doing something else. Once during a holiday he'd done an apprenticeship in a screw factory back home. He'd have liked to stay there. He enjoyed the orderly course of things, the unchanging rhythm of the machines, the unchanging nature of the conversations in the cafeteria. He liked the foreman he was assigned to, who answered his questions in monosyllables.

Everything changed with the new teacher. Until that point Henry had no interest in art.

There were a handful of drawings in his parents'
house, quick sketches made for tourists which
his father had bought from fly-by-night dealers
in Paris during their honeymoon. The only original came from Henry's grandfather and hung
over the bed in his boyhood room. It was of a
summer landscape in East Prussia; Henry could
feel the heat and the loneliness and he knew for
sure, though he had no grounds for it, that it was
a good picture. At school he had drawn figures
for his friend out of the fantasy novels; there were
scenes with dwarves, orcs and elves, and the way
Henry drew them gave them more life than the
language in the books did.

The teacher was almost sixty-five years old
and came from Alsace. She wore black-and-white
suits. Her upper lip wobbled a little when she
talked about art, and that's when you could hear
the faint traces of her French accent.

As always at the beginning of the school year,
she had the children paint a scene from their holidays. That afternoon she leafed through their
work, to see how far along they were. As she
took the pictures out of the folder one by one, she
was smoking, something she only did at home.
From time to time she made notes. Then she
held Henry's sheet of paper in her hands. It was a

drawing, just a few pencil strokes, of his mother collecting him at the station. She hadn't so much as noticed the boy in class, but now her hand began to tremble. She understood his drawing, it was all evident to her. She saw the struggles, the wounds and the fear, and suddenly she saw the boy himself. That evening, her entry in her diary consisted of two sentences. *Henry P is the greatest talent I have ever seen. He is the greatest gift of my life.*

They caught him shortly after the Christmas holiday.

An indoor swimming pool had been built on to the monastery in the 1970s. It was muggy in there, and smelled of chlorine and plastic. The boys used the anteroom to change. Henry had hurt his hand on the edge of the pool and was allowed to leave ahead of the others. A few minutes later another boy went to fetch his watch; he wanted to measure how long they could stay under water. As he came into the anteroom, he saw Henry taking money out of the other boys' pants, counting it and hiding it away. He watched him for several minutes, while the water dripped onto the tiled floor. At a certain point Henry noticed him and heard him say, 'You swine.' Henry saw the puddle of water beneath the boy's feet, his green-and-white swimming trunks, and the wet hair that hung down into his face. Suddenly the world slowed, he saw a single drop falling in slow motion, its surface perfect, the neon light on the ceiling refracted within it. As it splashed onto the floor, Henry did something he shouldn't have done and which later he couldn't explain to anyone: he kneeled. The other boy grinned down at him and repeated, 'You swine, you're going to pay for this.' Then he went back to the swimming pool.

The boy belonged to a little group in school who secretly called themselves the Illuminati. During his summer holiday he had read a book about defunct orders, the Templars and the Illuminati. He was sixteen and seeking explanations for the world. He gave the book to the others and after a few months they knew all the theories. There were three of them, they talked about the Holy Grail and world conspiracies, they met at night, searched for signs in the monastery, and finally they found symbols because they wanted to find them. The arches of the windows threw midday shadows that looked like pentagrams, they discovered an owl, the emblem of the Illuminati, in the dark portrait of the abbot who had founded the monastery, and they thought they saw a pyramid above the clock on the tower. They took it all seriously, and because they talked to nobody about it all, things took on a baseless significance. They ordered books on the internet, they went onto innumerable websites and gradually they came to believe what was said there.

When they got to exorcism, they decided to seek out a sacrificial victim, someone they could purify of his sins and make their disciple. Much later, after everything had happened, more than four hundred books were found in their cupboards and nightstands, books on Inquisition trials, Satanic rituals, secret societies and flagellants, and their computers were full of images of witches being tortured and sadistic pornography. They thought a girl would be ideal and they talked about what they would do with her. But when the thing with Henry happened at the swimming pool, the die was cast.

The teacher was careful with Henry. She let him draw what he wanted. Then she showed him pictures; she explained anatomy to him, and perspective and composition. Henry sucked it all in; none of it gave him any difficulty. He waited every week for the two hours of art class. When he had made some progress, he took his sketchpad outdoors. He drew what he saw, and he saw more than other people did. The only person the teacher talked to about Henry was the headmaster; they decided to let Henry continue to grow within the shelter provided by the school; he still seemed overly fragile. He began to grasp the pictures in the art books, and he slowly realised that he was not alone.

For the first few weeks they humiliated him in a haphazard way. He had to polish their shoes and buy sweets for them in the village. Henry did what they told him. Then came the carnival holiday before Lent; the boys had three days off, as every year, but for most of them it was too far to go home. They were bored, and things got worse for Henry. The monastery had an outbuilding; during the monks' time it had been the slaughter-house. There were two rooms inside, with yellow tiles that reached all the way to the ceiling. It had stood empty for many years, but the old chopping blocks were still there, as were the drainage channels in the floor for the blood.

He was made to sit naked on a chair, while the three boys circled round him screaming that he was a swine and a thief and a traitor to their community, and human garbage, and ugly. They talked about his acne and his penis. They beat him with wet towels. He was only allowed to move if he was on his knees, or they made him crawl on his stomach; and he had to keep repeating, 'I have brought great guilt upon myself.' They forced him into an iron butcher's barrel and banged on the metal until he almost went deaf. And they discussed what they should do with the pathetic creature. Shortly before supper, they stopped. They were friendly to him and told him to get dressed again; they would continue next weekend but for now they mustn't be late for supper.

That evening one of them wrote home about how the week had gone, and that he was looking forward to the holidays. He mentioned his marks in English and mathematics. The other two played soccer.

Henry went back to the slaughterhouse again after supper. He stood in the half-darkness and waited, but he didn't know what he was waiting for. He saw the streetlamp through the window, he thought about his mother and how he'd once eaten chocolate in the car and smeared it on the seat. When she discovered this, she got very angry. He spent the whole afternoon cleaning the car, not just the seats but the exterior too—he even scrubbed the tyres with a brush—till the car gleamed and his father complimented him. And then suddenly he took off his clothes, lay down on the floor, and spread his arms wide. He felt the cold rising up into his bones from the flagstones. He closed his eyes and listened to nothing except his own breath. Henry was happy.

...ascended into heaven
And sitteth at the right hand of God the Father Almighty
From thence he shall come to judge the quick and the dead...

It was the liturgy for Good Friday; attendance at the village church was compulsory for the boys. Originally it had been a Lady Chapel; now it was a baroque church full of gold, trompe l'oeil marble, angels and Madonnas.

Henry had long since drawn everything that was in here, but today he saw nothing. He groped for the piece of paper in his pocket. *Hodie te illuminatum inauguramus*, it said. 'Today we will consecrate you as one of the Illuminati.' He had waited for it, the piece of paper meant everything

to him, he'd found it this morning on his nightstand. Under the Latin text it said, '8 p.m. Old
Slaughterhouse.'

...and forgive us our trespasses...

'Yes,' he thought, 'today my trespasses will
be forgiven.' He was breathing so loudly that a
couple of the boys turned round to look at him.
They were already in the middle of the Lord's
Prayer, the liturgy would end at any moment.
'My trespasses will be forgiven,' he said half out
loud, and closed his eyes.

Henry was naked and was made to put the noose
around his neck himself. The others were wearing
black hoods that they had found in a forgotten
cupboard in the attic, rough monk's robes and
penitent's shirts made of goat's hair which hadn't
been worn in modern times. They had placed
candles around, and the flames were reflected in
the grimy film on the windows. Henry could no
longer recognise the boys' faces, but he saw all
the details: the fabric of the hoods, the thread the
buttons were sewn on with, the red bricks of the
window surrounds, the forced lock in the door,
the dust on the steps, the rust on the banisters.

They bound his hands behind his back. Using

watercolours from art class, one of the boys painted a red pentagram on Henry's chest to ward off evil; they'd seen it in some engraving. They took the rope around his neck and pulled it up to a hook in the ceiling using the old winch; Henry's toes could barely touch the floor. One of the boys read out the great exorcism, the *Rituale Romanum*, the papal instructions written in Latin in 1614. His words rang out in the room; nobody understood them. The boy's voice cracked; he was being carried away by himself. They really believed they were purifying Henry of his sins.

Henry didn't freeze. This time, this one time, he'd done everything right; they could no longer reject him. One of the boys swung at him with a whip he'd made himself, with knots in the leather. It wasn't a hard blow, but Henry lost his balance. The rope was made of hemp, it cut into his throat and blocked his air passages, he tripped, his toes could no longer find the floor. And then Henry got an erection.

A person being slowly hanged suffocates. In the first phase the rope cuts into the skin, the veins and arteries in the neck are closed off and the face turns violet-blue. The brain is no longer supplied with blood, consciousness is lost after about ten seconds, only if the windpipe is not totally blocked does it take longer. In the next phase, which lasts approximately one minute, the breathing muscles contract, the tongue protrudes from the mouth, and the hyoid bone and the larynx are damaged. This is followed by powerful, uncontrollable cramps; the legs and arms thrash eight or ten times, and the neck muscles often tear. Then suddenly the hanged man seems peaceful, he's no longer breathing, and after one or two minutes the last phase begins. Death is now almost inevitable. The mouth opens, the body gasps for air, but only in individual panting spasms, no more than ten in sixty seconds. Blood may issue from the mouth, nose and ears, the face is now congested, the right ventricle of the heart is distended. Death comes after approximately ten minutes. Erections during a hanging are not uncommon: in the fifteenth century people believed the mandrake, a solanaceous herb, grew from the sperm of hanged men.

But the young men knew nothing about the human body. They didn't understand that Henry was dying, they thought the blows were arousing him. The boy with the whip became furious, he struck harder and roared something that Henry didn't understand. He felt no pain. He remembered finding a deer that had been hit by a car on a country road. It was lying there in its own blood in the snow, and when he tried to touch it, it jerked its head round and stared at him. Now he was one of them. His trespasses had been wiped away, he would never be alone again, he was purified, and finally he was free.

The road from the art teacher's house to the only petrol station in the village ran between the monastery and the old slaughterhouse. She wanted to buy cigarettes there, and set off on her bike. She saw the light from the candles in the slaughterhouse and knew that no one was allowed to be there. She had been a teacher her whole life, she had supervised children and brought them up; it was probably this sense of responsibility that made her stop and climb the five worn steps. She opened the door. She saw the candles, she saw Henry, naked with a stiff penis, half-hanged in the noose, and she saw the three boys in their monk's hoods, one of them with a whip in his hand. She screamed, backed away, missed the stair, lost her balance, and hit her neck on the edge of the bottom step. Her neck snapped and she died instantly.

The rope around Henry's neck was made fast

to an iron chain that ran over a pulley in the ceiling and then to the winch. When he heard the teacher scream, the boy let go, the rope gave way, and Henry fell to the floor. The heavy chain raced over the pulley, yanking the plaster off the ceiling, and its weight shattered a flagstone next to Henry's head. While the boys ran into the school to fetch help, Henry lay there, then he slowly pulled in his knees, breathed, and when he opened his eyes, he saw the teacher's purse lying overturned in the doorway.

The headmaster had been put in touch with me by the school's lawyer. He told me what had happened and asked me to represent the interests of the school. He knew the teacher had had a particularly close relationship with Henry, closer than with any of the other pupils, and, although he'd always trusted her, he was now worried that her death might have something to do with this.

When I reached the school five days after the events, the old slaughterhouse was still blocked off with red-and-white crime tape. The prosecutor's office said the investigating authorities had no cause to suspect the art teacher. The detectives found her diary. I exercised my right to review the file and read it in my hotel room.

Then there were the pictures. The police found them in Henry's cupboard. He had recorded it all, rapid watercolour sketches on hundreds of sheets of paper; every humiliation was there, every humiliation of his and every desire of his torturers. The pictures would become the main evidence at trial; no one would be able to deny a thing. Not one of the sketches showed the art teacher; her death really had been an accident. I wasn't able to speak to Henry, who had been taken home, but there were almost fifty pages of interview transcripts, and I talked to his friends for many hours.

By the end of the week I was able to reassure the headmaster. Henry's parents were not going to sue the school; they didn't want their son's case to become public knowledge. The prosecutor's office didn't intend to put the school administration on trial. The criminal action against the students would not be a public one; they were just seventeen, and the only issue would be their guilt. My brief mandate was thus at an end.

A lawyer who was a friend of mine and was defending one of the young men told me later that they had all confessed and had been sentenced to three years in juvenile detention. They had not been charged with the death of the teacher.

Some years afterwards, when I was in the neighbourhood, I phoned the headmaster and he invited me to coffee at the monastery. The old slaughterhouse had been torn down and was now a carpark. Henry had not returned to the school. He was ill for a long time and now works in the screw factory where he had already served his apprenticeship. He has never gone back to drawing.

That evening I drove back down the same allée along which Henry had been driven to the school by his parents so many years before. I saw the dog too late. I braked and the car skidded on the gravel road. The dog was huge and black; it took its time crossing the road and didn't even look at me. In the Middle Ages such dogs were supposed to pull mandrake roots out of the ground; people believed the plants would scream when dug up and the scream would kill people. The dogs obviously didn't mind. I waited until it disappeared between the trees.

Children

Before they came to take him away, things had always gone well for Holbrecht. He had met Miriam at a supper given by friends. She was wearing a black dress and a silk shawl with brightly coloured birds of paradise on it. She taught at the primary school; he was the sales representative for an office furniture company. They fell in love and after that time was over they still got along well together. At family parties, everyone said they made such a good-looking couple, and most of them meant it.

A year after the wedding they bought a semi-detached house in one of the most respectable suburbs of Berlin, and five years later they had almost paid it off. 'Ahead of time,' as the local branch manager of the Volksbank said. He always stood up when he saw Miriam or Holbrecht at the counter. Holbrecht liked that. 'There's nothing to find fault with,' he thought.

Holbrecht wanted children. 'Next year,' said Miriam; 'let's enjoy life a little longer.' She was twenty-nine, he was nine years older. They were going to take a trip to the Maldives that winter, and whenever they talked about it Miriam looked at him and smiled.

Customers valued his straightforward manner; when his bonus was added in, he was making a comfortable ninety thousand a year. Driving back from meetings, he listened to jazz in the car, and his world was complete.

They came at seven in the morning. He'd been supposed to drive to Hanover that day: a new customer, complete office fit-out, good contract. They handcuffed him and led him out of the house. Miriam, still in the pyjamas that he liked so much, stared at the arrest warrant. 'Twenty-four counts of child abuse.' She knew the name of the girl from her primary school class. She stood in the kitchen with an officer as two of the policemen led Holbrecht down the narrow path to the police car. They had planted the boxwood hedge the year before; the jacket she'd given him last Christmas hung awkwardly, somehow, on his shoulders. The policeman said most wives had no idea. It was meant to sound comforting. Then they searched the house.

It wasn't a long trial. Holbrecht denied everything. The judge held up the fact that porn movies had been found on his computer. Admittedly there were no children in them and the films were legal, but the women were very young: one of them had barely any tits. The judge was sixty-three. He believed the girl. She said Holbrecht had always intercepted her on the way home. He had touched her 'down there'—she started to cry as she testified about that. The terrace of his house was where it took place. Another girl confirmed everything; she'd seen it all happen twice herself. The girls described the house and the little garden.

Miriam didn't attend the main hearing. Her lawyer sent the divorce papers to the remand centre. Holbrecht signed everything without reading it.

The court sentenced him to three and a half years. It stated in its opinion that it had no cause to doubt the girl's testimony. Holbrecht served out his sentence to the last day. The psychologist had wanted him to acknowledge his guilt. He said nothing.

His shoes were soaked by the rain; water had forced its way in over the rims and seeped into his socks. The bus shelter had a plastic roof, but Holbrecht preferred to stand outside. The rain ran down the back of his neck into his coat. Everything he owned fitted into the grey suitcase that was standing beside him. Some underwear, a few books, approximately 250 letters to his wife which he had never sent. In the pocket of his pants he had the addresses of his probation officer and a boarding house where he could stay to begin with. To tide him over, he had the money he'd earned in prison. Holbrecht was now forty-two years old.

The next five years passed quietly. He lived on his wages as a sandwich-board man for a tourist restaurant. He stood at the end of the Kurfürstendamm with colourful pictures of the various pizzas on the cardboard boxes. He wore a white hat. His trick was to give a little nod to people when he handed them the flyer. Most of them took one.

He lived in a one-and-a-half-room apartment in Schöneberg. His employer valued him; he was never ill. He didn't want to live on unemployment benefits and he didn't want any other job.

He recognised her at once. She must now be sixteen or seventeen, a carefree young woman in a close-fitting T-shirt. She was with her boyfriend, eating an ice cream. She tossed her hair back as she laughed. It was her.

He turned aside quickly, feeling ill. He pulled off the sandwich board and told the restaurant owner he was sick. He was so pale that no one asked him any questions.

In the suburban train someone had written *I love you* and someone else had written *pig* in the dirt on the window. Back home he lay on his bed in his clothes, and spread a wet kitchen cloth over his face. He slept for fourteen hours. Then he got up, made coffee, and sat down at the open window. A shoe was lying on the canopy of the building next door. Children were trying to reach it with a stick.

In the afternoon he met his friend, a homeless man, who was fishing in the Spree, and sat down beside him.

'It's about a woman,' said Holbrecht.

'It's always about a woman,' said his friend.

Then they fell silent. When his friend pulled a fish out of the water and killed it by smacking it against the concrete wall of the quay, he went home.

Back in the apartment he looked out of the window again. The shoe was still lying on the canopy. He fetched a beer from the refrigerator and pressed the bottle to his temples. The heat had barely eased at all.

She had walked past him and his sandwich board on the Kurfürstendamm every Saturday. He took the weekend off and waited. When she came he followed her; he waited in front of shops and cafés and restaurants. Nobody noticed him. On the fourth Saturday she bought movie tickets. He found a seat directly behind her. His plan was going to work. She had put her hand on her boyfriend's thigh. Holbrecht sat down. He smelled her perfume and heard her whispering. He pulled the kitchen knife out of the waistband of his pants and clutched it under his jacket. She had pinned her hair up; he saw the blond fuzz on the back of her slender neck. He could almost count the individual tiny hairs.

He thought he had every right.

I don't know why Holbrecht came straight to my office. I have no walk-in clients, but the office is not far from the cinema: maybe that's the only reason. My secretary called me early in the morning; a man was waiting without an appointment, he'd been sitting on the steps outside the office, and he had a knife. My secretary has been with me for years. Now she was afraid.

Holbrecht sat hunched in a chair, staring at the knife in front of him on the table. He didn't move. I asked him if I might take the knife. Holbrecht nodded without looking up. I put it in an envelope and carried it to the secretary's office. Then I sat down with him and waited. At some point he looked at me. The first thing he said was, 'I didn't do it.' I nodded; sometimes it's hard for clients to talk. I offered him a coffee, then we sat there and smoked. It was midsummer, and through the large open windows of the conference room you could hear high voices—children on a class outing. Young people were laughing in the café across the way. I closed the window. It was quiet and warm.

It took a long time before he told me his story. He had a strange way of talking: he nodded after every sentence, as if he had to reaffirm personally everything he said. And there were long pauses. At the end he said he'd followed the girl into the cinema but he hadn't stabbed her; he couldn't bring himself to do it. He was trembling. He had sat all night in front of my office and he was exhausted. My secretary called the cinema: there had been no incident.

Next day Holbrecht brought the documents from the old trial. The young woman's address was in the phone book. I wrote to her and asked if she would talk to me. It was the only possibility we had. I was surprised when she actually came.

She was young, training in the hospitality business. Freckled, nervous. Her boyfriend came with her. I asked him to wait in another room. When I told her Holbrecht's story, she went quiet and looked out of the window. I told her we couldn't win the right to a new hearing unless she testified. She didn't look at me, and she didn't answer. I wasn't sure if she would help Holbrecht, but when she held out her hand to say goodbye, I saw that she had been crying.

A few days later, she mailed me her old diary. It was pink, with horses and hearts printed on the cloth cover. She had started to write it a few years after the events; it really had a grip on her. She had stuck yellow Post-its on some of the pages for me. She had come up with the whole plan when she was eight. She wanted to have Miriam, her teacher, all for herself: she was jealous of Holbrecht, who sometimes came to pick up his wife. It was a little girl's fantasy. She had persuaded her girlfriend to back up her story. That was all.

A new trial was granted, the girlfriend admitted what the two of them had done back then, and Holbrecht was exonerated at the new hearing. It wasn't easy for the young women to testify. They apologised to Holbrecht in open court. He didn't care. We managed to keep the press out of it. He was awarded damages for the time he'd spent in prison as an innocent man. They amounted to a bit more than thirty thousand euros.

★ ★ ★

Holbrecht bought a little café in Charlottenburg; it sells homemade chocolates and good coffee. He lives with an Italian woman who loves him. Sometimes I drink an espresso there. We never discuss the affair.

Anatomy

He sat in the car. He had fallen asleep briefly, not a deep sleep, just a dreamless nodding-off for a few seconds. He waited and drank from the bottle of schnapps he'd bought in the supermarket. The wind blew sand against the car. There was sand everywhere here, a few centimetres under the grass. He was familiar with it all; he'd grown up here. At some point she would come out of the house and walk to the bus stop. Maybe she'd be wearing a dress again, a thin one, preferably the one with yellow and green flowers on it.

He thought about how he'd spoken to her. About her face, her skin under her dress, about how tall she was and how beautiful. She had barely looked at him. He had asked if she would like something to drink. He wasn't sure if she'd understood. She'd laughed at him. 'You're not my type,' she'd yelled, because the music was too loud. 'I'm sorry,' she added. He'd shrugged, as if it didn't matter. And grinned. What else was he supposed to do. Then he'd gone back to his table.

She wasn't going to make fun of him today. She would do what he wanted. He would possess her. He imagined her fear. The animals he'd killed had felt fear as well. He'd been able to see it. They smelled different just before they died. The larger they were, the more fear they felt. Birds were boring. Cats and dogs were better; they knew when death was coming. But animals couldn't talk. She would talk. It would be crucial to do it slowly so as to get the most out of it. That was the problem. Things mustn't move too fast. If he was too excited, it would go wrong. The way it did with the very first cat. He'd lost control right after he'd amputated the ears, and he'd stabbed it convulsively much too soon.

The set of dissecting instruments had been expensive, but it was complete, including bone shears, a Stryker saw to open the skull, the knife for cutting through cartilage and the knife for severing the head. He'd ordered it on the internet. He knew the anatomical atlas almost by heart. He'd written everything down in his diary, from the first meeting in the nightclub until today.

He'd taken photos of her secretly and glued her head on to pornographic pictures. He'd drawn in the line where he wanted to cut, with black dashes, like in the anatomical atlas.

She came out of the front door, and he got ready. As she shut the garden door behind her, he climbed out of the car. This would be the hardest part. He had to compel her to come with him, but she mustn't cry out. He had written down all the possible variants. Later the police found the notes, the pictures of the young woman, the slaughtered animals, and hundreds of splatter films in his parents' cellar. The officers had searched the house when they found his diary and the dissecting tools in his car. He also had a small chemistry lab in the cellar—his attempts to make chloroform had been unsuccessful.

The right side of the Mercedes hit him as he got out of his car. He flew over the hood, slammed his head onto the windshield, and landed on the ground on the left side of the car. He died on the way to the hospital. He was twenty-one.

I defended the driver of the Mercedes. He got an eighteen-month suspended sentence for negligent homicide.

The Other Man

Paulsberg stood next to his car. As he did every evening, he had turned off on the way home and driven up the little hill to his old ash tree. He had often sat here as a child in the shadow of the branches, carving figures out of wood and playing truant. He lowered the window; the days were already getting shorter again and the air was cooler. It was quiet. For the only moment in the day. His mobile phone was switched off. From here he could see his house, the house where he had grown up, built by his grandfather. It shone brightly, the trees in the garden lit by the sun; he could see the cars parked by the road. He would be there in a few minutes, his guests would already be waiting, and he would have to talk about all the idiocies that go to make up social life.

Paulsberg was forty-eight now. He owned

seventeen major retail businesses in Germany and Austria that sold expensive men's clothing. His great-grandfather had established the knitwear factory back there in the valley; Paulsberg had already learned everything about fabric and cut when he was a child. He had sold the factory.

He thought about his wife. Slim, elegant, enchanting, she would make conversation with everyone. She was thirty-six, a lawyer in an international firm, black suit, hair loose. He had met her in the airport in Zurich. They had both been waiting for their delayed flight in the café bar and he'd made her laugh. They made a date. Two years later they got married. That was eight years ago. Things could have gone well.

But then the thing in the hotel sauna happened, and it changed everything.

Every year after their marriage, they spent a few days in a mountain hotel in Upper Bavaria. They liked this way of unwinding, sleeping, walking, eating. The hotel was much cited for its 'wellness environment'. There were steam baths and Finnish saunas, indoor and outdoor pools, massages and mud packs. The garage was full of Mercedes, BMWs and Porsches. Everyone belonged.

Like most men of his age, Paulsberg had a paunch. His wife had kept herself in better shape. He was proud of her. As they sat in the sauna he observed the young man staring at her. A southerner, black hair, Italian perhaps, good-looking, smooth skin, tanned, around twenty-five. The stranger was looking at his wife as if she were some beautiful animal. It irritated her. He smiled at her; she looked away. Then he stood up with his penis half-erect, walked towards the exit, and stopped in front of her, turning towards her so that his member was right in her face. Paulsberg was about to intervene when the young man wrapped a towel around his hips and nodded to him.

Later, when they were back in their room, they made jokes about it. They saw the stranger at dinner; Paulsberg's wife smiled at him and blushed. They talked about him for the rest of the evening, and during the night they imagined what it would be like with him. They had sex for the first time in a long time. They were afraid, and they were turned on.

Next day at the same time they went back to the sauna, and the stranger was already waiting there. She opened her towel while she was still at the door, and walked slowly past him, naked, knowing exactly what she was doing and wanting him to know too. He got to his feet and stood in front of her again. She sat on the bench, and looked first at him, then at Paulsberg. Paulsberg nodded and said 'Yes' in a loud voice. She took the stranger's penis in her hand. Paulsberg saw the rhythmic motions of her arm through the steam in the sauna, he saw the young man's back in front of his wife, olive-skinned and shining wet. Nobody spoke; he heard the stranger panting; the movements of his wife's arm became slower. Then she turned to Paulsberg and showed him the stranger's semen on her face and body. The stranger picked up his towel and left the sauna without saying a word. They stayed behind in the heat.

First they experimented in public saunas, then in swinger clubs, and finally they advertised on the internet. They established rules: no violence, no love, no encounters at home. They would stop it all if either of them started to feel uncomfortable. They never stopped once. At the beginning he was the one who wrote the copy, then she took over; they posted masked photos on websites. After four years they had it down to a science. They'd found a discreet country hotel. There they would meet men at weekends who'd answered their ads. He said he was making his wife available. They thought it was a game, but after so many encounters it wasn't a game anymore, it had become a part of them. His wife was still a lawyer, she was still radiant and unapproachable, but at weekends she became an object used by other people. That was how they wanted it. It had simply presented itself; there was no explanation.

The name in the email had meant nothing to him, nor could he connect the photo with anyone; he had stopped looking at the photos the men sent a long time ago. His wife had written back to the man and now he was standing in front of them in the hotel reception hall. Paulsberg knew him fleetingly from school thirty-five years before. They had had nothing to do with each other there. He was in the same year, but a different class. They sat on the barstools in the lobby and told each other the things people who've been at school together always tell each other, they talked about former teachers, the friends they'd both known, and tried to ignore the situation. But it didn't get any better. The other man ordered whisky instead of beer and spoke too loudly. Paulsberg knew the firm he worked for, he was in the same business. The three of them ate dinner together, and the other man drank too much. He flirted with Paulsberg's wife, saying she was young and beautiful and Paulsberg was to be envied, and he kept on drinking. Paulsberg wanted to leave. She began to talk about sex and about the men who sent her pictures and whom they met. At a certain point she laid her hand on the other man's hand, and they went to the room they always booked.

While the other man was having sex with his wife, Paulsberg sat on the sofa. He looked at the picture that hung over the bed: a young woman standing on the seashore. The artist had painted her from behind, in a blue-and-white bathing suit of the kind worn in the twenties. 'She must be beautiful,' he thought. At some point she would turn around, smile at the artist, and they would go home together. Paulsberg thought about the fact that he and his wife had been married for eight years now.

Later, when they were alone in the car, neither of them said a word. She stared out of the passenger window into the darkness until they reached home. During the night he went to the kitchen to drink a glass of water, and when he came back he saw the display on her phone light up.

She had been taking Prozac for a long time.
She thought she was dependent on it and never
left the house without the green-and-white pills.
She didn't know why she satisfied men. Sometimes in the night, when the house was still and
Paulsberg was asleep and she couldn't stand the
bright green numbers on her alarm clock, she got
dressed and went out into the garden. She would
lie down on one of the lounge chairs by the pool
and look up at the sky, waiting for the feeling
that she'd known ever since her father died. She
could hardly bear it. There were billions of solar
systems in the Milky Way and billions of Milky
Ways. And, in between, nothing but cold and the
void. She had lost control.

Paulsberg had long since forgotten about the other
man. He was at the annual Association conference
in Cologne, standing at the buffet in the breakfast
room, when the man called his name. Paulsberg
turned around.

Suddenly the world slowed down, and became
viscous. Later he would remember every image,
the butter floating in ice water, the colourful
yoghurt cartons, the red napkins and the slices
of sausage on the white hotel plates. Paulsberg

thought the other man looked like one of those blind amphibians he'd seen as a child in caves in Yugoslavia. He'd caught one and carried it all the way back to the hotel, wanting to show his mother. When he opened his hand, it was dead. The other man's head was shaved bald; watery eyes, thin eyebrows, thick lips, almost blue. The lips had kissed his wife. The other man's tongue moved in slow motion, pushing against the inner surface of his front teeth as he said his name. Paulsberg saw the colourless threads of spittle, the pores on his tongue, the long thin hairs in his nostrils, the larynx pressing hard against the reddened skin from the inside. Paulsberg didn't understand what the other man was saying. He saw the girl in the blue-and-white bathing suit from the picture in the hotel; she turned around towards him, smiled, then pointed to the thin man kneeling over his wife. Paulsberg felt his heartbeat stop; he imagined himself falling over, dragging the tablecloth down with him. He saw himself lying dead between the sliced oranges, the white sausages and the cream cheese. But he didn't fall. It was only a moment. He nodded at the other man.

★ ★ ★

There were all the usual speeches at the Association meeting. They looked at presentations, and there was filter coffee out of silver vacuum jugs. After a few hours nobody was listening anymore. It was nothing special.

That afternoon the other man came to his room. They drank the beer he'd brought with him. He also had some cocaine and offered Paulsberg a line; he tipped the powder onto the glass table and inhaled it through a rolled-up banknote. When he went to the bathroom to wash his hands, Paulsberg followed him. The other man was standing at the basin, bent over to wash his face. Paulsberg saw his ears and the yellowed edge of his white shirt collar.

He couldn't help himself.

Now Paulsberg was sitting on the bed. The hotel room was like a thousand others he had slept in. Two slabs of chocolate in the brown mini-bar, vacuum-packed peanuts, yellow plastic bottle opener. A smell of disinfectant, liquid soap in the bathroom, the sign on the tiles saying Please support the environment by re-using your towels.

He closed his eyes and thought about the horse. He had walked across the bridge that morning and then to the stone steps leading to the water

CRIME & GUILT

meadows by the Rhine in the early mist that was coming off the river. And suddenly there it was, right in front of him, steam rising from its coat, its nostrils soft and bright red.

He would have to call her at some point. She would ask him when he was coming back. She would tell him about her day, the people in the office, the cleaning lady who banged around the rubbish bins too loudly, and all the other things that made up her life. He would say nothing about the other man. And then they would hang up and try to go on with their lives.

Paulsberg heard the other man in the bathroom, groaning. He threw the cigarette into a half-full glass of water, took his travelling bag, and left the room. When he was paying his bill at reception, he said it would be a good idea for the room to be made up quickly. The girl behind the counter looked at him, but he didn't say anything else.

They found the other man twenty minutes later. He survived.

Paulsberg had done it with the ashtray in the bathroom.

It was a 1970s piece, thick and heavy, made of

dark smoked glass. The pathologist later catego-
rised it as blunt-force trauma; the edges of the
wounds could not be clearly distinguished. The
ashtray was identified as the weapon.

Paulsberg had seen the holes in the other man's
head as the blood poured out of them, brighter
than he had expected. 'He's not dying,' he thought
as he kept hitting the skull, 'he's bleeding but he's
not dying.'

Paulsberg finally jammed the other man in
between the bathtub and the toilet and laid him
face down on the lid of the toilet. He'd wanted to
hit him one last time, and raised his arm to strike.
The other man's hair had clumped together; it
looked stiff with blood, black wires like pencils
on the pale skin of his head. Suddenly Paulsberg
found himself thinking about his wife, and the
way they'd said goodbye for the first time, in
January ten years ago; the sky was made of ice
and they'd stood on the road outside the airport,
freezing. He thought of her thin shoes in the
slush, and of her blue coat with the big buttons,
and the way she'd turned up the collar, holding
the lapels together with one hand. She'd laughed;
she was lonely and beautiful and wounded. After
she'd got into the taxi, he'd known she belonged
to him.

Paulsberg set the ashtray down on the floor. The officers found it later among the red smears on the tiles. The other man had groaned quietly again as he left. Paulsberg no longer wanted to kill him.

The trial began five months later. Paulsberg was accused of attempted murder. According to the prosecutor, he'd tried to kill the man from behind. The indictment stated that at issue was cocaine. The prosecutor couldn't have known better.

Paulsberg gave no reason for his act and said nothing about the other man. 'Call my wife,' were his only words to the policeman after his arrest. Nothing more. The judges were casting around for a motive. Nobody simply batters another man in his hotel room. The prosecutor had been unable to find any connection between the men. The psychiatrist said Paulsberg was 'absolutely normal'; no drugs were found in his system and nobody believed he'd tried to kill out of sheer blood lust.

The only person who could have provided the information was the other man. But he kept silent too. The judges couldn't force him to testify. The police had found cocaine in his pocket and on the glass table; preliminary proceedings had been initiated against him, and this allowed him to remain silent—he could have incriminated himself by making any statement.

Of course judges do not have to know the motives of a defendant in order to sentence him. But they want to know why people do what they do. And only when they understand can they punish the defendant in a way that is commensurate with his guilt. If that understanding is lacking, the sentence will almost always be longer. The judges didn't know that Paulsberg wished to protect his wife. She was a lawyer; he had committed a crime. Her office had not yet fired her: no one can do anything about an insane husband. But the partners in the law firm would not be able to accept the truth about all the unknown men, and so she would have been unable to continue in her job. Paulsberg left the decision up to his wife. She was to do what she thought was right.

She appeared as a witness without legal counsel. She seemed fragile, too delicately spun a creature to belong with Paulsberg. The judge instructed her that she had the right to remain silent. Nobody believed anything new was now going to come out in this trial. But then she started to speak and it all changed.

In almost every jury trial there is this one moment when everything suddenly becomes clear. I thought she was going to talk about the unknown men. But she told a different story. She spoke for forty-five minutes without interruption, she was clear, explicit, and did not contradict herself. She said she had had an affair with the other man and Paulsberg had found out. He had wanted to separate; he was crazed with jealousy. The guilt was hers, not his. She said her husband had found the film she and her lover had made. She handed the court usher a DVD. Paulsberg and she had often made similar films. This one came from the encounter with the other man. The video camera had been on a tripod next to the bed. The public was asked to leave, as we had to view it. You can find such films on countless sites on the internet. There was no doubt: it was the other man who was having sex with her. The prosecutor observed Paulsberg while the film was running. He remained calm.

The prosecutor had made yet another mistake. Our criminal law is more than 130 years old. It is an intelligent law. Sometimes things don't go the way the perpetrator wants. His revolver is loaded. He has five bullets. He approaches a woman, he shoots, he wants to kill her. He misses four times, only a single shot grazes her arm. Then he's standing right in front of her. He pushes the barrel of the revolver against her stomach, he cocks it, he sees the blood running down her arm, and he sees her fear. Perhaps he has second thoughts. A bad law would sentence the man for attempted murder; an intelligent law wants to save the woman. Our criminal code says that he can step back from his attempt to murder without incurring punishment. Which is to say: if he stops now, if he doesn't kill her, his only punishment will be for endangering her by inflicting bodily injury— not for attempted murder. So it's up to him: the law will be friendly to him if he does the right thing at this point and lets his victim live. Professors call this 'the golden bridge'. I never liked this expression. The things that go on inside people at such moments are too complicated, and a golden bridge belongs more in a Chinese garden. But the idea behind the law is right.

Paulsberg had stopped beating in the other man's skull. At the end, he no longer wanted to kill him. This meant that he stepped back from attempted murder; the judges could only convict him of endangering someone by inflicting bodily injury.

The court could refute neither Paulsberg's

statement nor his wife's testimony and hence
could not refute his motive. He was sentenced to
three and a half years.

His wife visited him regularly in prison,
then he was transferred to the daytime release
program. Two years after the trial the remainder
of the sentence was commuted to probation. She
resigned from her position in the law firm and
they moved back to the town where she'd grown
up in Schleswig-Holstein; she opened a small law
practice there. He sold his shops and the house
and began to take photographs. Not long ago he
had his first exhibition in Berlin. All the photos
were of a faceless naked woman.

The Briefcase

The police sergeant was standing in a carpark on the Berlin Ring Road. She and her colleagues were the last checkpoint in a routine traffic control operation, a boring job, and she would have preferred to be one of the drivers sitting in the warmth, only having to open their windows a crack. It was nine degrees below; only the occasional frozen blade of grass broke through the crusted snow cover, and the damp cold crawled through her uniform and into her bones. She wished she were up at the front, choosing which cars would be checked, but that job belonged to her superiors. She had moved from Cologne to Berlin only two months before. Now she was longing for her bathtub. She just couldn't take the cold; it had never been as bad as this in Cologne.

The next vehicle was an Opel Omega, silver

grey, Polish plates. The car looked well cared for, no dents, all its lights in order. The driver lowered the window and handed out his licence and registration. Everything seemed normal, he didn't smell of alcohol, and his smile was friendly. The policewoman didn't know why, but she had a strange feeling. While she read his papers she tried to identify it. At the police academy they had taught her to trust her instincts, but that she had to find a logical reason for them.

It was a rental car from an international company; the rental agreement was made out to the driver and all the papers were right there. And then she realised what was bothering her: the car was empty. There was nothing lying in it, no crumpled chewing gum paper, no newspapers, no suitcase, no cigarette lighters, no gloves, nothing. The car was as empty as if it had just been delivered from the factory. The driver spoke no German. She waved over a colleague who spoke a little Polish. They told the man, who was still smiling, to get out of the car and asked him to open the boot. The driver nodded and pressed the button. Everything in here was clean to the point of sterility too; the only thing lying in the middle was a briefcase made of red imitation leather. The policewoman pointed to it and made a sign to the man to open it. He shrugged and shook his head. She bent forward to look at the locks. They were simple combination locks, set to zero, and opened immediately. She lifted the lid of the case, and recoiled so violently that she banged the back of her head against the lid of the boot. She managed to turn away, then she threw up on the road. Her colleague, who hadn't seen what was in the case, drew his weapon and yelled at the driver to put his hands on the roof of the car. Other police officers came running and the driver was over-powered. The policewoman was white; traces of vomit clung to the corners of her mouth. She said, 'Oh my God,' and then she threw up again.

The police took the man to Keithstrasse, which houses the Major Case Department. The red briefcase was sent to forensics. Although it was Saturday, a call was made to Lanninger, the chief coroner. The briefcase contained eighteen colour photocopies of corpses, all apparently laser prints. All of their faces looked the same: mouths wide open, eyeballs protruding. People die, and pathologists deal with them; it's their job. But the pictures were unusual, eleven men and seven women were all lying on their backs in the same twisted pose. They all looked strangely similar:

they were naked and the rough point of a wooden stake was sticking out of each stomach.

Jan Bathowitz was the name on the Polish passport. When he was brought in, they wanted to question him at once; the police interpreter was standing ready. Bathowitz was polite, almost meek, but he kept repeating he wanted to call his embassy first. It was his right and finally they allowed him to make the call. He said his name and the legal staff at the embassy advised him to remain silent until a lawyer could get there. That too was his right, and Bathowitz exercised it.

Chief Inspector Pätzold could hold the suspect until the end of the following day, and this he did. So the man was taken to the holding pen and locked in a cell. As they did with every prisoner, they took away his shoelaces and his belt in case he tried to hang himself. When I got there at two o'clock the next day, the questioning could proceed. I advised Bathowitz not to answer. Nonetheless he wanted to make a statement.

'Your name?' Chief Inspector Pätzold looked bored, but he was wide awake. The interpreter translated every question and every answer.

'Jan Bathowitz.'

Pätzold went through the man's particulars; he had had the passport checked out and it appeared to be genuine. A message had been sent to the Polish authorities the day before, asking if there were any charges against Bathowitz, but as always such enquiries took forever.

'Mr Bathowitz, you know why you're here.'

'Your police brought me here.'

'Yes. Do you know why?'

'No.'

'Where did you get the photos?'

'What photos?'

'We found eighteen photos in your briefcase.'

'It's not my briefcase.'

'Aha. So whose is it?'

'A businessman from Witoslaw, my hometown.'

'What's the name of this businessman?'

'I don't know. He gave me the briefcase and said I was to bring it to Berlin.'

'But you have to know what his name is.'

'No, I didn't have to know that.'

'Why?'

'I met him in a bar. He spoke to me, he paid me right up front and in cash.'

'Did you know what's in the photos?'

'No, the briefcase was closed when I got it. I have no idea.'

'You didn't look inside?'

'It was shut.'

'But it wasn't locked. You could have looked inside.'

'I don't do things like that,' said Bathowitz.

'Mr Pätzold,' I said, 'what is the actual charge against my client?'

Pätzold looked at me. That was the point, and of course he knew it.

'We've had the photographs examined. Professor Lanninger says the corpses are most likely genuine.'

'Yes?' I said.

'What do you mean, *yes*? Your client had photos of corpses in his briefcase. Corpses with stakes through them.'

'I still haven't found out what the charge is. Transporting colour photocopies of photographs of corpses made by a laser printer? Lanninger is no Photoshop expert, and "most likely" is not the same as "definitely". And even if they were genuine corpses, there is no law against having pictures of them. There's nothing here that constitutes a criminal offence.'

Pätzold knew I was right. Nonetheless, I could understand his position.

At that moment, we could have left. I stood

up and took my briefcase. But then my client did something I didn't understand. He laid a hand on my forearm and said he didn't mind the chief inspector's questions. I wanted a break, but Bathowitz shook his head and said, 'It's fine.'

Pätzold's questions continued. 'To whom does the briefcase belong?'

'The man in the bar.'

'What were you supposed to do with it?'

'I already said I was supposed to bring it to Berlin.'

'Did the man say what was in the case?'

'Yes he did.'

'What?'

'He said it was blueprints for a big project. There was a lot of money involved.'

'Blueprints?'

'Yes.'

'Why didn't he send the plans by courier?'

'I didn't ask. He said he didn't trust couriers.'

'Why?'

'He said couriers in Poland are always working for both sides. He preferred to have a stranger whom nobody knew transport the things.'

'Where were you to take the pictures?'

Bathowitz didn't hesitate for second. He said, 'To Kreuzberg.'

Pätzold nodded; he seemed to have achieved his aim.

'To whom in Kreuzberg? What's his name?'

I don't understand Polish, but I understood the tone in Bathowitz's voice. He was totally calm. 'I don't know. I was supposed to go to a phone booth at five o'clock.'

'Excuse me?'

'Mehringdamm, Yorckstrasse.' He said these words first in German, then in Polish. 'There's apparently a phone booth there. I'm to be there at five o'clock tomorrow afternoon, and the phone will ring, and I'll be told the rest of it.'

Pätzold continued questioning him for another hour. The story didn't change. Bathowitz remained friendly, he answered every question politely, nothing made him tense. Pätzold couldn't find holes in any of his statements.

Bathowitz was fingerprinted and photographed. The computer had no trace of him. The enquiry to Poland was answered: everything appeared to be in order. Pätzold must either release Bathowitz or go before a judge. The prosecutor's office declined to make a request for an arrest warrant; Pätzold had no choice. He asked Bathowitz if he'd agree to leave the briefcase with the police. Bathowitz shrugged; all he asked was a receipt for it. At seven that evening he was allowed to leave the police station. He said goodbye to me on the steps of the old building, walked to his car, and disappeared.

Twenty policemen were posted around the phone booth next day and the police cars in the neighbourhood were on alert. A Polish-born plainclothes officer who had roughly the same build as Bathowitz and was wearing similar clothes stood in the phone booth at 5 p.m. with the red briefcase. A judge had granted a warrant to tap the phone line. The phone didn't ring.

A jogger found the body on Tuesday morning at a parking spot in the woods. The 6.35 millimetre Browning had made only small entry wounds, circular, barely half a centimetre across. It was an execution. Pätzold could only start a new file and notify his colleagues in Poland. The cause of Bathowitz's death was never determined.

Desire

She had positioned the chair in front of the window. She liked to drink her tea there, because she could see into the playground. A girl was doing cartwheels while two boys watched. The girl was a little older than the boys. When she fell down, she started to cry. She ran to her mother and showed her the scrape on her elbow. The mother had a bottle of water and a handkerchief and swabbed the wound clean. The girl looked over to the boys as she stood between her mother's legs holding the arm out to her. It was Sunday. He would be coming back with the children in an hour. She would set the table; friends were coming to visit. It was silent in the apartment. She stared into the playground again without seeing what was happening there.

They were fine. She did everything the way

she'd always done it: conversations with her husband about work, shopping at the super-market, tennis lessons for the children, Christmas with her parents or parents-in-law. She uttered the same sentences she always uttered; she wore the same clothes she always wore. She went shop-ping for shoes with her girlfriends, and went to the movies once a month if she could get a baby-sitter. She kept up to date with exhibitions and plays. She watched the news, read the political section of the paper, paid attention to the chil-dren, attended parent–teacher days at school. She didn't do any exercise, but she hadn't put on weight.

Her husband suited her; she'd always believed that. But it wasn't his fault. It was nobody's fault. It had just happened. She hadn't been able to do anything about it. She could remember every detail of the evening when it all became clear.

'Are you ill?' he had said. 'You look pale.'

'No.'

'What's the matter?'

'Nothing, darling, I'm just going to go to bed now. It was a long day.'

Much later, when they were lying in bed, she'd suddenly been unable to breathe. She'd lain awake until morning, rigid with anxiety and guilt, her

thighs cramping. She didn't want it that way, but
it had stayed that way. And, while making breakfast for the children next day and checking their
schoolbags, she had known she would never feel
any different again: she was totally empty inside.
She would have to keep living with that.

That was two years ago. They went on living
together; he didn't notice. Nobody noticed. They
rarely had sex, and when they did she was affable
about it.

Gradually everything disappeared, until she
was a mere shell. The world became alien to her;
she no longer belonged in it. The children laughed,
her husband got excited, their friends argued—but
nothing touched her. She was serious, she laughed,
she cried, she comforted—everything the way it
usually was, and all on cue. But when things were
quiet and she looked at other people in cafés or on
the tram, she felt none of it had anything to do
with her anymore.

At some point she started. She stood for half
an hour in front of the shelves with the stockings, went away, came back. Then she grabbed.
It didn't matter what size or what colour. She
shoved the packs under her coat too hastily and
the stockings slid to the floor. She bent down,
then ran. Her heart was racing, she could feel the

pulse in her neck and stains on her hands. Her whole body was wet. She didn't feel her legs, she was trembling, then she was past the checkout. Someone bumped into her. Then the ice-cold evening air, and rain. Adrenaline flooded her; she wanted to scream. Two corners further on, she threw the stockings into a rubbish bin. Taking off her shoes, she ran home in the rain. Outside her front door she looked up into the sky. The water splashed onto her forehead, her eyes, her mouth. She was alive.

She only ever stole things she didn't need, and only when she couldn't bear it any longer. She wouldn't always get away with it, she knew that. Her husband would say that was in the nature of things. He always made remarks like that. He was right. When the detective stopped her, she confessed immediately, right there on the street. People passing by stopped to stare at her, a child pointed and said, 'That woman stole things.' The detective was holding her tight by the arm. He took her to his office and wrote up a report for the police: name, address, identity card number, sequence of events, value of goods 12.99 euros, tick the relevant box 'admitted: yes/no'. He was wearing a checked shirt and smelled of sweat. She was the woman with the Louis Vuitton handbag and the Gucci wallet, credit cards, and 845.36 euros in cash. He showed her where to sign. She read the sheet and wondered for a moment if she could correct his spelling mistakes, the way she did with her children. He said she would get something from the police in the mail, and grinned at her. The remains of a sausage roll were lying on the table. She thought of her husband, and imagined the trial, with the judge questioning her. The detective took her out through a side door.

The police asked her to make a written statement. She came to my office with it. It didn't take long to settle. It was the first time, the value of the goods was minimal, she had no previous convictions. The prosecutor's office stopped the proceedings. No one in the family learned of it.

Things settled down, the way everything in her life had always settled down.

Snow

The old man stood in the kitchen and smoked. It was August, the day was warm, and he'd opened the window wide. He looked at the ashtray: a naked mermaid with a green fishtail and underneath, in script, 'Welcome to the Reeperbahn'. He didn't know where he'd got it. The colour on the girl had faded and the 'R' of Reeperbahn had disappeared. The drops of water splashed into the metal sink, slow and hard. It calmed him. He would remain standing at the window, smoking and doing nothing.

The special task force had assembled in front of the building. The policemen were wearing uniforms that looked too big, and black helmets; they carried riot shields. They were brought in when things got too difficult for the others, and armed resistance was anticipated. They were hard men with a hard code. The task force had sustained deaths and injuries, which meant the adrenaline was building up in them. They had their orders: *Drug den, suspects thought to be armed, arrest.* They were now standing silently by the rubbish bins in the courtyard and waiting both on the staircase and in front of the apartment. It was too hot under their helmets and riot masks. They were waiting for the word from the leader of the task force; everyone was eager to hear it now. At some point he would yell, 'Go, go, go,' and then they'd do what they had been trained to do.

The old man at the window thought about Hassan and his friends. They had the key to his apartment and when they came during the night they made up the little packages in his kitchen, 'stretching', they called it, two-thirds heroin, one-third lidocaine. They compressed it into rectangular lumps with a jack. Each lump weighed a kilo. Hassan paid the old man a thousand euros every month, and he did it punctually.

Of course it was too much money for one and a half rooms in the back of a building, fourth floor, too dark. But they wanted the old man's apartment, nothing would serve them better as what they called their 'bunker'. The kitchen was big enough and that was all they needed. The old man slept in the room and when they came he switched on the television so that he didn't have to listen to them. The only thing was, he couldn't cook anymore: the kitchen was crammed with plastic wrappers, precision scales, spatulas and rolls of adhesive tape. The worst thing was the white dust that settled in a film on everything. Hassan had explained the risk to the old man, but he didn't care. He had nothing to lose. It was a good business arrangement, and he'd never cooked anyway. He drew on his cigarette and looked up at the sky: not a cloud to be seen, it would get even hotter before evening.

He first heard the policemen when they broke down the door. It all went fast, and there was no point in fighting back. He was thrown to the floor, fell over the kitchen stool, and broke two ribs. Then they yelled that he was to tell them where the Arabs were. Because they were so loud, he said nothing. And also because his ribs hurt. He kept silent later in front of the examining magistrate too—he had been in prison too often, and he knew it was too early to talk. They wouldn't let him go now if he did.

The old man lay on his bed, cell number 178, C block, in the prison where detainees await trial. He heard the key and knew he had to say something to the female guard now, or nod, or move a foot; otherwise she wouldn't leave. She came every morning at 6.15; it was called 'life check'. They were looking to see if any of the prisoners had died in the night or killed themselves. The old man said everything was in order. The guard would also have collected his mail except that he had no one to write to, and she no longer asked. When he was alone again, he turned to the wall. He stared at the bright yellow oil paint that reached two-thirds of the way up, until it got to a white stripe. The floors were light grey. Everything here looked the same.

As soon as he woke up, he had thought about the fact that today was their wedding anniversary. And now he thought again about the man who was sleeping with his wife. His wife.

It had all started with the singlet. He remembered the summer evening twenty-two years ago when he found it under the bed. It was lying there all crumpled up and somehow dirty. It wasn't his singlet, although that was what his wife kept saying. He knew it belonged to the other man. After that nothing was the same. In the end he used it to clean his shoes, but that didn't change things either, and at a certain point he'd had to move out or else he'd have fallen apart. His wife cried. He didn't take anything with him; he left the money and the car and even the watch she'd given him. He quit his job. It was a good one, but he couldn't keep going there; he couldn't bear it any longer. He got drunk every evening, silently and systematically. At a certain point it became a habit, and he sank into a world of schnapps, petty crime and social security. He didn't want anything else. He was just waiting for the end.

But today was different. The woman who wanted to talk to him was called Jana, plus a last name that had too many letters in it. They told him there must have been a mix-up, she had applied for a visitor's permit. She didn't need his permission for that. So he went to the visiting room at the appointed time and sat down with her at the table covered with green plastic. The officer who was supervising the conversation sat in the corner and tried not to disturb them.

She looked at him. He knew he was ugly. His nose and his chin had been growing towards each other for years until they almost formed a semicircle, his hair was just about gone, and his stubble was grey. She looked at him anyway. She looked at him in a way no one had looked at him for years. He scratched his neck. Then she said in a strong Polish accent that he had beautiful hands, and he knew she was lying, but it was okay that she said it. She was beautiful. Like the Madonna in the village church, he thought. As a boy he had always stared at her during Mass, and imagined that God was inside her stomach, and that it was a riddle how he'd managed to get in there. Jana was in her seventh month, everything about her was round and radiant and full of life. She leaned over the table and touched his sunken cheek with her fingertips. He stared at her breasts and then was ashamed and said, 'I've lost all my teeth.' He tried to smile. She nodded in a friendly way. They sat at the table for twenty minutes and didn't utter another word. The officer was familiar with this; it often happened that prisoner and visitor had nothing to say to each other. When the officer said that visiting time was over she stood up, leaned forward quickly again and whispered in the old man's ear, 'Hassan is the father of my child.' He smelled her perfume, and felt her hair on his old face. She blushed. That was all. Then she left and he was taken back to his cell. He sat on his bed and stared at his hands with their age spots and scars, he thought about Jana and the baby in her stomach, he thought about how warm and safe it was in there, and he knew what he had to do.

When Jana got home, Hassan was asleep. She undressed, lay down beside him and felt his breath on the back of her neck. She loved this man whom she couldn't make sense of. He was different from the boys in her village in Poland, he was grown up, and his skin seemed to be made of velvet.

Later, when he woke up for a moment, she told him the old man wouldn't testify against him; he could stop worrying. But he had to do something for him, buy him new teeth, she'd already spoken to a social worker who could take care of it. No one would find out. She was all worked up and talking too fast. Hassan stroked her stomach till she fell asleep.

'Does your client wish to make a statement about the men behind this? If so, the court could consider sparing him any further pre-trial detention.' I had taken on the defence on a pro bono basis and applied for a review of his remand. Everything had been negotiated with the court; the man would be released. It was not a complicated set of proceedings. The police had found 200 grams of heroin in the apartment. Worse still: the old man had had a knife in his pocket. The law calls this trafficking with weapons; the minimum sentence—the same as for manslaughter—is five years. The intention of the law is to protect officers from attack. The old man had to provide the name of the actual perpetrator: it seemed to be his only chance. But he remained silent. 'In which case pre-trial detention will continue,' said the judge, shaking his head.

The old man was happy. The Polish girl must not have her baby alone. 'That's more important than me,' he thought, and even as he was thinking it he knew that he'd won something distinct from—and more important than—his freedom.

The trial began four months later. They fetched the old man from his cell and led him to the courtroom. They had to pause for a moment in front of the Christmas tree. It was standing in the main corridor of the prison, as enormous as it was foreign, the electric candles reflected in the decorative balls which hung in orderly gradation, the largest ones at the foot, the smaller ones above. The power cord from the bright red drum was attached to the floor with black-and-yellow warning stickers. There are safety precautions for things like that.

It rapidly became clear to the judges that the old man could not be the owner of the drugs; he simply didn't have the money for that. Nonetheless what was at issue was the five-year minimum term. No one wanted to sentence him to something that long—it would have been unjust—but there seemed to be no way out.

During a recess something strange happened: the old man was eating some bread and cheese which he was cutting into tiny little pieces with a plastic knife. As I was looking at him he apologised: he didn't have his teeth anymore and had to cut up everything he ate into these little morsels. The rest of it was simple. That was why, indeed it was the only reason why, he had had the knife in his pocket. He needed it so as to be able to eat. There was a decision handed down by the Federal Court that said trafficking with a weapon didn't apply if the knife was clearly intended for another use.

The business with the teeth was perhaps an odd explanation, but this was also the last trial of the year. Everyone was relaxed, during the recesses the prosecutor was talking about the presents he hadn't yet bought, and we were all wondering if it was going to snow. Finally the old man was given a two-year suspended sentence, and he was released from prison.

I wondered where he would spend Christmas; the lease on his apartment had been terminated and he had no one he could go to. I stood on one of the higher landings and watched him walk slowly down the stairs.

On the 24th of December the old man was lying in the hospital. The operation wasn't due to take place until the second of January, but the clinic had insisted that he go directly from jail to hospital. They were afraid of an alcoholic relapse. The social worker had organised every-thing, and, when the old man was first told of it, he didn't want to do it. But then he heard that someone called Jana, or so the social worker said, had already paid for his new teeth at the clinic. Because they came from her he pretended she was a relative and agreed.

The hospital bed was clean, he'd showered and shaved, and they'd given him a gown with a yellow pattern on it. There was a Santa Claus made of chocolate on his nightstand. Its chest was squashed in and it looked oddly lopsided. He liked that. 'He's just like me,' he thought. He was somewhat afraid of the operation; they were going to take a piece of bone from his hip. But he was excited about the new teeth. In a few months he would finally be able to eat normally again. As he went to sleep, he no longer dreamed of the singlet under his bed. He dreamed of Jana, her hair, her smell, her stomach, and he was happy.

About two kilometres away Jana was sitting on the sofa telling her sleeping baby the Christmas story. She had cooked borscht for Hassan. It was a lot of work, but she knew how to do it; after her father died, that was how her mother had kept the little family's heads above water in Karpacz in south-western Poland. Borscht made with brisket of beef and beetroot for the tourists who hiked over the mountain and were hungry. That had been her childhood, her mother standing out in the cold every day with her pots and her Bunsen burners among the other women, as they all squeezed the last of the goodness out of the vegetables and then threw them behind them into the snow. Jana told the baby about the red snow you could see from a long way away, and the fine smell of the soup and the gas burners. She thought about her village there in the mountains, and her family, and she told stories about Christmas, the yellow lights, roast goose and Uncle Malek who owned the bakery and certainly had baked the biggest cake again today.

Hassan was not coming back, she knew that. But he had been there with her when the baby came, he had held her hand and wiped the sweat from her forehead. He had stayed calm when she screamed, he was always calm when it came right down to it, and she believed nothing would happen to her as long as he was there. But she had also always sensed that he would go; he was far too young. She could only live in peace if she loved him from a distance. Suddenly she felt alone, she missed the village and her family, she missed it all so much it hurt, and she decided to take the train to Poland the next morning.

Hassan was driving through the city. He couldn't go to see her; he didn't know what to say. He was engaged to another woman in Lebanon; he had to marry her, his parents had arranged it while he was still a child. Jana was a good woman; she had saved him from prison; she was clear and direct in every way. He slowly worked himself into a fury, at himself and his family and the world in general. And then he saw him.

The man was just coming out of a shop where he had been buying his last presents. He owed Hassan 20,000 euros and had simply disappeared. Hassan had been looking for him for weeks. He stopped the car, took the hammer out of the glove compartment, and followed the man to the entrance of a building. Seizing him by the throat, he threw him against the wall. The shopping bags fell to the ground. The other man said he wanted to pay but it was taking a little time. He begged. Hassan wasn't listening to him anymore; he was staring at the little gift parcels lying in the hallway. He saw the printed Father Christmases and the golden gift ribbons and suddenly it all came together in his head: Jana and the baby, the heat of Lebanon, his father and his future wife. He realised he couldn't change any of it now.

It took far too long and a neighbour said later he'd heard the blows interspersed with the screams, a dull, wet sound like you hear at the butcher's. When the police were eventually able to pull Hassan off the man's upper body, his victim's mouth was a mass of blood. Hassan had smashed eleven of his teeth with the hammer.

Snow did fall that night. It was Christmas.

The Key

The Russian spoke German with a heavy accent.
The three of them were sitting on three red sofas
in a café in Amsterdam. The Russian had been
drinking vodka for hours while Frank and Atris
drank beer. They couldn't work out the Russian's
age, maybe he was fifty; his left eyelid drooped
since his stroke, and his right hand was missing
two fingers. He said he'd been a career soldier in
the Red Army. 'Chechnya and all that.' He held
up his mutilated hand. He liked talking about the
war. 'Yeltsin is a woman, but Putin, Putin's a man,'
he said. It was a market economy now, everyone
understood that. A market economy meant you
could buy anything. A seat in parliament cost $3
million, a ministerial post $7 million. Everything
had been better during the war with Chechnya,
and more honourable; men had been men. He had

respected the Chechens. He'd killed a lot of them. Their children would already be playing with Kalashnikovs, they were good fighters, tenacious. They should drink to them. A lot of alcohol was drunk that evening.

They'd had to listen to the Russian for a long time. Finally he got around to the pills. Ukrainian chemists were going to make them; they'd lost their state jobs and were out of work. They'd had to privatise; their wives and children had to eat. The Russian had also offered Frank and Atris everything imaginable: machine guns, howitzers, grenades. He even had a photo of a tank in his wallet. He looked at it tenderly and passed it around. He said he could get viruses too, but that was a dirty business. They all nodded.

Frank and Atris didn't want weapons. They wanted the pills. The previous night they'd tried out the drugs on three girls they'd brought back from a nightclub. The girls had told them in a mixture of English and German that they were going to study history and politics. They had all driven to the hotel where they drank and fooled around. Frank and Atris had given them the pills. Atris found himself thinking repeatedly about the things they did next. The red-haired one had lain down on the table in front of Frank and tipped the ice from the champagne bucket on her face. She'd screamed it was too hot for her and they were to hit her, but Frank didn't want to. He had faced the table with his trousers down, smoking an enormous cigar while his hips moved rhythmically and the girl's legs rested on his chest, as he kept up a complicated monologue about the dissolution of Communism and its consequences for the drug trade. The cigar made it hard to understand him. Atris lay on the bed and watched him. After he'd told the two girls between his legs not to keep going, they'd fallen asleep, one of them with his big toe still in her mouth. Atris realised the pills would be perfect for Berlin.

Now the Russian was talking about the drug-sniffing dogs. He knew everything about them. 'In South Korea they even clone them because they're so expensive,' he said. You had to weld a metal box into the car and then prepare it by stuffing bags of garbage, coffee, and washing powder into it, all separated by thick wrappers; it was your only chance to stop the dogs smelling something. Then he went back to talking about the war. He asked Atris and Frank if they'd ever killed anyone. Frank shook his head.

'With the Chechens it's like potato chips,' the Russian said.

'What?' said Frank.

'Potato chips. With the Chechens it's like a bag of potato chips.'

'I don't get it,' said Frank.

'Once you start killing them, you can't stop till they're all gone. You have to kill them all. Every single one of them.' The Russian laughed. Then suddenly he turned serious, and stared at his crippled hand. 'Otherwise they come back,' he said.

'Ah,' said Frank. 'The revenge of the chips... Now could we talk about the pills again?' He wanted to go home.

The Russian screamed at Frank, 'You stupid arsehole, why don't you listen? Look at your friend. He's a lump of meat but at least he's paying attention.'

Frank looked over at Atris, who was sitting in the corner of the sofa. A dark blue vein was standing out on his forehead. Frank knew that vein, and knew what was going to happen next.

'We're talking about the war here, and you don't have time to listen? We can't do business this way. You're idiots,' said the Russian.

Atris stood up. He weighed 105 kilos. He lifted one side of the glass table until it was on edge. Bottles, glasses and ashtrays landed on the floor. He went for the Russian, who was faster than they'd expected and sprang to his feet, pulling a pistol out of his waistband and pressing the muzzle to Atris's forehead.

'Easy, my friend,' he said. 'This is a Makarov. It makes big holes, big ones, better than those American toys. So sit down or there's going to be one hell of a mess.'

Atris's face had flushed a deep crimson. He took a step back. The mouth of the pistol had left a white mark on his forehead.

'So. Sit down again. We have to drink,' said the Russian. He summoned a waiter. They sat down and started drinking again.

It would be a good piece of business. They would make a lot of money and there would be no problems. They just had to pull themselves together, thought Atris.

There was a bus stop opposite the café. Nobody noticed the woman sitting on the bench. She had pulled the hood of her black sweater over her head; in the darkness she was hard to distinguish from her surroundings. She didn't get into any of the buses. She seemed to be asleep. Only when Atris leapt to his feet did she open her eyes for a moment. Otherwise she didn't move.

Atris and Frank didn't notice her. They also didn't see the Russian give her a brief signal.

Atris stood on the balcony of the apartment on the Kurfürstendamm looking out for the dark blue Golf. It was drizzling. Frank would be back from Amsterdam in twenty-four hours and they would have the new designer drugs, better than anything on the market. The Russian had said he would give them the pills on commission. They would have three weeks to pay him the 250,000 euros.

Atris turned around and went back into Frank's apartment. It was built in the classic old Berlin way: four-metre ceilings, mouldings, parquet floors, five rooms. They were almost empty. Frank's girlfriend was an interior designer. She'd said, 'The spaces have to work.' Then she'd had the sofas and chairs and everything else taken out. Now everyone had to sit on grey felt cubes with tiny backs. Atris found it uncomfortable.

Before he left, Frank had told Atris what he had to do. His instructions had been clear and very simple. Frank always spoke clearly and simply to him. 'It's not hard, Atris, you just have to listen really carefully. First: don't let the key out of your sight. Second: keep an eye on the Maserati. Third: only leave the apartment when Buddy has to shit.' Buddy was Frank's mastiff. Frank made him repeat it. Five times. 'Key, Maserati, Buddy.' He wouldn't forget. Atris admired Frank. Frank never made fun of him. He'd always told him what he had to do and Atris had always done it. Always.

When he was fourteen, Atris was the weakest boy in his class, and in Wedding the weakest got beaten up. Frank had protected him. Frank had also got him his first anabolic steroids; he'd said they would make Atris strong. Atris didn't know where Frank got the stuff. When he was twenty, the doctor diagnosed liver damage. His face was covered with pustules and oozing lumps. When he was twenty-two, his testicles had almost disappeared. But Atris had become strong in the meantime, nobody beat him up anymore, and he didn't believe the rumours that steroids came from cattle breeding.

Today he was going to watch some DVDs, drink beer and go out with the mastiff now and then. The Maserati was downstairs in the underground carpark. The key to the locker was on the kitchen table. Frank had written it all down on a piece of paper. *6 p.m. Feed Buddy*. Atris didn't like the huge animal; it always looked at him in such

a peculiar way. Frank had once said he'd given
Buddy steroids too, something had gone wrong,
and the animal just wasn't the same as before.
Everyone thought Atris was dumb, but nothing
was going to go wrong for him this time.

He went back into the empty living room and
tried to switch on the Bang & Olufsen TV. He
sat down on a felt cube and took a long time to
work out how to use the remote. Atris was proud
that he was the one Frank had entrusted with
his apartment, his dog and the locker in the new
main station. He picked up a joint from the table
and lit it. They were going to be rich, he thought.
He would buy his mother a new kitchen, the one
with the double-width range he'd seen in a high-
end decorating magazine of Frank's. He blew
a smoke ring and sucked it right back in again.
Then he put his feet on the table and tried to
follow the talk show.

The dog food consisted of pieces of beef
chopped up small; the bowl was on the kitchen
table. The mastiff was lying on the black-and-
white tiled floor. It was hungry. Smelling the meat
it got up, growled, and then began to bark. Atris
dropped the remote in the living room as he ran
to the kitchen. He got there too late. The mastiff
had pulled the tablecloth to the floor. The chunks

of flesh were flying through the air in a sticky clump, and Atris saw the mastiff go up on its hind legs, mouth open, waiting. Suddenly something glinted amid the bits of meat and it took a mere fraction of a second for Atris to understand. He screamed, 'Out...' and leapt from his position in the doorway. The mastiff was quicker. It didn't so much as look at him. The mass of meat landed in the dog's jaws with a smack. It didn't even chew; it just swallowed. Atris skidded across the floor and hit the wall in front of the dog. The dog licked the flagstones clean. Atris yelled at him, yanked open his mouth, and looked into his maw, got him in a headlock and throttled him. The dog growled and snapped at him. Atris wasn't fast enough; the dog got his left earlobe and tore it off. Atris slammed his fist against the dog's muzzle, then sat on the floor, his blood dripping on the flagstones and his shirt torn. He stared at the dog and the dog stared back. Frank hadn't been gone for more than two hours and he'd already screwed things up: the dog had swallowed the key to the locker.

They almost beat him to death. It was an oversight.

Once past the border, Frank had been followed by members of a special task force. He needed to use the toilet so he drove to a rest stop. The leader of the task force was nervous. He made the wrong decision and gave the order for an arrest. Later the state police had to reimburse the owner of the petrol station for both broken washbasins, the lock on the toilet door, the door itself, which had been smashed in, the air dryer and the cleanup. They put a sack over Frank's head, dragged him out of the toilet and took him to Berlin. He put up a fight.

The woman in the hoodie had followed Frank's Golf since he left Amsterdam. She had watched the task force with a little pair of binoculars. Once it was all over, she used a phone booth to call the number of a stolen mobile in Amsterdam. The conversation lasted twelve seconds. Then she went back to her car, typed an address into the GPS unit, pushed back the hood of her sweater and drove onto the autobahn again.

Atris waited eight hours to see if the dog would spit the key out again. Then he gave up and dragged Buddy down into the street. The rain had started coming down more heavily in the meantime, the dog got wet, and when he finally got it into the

Maserati, it stank up the car. He would have to clean the upholstery later, but first he needed the key. The vet had said on the phone that he had to come. Atris started the car. He was in a rage. He gave it too much throttle, and the car shot out of the parking space, its right wing making contact with the bumper of the Mercedes in front of it with a metallic sound. Atris got out, cursing, to look at the scrape in the paintwork. He tried polishing the damage with his finger but a splinter of the lacquer tore his skin and he started bleeding. Atris gave the Mercedes a kick, got back in the car, and drove off. The blood on his finger stained the pale leather on the steering wheel.

The vet's offices were on the ground floor of a building in Moabit. The blue sign outside said SMALL ANIMAL PRACTICE. Atris couldn't read very well. After he'd deciphered the sign, he wondered if Buddy qualified as a small dog. He hauled the beast out of the car onto the street and gave him a kick in the backside. Buddy snapped at him but missed. 'Filthy monster, you small animal,' said Atris. He didn't want to wait, so he yelled at the nurse. She let him jump the queue because he was making so much noise. When he got into the examination room, he put a thousand euros in fifty-euro notes on the vet's steel table.

'Doctor, this damn fucking dog swallowed a key. I need the key but I need the dog too. Cut the beast open, get the key out, then close him up again,' said Atris.

'I have to X-ray him first,' said the vet.

'I don't give a fuck what you do. I need the key. I have to leave. I need the key and the damn dog.'

'You can't take him with you if I cut him open. He'll need to lie flat, undisturbed, for at least two days. You have to leave him here.'

'Open him up, and he's coming with me afterwards. He's tough: he'll survive,' said Atris.

'No.'

'I'll give you more money,' said Atris.

'No. Money won't heal the dog.'

'Crap,' said Atris. 'Money heals everything. I'm not giving the money to the damn dog, I'm giving it to you. You open him up, you take the key out, you close him up again. You take the money. Everyone goes home happy.'

'It's impossible. Please try to understand. It's simply impossible—no matter how much money you give me.'

Atris paced up and down the examination room and thought. 'Okay. Next possibility. Can the damn dog just shit the key out again?'

'If you're lucky, yes.'

'Can you give him something to make him shit quicker?

'You mean a laxative? Yes, that could work.'

'Right. So how stupid are you anyway? Why do I have to explain everything to you, you're the doctor. Give him the stuff to make him shit. A lot, enough to work on an elephant.'

'You have to give him natural laxatives. Liver, lungs, or udders.'

'What?'

'It helps.'

'Are you out of your mind? Where am I going to get udders? I can't set the dog on a cow to rip off her udders.' Atris looked at the nurse's tits.

'You can get these things at the butcher's.'

'Give him a pill. Now. You're a doctor. You give people pills. A butcher gives people udders. Everyone has their own job. Do you get it?'

The vet didn't want any more argument. The week before, he'd had a letter from the bank to say that he needed to balance his account. There was a thousand euros lying on the table. In the end he gave the mastiff Animalax and, because Atris put another two hundred euros on the table, he gave it five times the manufacturer's recommended dose.

Atris dragged Buddy out into the street again.

The rain was sheeting down. He cursed. The vet had said the dog needed to be kept moving; it would make the medicine work quicker. He had no desire to get wet, so he jammed the lead into the passenger door and drove off slowly. The dog trotted along beside the Maserati. Other cars honked. Atris turned the music up louder. A policeman stopped him. Atris said the dog was sick. The policeman yelled at him, so he pulled the mastiff into the car and drove on.

At the next corner he heard it. It was a dark, ominous rumbling. The mastiff suddenly opened its jaws, panted, howled in pain, then voided itself. It hunched over in the front seat, forced its rear end backwards and up between the armrests, bit into the upholstery, and tore out a large mouthful. The liquid shit sprayed over the seats, the windows, the floor and the parcel shelf. The dog spread it around with its paws. Atris braked and leapt out of the car, closing the driver's door. It lasted twenty minutes. Atris stood in the rain while the car windows steamed up from inside. He kept getting glimpses of the dog's nose, its red gums and its tail; he heard its high-pitched yowling, and waves of shit kept hitting the windows. Atris thought about Frank. And about his father, who'd told him while he was still a child that he was too stupid even to walk in a straight line. Atris thought that maybe his father had been right.

Frank woke out of the coma in the prison hospital in Berlin. The task force had overdone it; he had a severely fractured skull, bruises all over his body, and they'd broken his collarbone and his right upper arm. The examining magistrate read him the warrant at his bedside; the only charges were resisting arrest and bodily harm—one of the eight officers had had his little finger broken. The police had found no drugs, but they were convinced these must be somewhere.

I took over his defence. Frank would remain silent. The prosecutor's office would have a hard time proving drug-trafficking. The custody hearing was in thirteen days' time and, if nothing new turned up, he would be released.

'You stink of shit,' said Hassan.

Atris had called him. Before that he had searched the Maserati for an hour, and his shirt and pants were smeared with it. He hadn't found the key; it must still be inside the mastiff. Atris hadn't known what to do. Hassan was his cousin; in the family he was rated as intelligent.

'I know I stink of shit. The car stinks of shit, Buddy stinks of shit, I stink of shit. I know that. You don't have to say it.'

'Atris, you *really* stink of shit,' said Hassan.

Hassan did business out of one of the countless converted spaces under the arches of the Berlin suburban railway. The railway company rented out these spaces. There were car body shops, storerooms and junk dealers. Hassan recycled old tyres. He got paid to get rid of them, loaded them onto a truck and threw them into a ravine he'd discovered in a forest in Brandenburg. He earned good money. Everyone said he was a talented businessman.

Atris told Hassan about the thing with the dog. Hassan said he should bring Buddy inside. The mastiff looked wretched, and its white coat was all brown.

'The damn dog stinks too,' said Hassan.

Atris groaned.

'Tie him to the steel post,' said Hassan.

He showed Atris the shower in the back room, giving him a freshly washed set of coveralls from the city garbage collectors. They were orange.

'What's this?' said Atris.

'I need it for the recycling work,' said Hassan.

Atris undressed and packed his old things into a garbage bag. Twenty minutes later when he came out of the shower, the first thing he saw was the car jack, lying in a pool of blood. Hassan was sitting on a chair, smoking. He pointed to the body of the dog on the floor.

'Sorry, but you'd better get undressed again. If you cut him open you'll get a mess all over you again. That's the last clean set of coveralls.'

'Shit.'

'It's the only way. The key would never have come out—it's caught in his stomach. We'll get another dog.'

'And the Maserati?'

'I've already made a phone call. The boys are going to steal another one, exactly the same model. We just have to wait. You'll get the new one.'

Atris came back to the apartment on the Kurfürstendamm at two o'clock in the morning. He had parked the new Maserati in the underground carpark. It looked completely different; it was red, not blue, and the seats were black instead of beige. It was going to be hard to explain to Frank.

Atris took the lift up. The key seemed to stick a little in the door of the apartment, but he was too tired to notice. He couldn't fight back; he didn't even try. The woman was small-built, she was wearing a hoodie, and he couldn't see her face. Her pistol was enormous.

'Open your mouth,' she said. Her voice was warm.

She shoved the barrel between Atris's teeth. It tasted of oil.

'Walk backwards slowly. If you make a false move or I stumble, the back of your head will blow off, so you'd better be careful. Do you understand?'

Atris nodded carefully. Inside his mouth, the bead on the barrel struck his teeth. They went into the living room.

'I'm going to sit down on the stool. You are going to kneel in front of me. Very slowly.' She was talking to him the way a doctor talks to a patient. The woman sat on one of the felt cubes. Atris kneeled down next to her. He still had the barrel in his mouth.

'Very good. Now if you do everything right, nothing's going to happen. I don't want to kill you, but it doesn't matter to me whether I do or not. Do you understand?'

Atris nodded again.

'So, I'm going to explain it to you.'

She spoke slowly, slowly enough for Atris to understand it all, and leaned back on the stool, crossing her legs. Atris had to follow her movements and bend his head forward.

'You and your partner bought pills from us. You need to give us 250,000 euros for them. Your partner was arrested on the autobahn. We're sorry about that. But you still have to pay the money.'

Atris swallowed. Frank got caught, he thought. He nodded. She waited till she could be sure Atris had got it.

'I'm glad you understand. Now I'm going to ask you a question. After I'm done, you can take the barrel out of your mouth so you can answer. When you've finished answering, you put the barrel back in your mouth. It's quite simple.'

Atris was getting used to the voice. He didn't have to think. He was just going to do everything the voice said.

'Where is the money?' she said.

Atris opened his mouth and said: 'The money's at the station. Buddy swallowed the key, he shat all over everything, I had to...'

'Quiet,' said the woman. Her voice was sharp. 'Put the barrel back in your mouth immediately.'

Atris stopped talking and did as he was told.

'Your story's too long. I don't want to listen to a whole novel. All I want is to know where the money is. I'm going to ask you again. I want you to answer in a single sentence. You can take your time to work out the answer. When you know what you want to say, open your mouth and say the sentence. But only one sentence. If you say more than one sentence, I'll cut your balls off. Do you understand?'

Her voice hadn't changed. Atris began to sweat.

'Where is the money?'

'In a locker in the main station,' said Atris, and immediately bit down on the steel again.

'Very good, now you've got it, this is exactly the way it goes. Now comes the next question. Think about it, open your mouth, say one sentence, and shut it again. Work out your answer. So, here's the question. Who has the key to the locker?'

'Me,' said Atris and closed his mouth again.

'Do you have it here?'

'Yes.'

'I'm proud of you. We're getting somewhere. Now comes the next question. Where is your car?'

'In the underground carpark.'

'I see we're getting on with each other. Now it gets a little more complicated. Here's what we're going to do. You're going to stand up, but you're going to do it very slowly. Do you understand? What matters is doing it all really slowly. We don't want the thing to go off because I get a fright. If we're careful nothing's going to happen.'

Atris slowly got to his feet. He still had the pistol in his mouth.

'I'm going to take it out of your mouth now. Then you're going to turn around and walk to the door. I'm behind you. We're going to drive together to the station now. If the money is there, you can go.'

Atris opened his mouth and she pulled out the barrel.

'Before we go, there's one thing you need to know. There are special cartridges in the pistol. They contain a drop of nitro-glycerine. You're going to walk ahead of me. If you run, I'll have to shoot. The nitro will explode in your body. There will be nothing left of you that anyone can recognise. Do you understand?'

'Yes,' said Atris. Nothing would make him run.

They took the lift down. Atris went ahead

and opened the door to the underground carpark. Someone yelled, 'That's the pig.' The last thing Atris saw was the metal baseball bat. It shone red.

They'd stolen the wrong Maserati. The car belonged to a rapper. He'd been having dinner with his girlfriend in Schlüterstrasse. Afterwards when he couldn't find his car, he'd called the police, but the car hadn't been towed away. His girlfriend got in a bad mood. She wound him up till he called his old friends from Kreuzberg. Muhar El Keitar promised to take care of it.

If you didn't belong to the police force, it wasn't hard to find out who now had the car. El Keitar was the head of a large family. They all came from the same village, and they were Lebanese Kurds. El Keitar wanted the car. He made that clear. His friend the rapper was a famous man now, and he absolutely wanted to help him. The four men who paid Hassan a visit on Muhar El Keitar's orders didn't want to kill him; all they wanted to know was who the car had been for. But something went wrong. When they came back, the men said Hassan had tried to fight back. He'd said where the car was, but then it was all over.

When Atris regained consciousness, he was on a wooden chair, bound and naked. It was a damp, windowless room. Atris got scared. Everyone in Kreuzberg had heard of this cellar. It belonged to Muhar El Keitar. Everyone knew that El Keitar liked to torture people. They said he'd learned the technique during the war in Lebanon. There were a lot of stories about it.

'What's going on?' Atris asked the two men sitting on a table in front of him. His tongue was all furred and swollen. Between his legs was a car battery with two cables.

'Wait,' said the younger man.

'What am I waiting for?'

'Just wait,' said the older one.

Ten minutes later Muhar El Keitar came down the stairs. He looked at Atris. Then he screamed at the two men.

'I've told you a thousand times you're to put the tarp under the chair. Why don't you ever get it? Next time I won't say anything and you can see how you get all the shit cleaned up.'

In fact, Muhar El Keitar didn't want to torture people. That sentence was almost always enough to get his victims to talk.

'What do you want, Muhar?' asked Atris. 'What should I do?'

'You stole a car,' said El Keitar.

'No, I haven't stolen any car. The boys stole it. The other Maserati was full of shit.'

'Good, I understand,' said El Keitar, although he didn't understand at all. 'You have to pay for the car. It belongs to a friend.'

'I'll pay.'

'And you'll pay compensation for my costs.'

'Of course.'

'Where's your money?'

'In a locker in the main station.' Atris had already learned that there was no sense in telling long stories.

'Where's the key?' asked Muhar El Keitar.

'In my wallet.'

'You're morons,' Muhar El Keitar said to the two men. 'Why didn't you check it? I have to do everything myself.' El Keitar went over to Atris's orange garbage company coveralls. 'Why do you have garbage company coveralls?' said Muhar El Keitar.

'It's a long story.'

Muhar El Keitar found the wallet and inside it the key.

'I'm going to the station myself. You guys keep an eye on him,' he said to his men, and then to Atris: 'If the money's there, you can go.'

He went back up the stairs. Then he came

down again backwards. He had a pistol in his mouth. El Keitar's two men reached for the baseball bats.

'Put them down,' said the woman with the pistol.

Muhar El Keitar nodded vigorously.

'If we all stay calm, nothing's going to happen to anyone,' said the woman. 'We're going to solve our problems together.'

Half an hour later Muhar El Keitar and the older of his two men were sitting on the floor of the cellar, bound to each other with zip ties. Their mouths were sealed with parcel tape. The older one still had his underpants on; Atris was now wearing his clothes. The younger one was sitting in a huge pool of blood. He'd made a mistake and pulled a cosh out of his pocket. The woman's pistol had still been in El Keitar's mouth. With her left hand she'd pulled a switchblade out of the front pocket of her of her hoodie, opened it, and plunged it deep into the inner part of his right thigh. It was over quickly: he registered almost nothing. He had dropped to the floor at once.

'I severed your femoral artery,' she said. 'You're going to bleed out, it'll take six minutes.

Your heart will keep pumping the blood out of your body. Your brain will be the first to go; you'll lose consciousness.'

'Help me,' he said.

'Now for the good news. You can survive. It's simple. You have to reach into the wound and find the end of the artery. Then you have to squeeze it shut between your thumb and your forefinger.'

The man looked at her in disbelief. The pool of blood was getting bigger.

'If I were you, I'd get a move on,' she said.

He'd groped around in his wound. 'I can't find it, dammit, I can't find it.' Then the bleeding suddenly stopped. 'I got it.'

'Now you can't let go. If you want to live, you have to stay sitting down. At some point a doctor will get here. He'll close off the artery again with a little steel clip. So keep still.'

And to Atris she said, 'Let's go.'

Atris and the woman drove to the main station in the stolen Maserati. Atris went to the locker and opened it. He set down two bags in front of the woman and opened them.

'How much money is that?' she asked.

'Two hundred and twenty thousand euros,' said Atris.

'And what's in the other one?'

'One point one kilos of cocaine,' said Atris.

'Good. I'll take both. The thing is all settled. I'm leaving now, you'll never see me again, and you've never seen me,' she said.

'Yes.'

'Repeat it.'

'I've never seen you,' said Atris.

The woman turned, picked up both bags, and headed for the escalator. Atris waited for a moment or two, then ran to the nearest phone booth. He picked up the receiver and dialed the police emergency number.

'A woman in a black hoodie, 170 centimetres tall, slim, is in the main station, heading for the exit.' He knew how the police talk. 'She's armed, she's carrying a bag of counterfeit money and a kilogram of cocaine. She's stolen a blue, no, a red Maserati. It's in carpark number two,' he said and hung up.

He went back to the locker and reached into it. Behind the coin slot—invisible from the outside—a second key was taped. He used it to open the next-door locker and took out a bag. He looked into it for a moment. The money was still there. Then he went back into the main hall and took the escalator up to the suburban train platforms. Down on the lowest level he saw the woman lying on the ground, surrounded by eight policemen.

Atris took the first train to Charlottenburg. As it came in, he leaned back. He had the money. Tomorrow the big package from Amsterdam with the pills in it would reach his mother. Frank had even included a windmill in the package that lit up red and green. She loved things like that. The post office didn't have drug-sniffing dogs yet, the Russian had said; they cost too much money.

The woman would be sentenced to four or five years. The cocaine was admittedly only sugar, but Frank and Atris had once fallen for the counterfeit money trick themselves. Aside from which there was still possession of a weapon and the theft of a car.

Frank would be set free in a few days; nothing could be proved against him. The pills would find a ready market. When Frank got out, he'd give him a puppy, or definitely a smaller dog. They had saved 250,000 euros, and the woman's arrest was the Russian's problem: these were the rules. Frank would be able to buy himself the new four-door Maserati.

After he'd told me the whole story, Atris said, 'You just can't trust women.'

Lonely

Today she walked past the house again for the first time in a long time. It had all happened fifteen years ago.

She took a seat in a café and called me. Did I remember her? she asked. She was a grown-up now, with a husband and two children. Both girls, ten and nine years old, pretty children. The younger one looked like her. She didn't know who else to call.

'Do you still remember it all?' she asked.

Yes, I still remembered it all. Every detail.

Larissa was fourteen. She lived at home. The family's only income was from welfare; her father had been out of work for twenty years, her mother had once been a cleaning lady, and both drank. Her parents often came home late. Sometimes they didn't come home at all. Larissa had got used to this, and to the beatings, the way children get used to anything. Her brother had moved out when he was sixteen and never been heard from again. She was going to do the same.

It was a Monday. Her parents were in the bar on the corner. That's where they were almost always to be found. Larissa was alone in the apartment, sitting on the bed, listening to music. When the bell rang she went to the door and peered through the peephole. It was her father's friend Lackner, who lived next door. She was wearing nothing but a T-shirt and briefs. He asked where her parents were, came into the apartment, and checked that she really was alone. Then he pulled the knife. He told her to get dressed and come with him or he'd slit her throat. Larissa obeyed; there was nothing else she could do. She went with Lackner, who wanted to be in his apartment where no one could disturb him.

Frau Halbert, the neighbour who lived in the apartment across the hall, was coming up the stairs towards them. Larissa tore herself free, screamed, and ran into her arms. Much later, when it was all over, the judge would ask Frau Halbert why she hadn't protected Larissa. Why she had detached herself from Larissa's embrace and had left her to Lackner. The judge would ask her why she had watched as the man took the girl away although she was begging and crying. And Frau Halbert would always answer in the same way. To every question she replied, 'It wasn't my business; it was nothing to do with me.'

Lackner took Larissa into his apartment. She was still a virgin. When he had finished, he sent her home. 'Say hi to the old guys,' were his farewell words. Back in the apartment, Larissa took a shower under water so hot that it almost scalded her skin. She closed the curtains in her room. She was in pain, she was terrified, and there was no one she could tell.

In the next few months things went badly for Larissa. She was tired, she threw up, and she couldn't concentrate. Her mother said she shouldn't eat so many sweets, it caused her heartburn. Larissa gained almost ten kilos. She was in the middle of puberty. She had only just taken the pictures of horses down from her wall and hung up photos from teen magazines. Things got worse, particularly the pains in her stomach. 'Colic,' said her father. Her periods had stopped coming: she thought it was because of the revulsion.

On the twelfth of April she barely made it

to the toilet. She thought her bowels would explode—she'd had cramps in her stomach all morning. It was something else. She reached between her legs and felt something strange that was growing out of her. She touched sticky hair and a tiny head. 'It mustn't be inside me,' she said later. This had been her only thought, over and over again: 'It mustn't be inside me.' A few minutes later the baby dropped down into the toilet bowl; she heard the water splash. She stayed sitting. She lost all track of time.

At some point she stood up. The baby was lying down there in the toilet bowl, white and red and greasy and dead. She reached up to the shelf above the washbasin, took the nail scissors, and cut the umbilical cord. She dried herself off with toilet paper but she couldn't throw that on top of the baby, so she stuffed it into the plastic bucket in the bath, then sat on the floor till she got cold. When she tried to walk, she wobbled, but she fetched a garbage bag from the kitchen, supporting herself against the wall and leaving a bloody handprint. She pulled the baby out of the toilet, its tiny legs as thin as her fingers. She laid it on a towel. She looked at it, a brief look that was far too long; it lay there, its face blue and its eyes closed. Then she folded the towel over the baby and pushed it into the bag. Carefully, like a loaf of bread, she thought. She took the bag down to the cellar, carrying it with both hands, and set it between the bicycles, weeping silently. On the steps back up she began to bleed. It ran down her thigh, but she didn't notice. She made it as far as the apartment, then collapsed in the hall. Her mother, who had come home, called the fire brigade. In the hospital the doctors took care of the afterbirth and alerted the police.

The policewoman was friendly, she wasn't in uniform, and she stroked the girl's forehead. Larissa lay in a clean bed; one of the nurses had brought her a few flowers. She told them everything. 'It's in the cellar,' she said. And then she said something that no one could believe: 'I didn't know I was pregnant.'

I visited Larissa in the women's prison. A judge who was a friend of mine had asked me to take her on as a client. She was fifteen. Her father gave an interview to the tabloids, saying she'd always been a good girl and he just couldn't understand it. He was paid fifty euros.

There have always been repressed pregnancies. Every year in Germany alone, 1500 women recognise too late that they're pregnant. And, year after year, almost 300 women only realise it when they give birth. They misinterpret all the signs: menstruation has ceased because of stress, the stomach is distended because of overeating, the breasts are enlarging as a result of some hormonal disturbance. These woman are either very young or over the age of forty. Many have already had children. People can repress things, though nobody knows how the mechanism works. Sometimes it's completely successful: even doctors are deceived and see no need for further physical exams.

Larissa was set free. The judge said the child had been born alive, it had drowned, its lungs had been fully developed, and *E. coli* bacteria had been found in them. He said he believed Larissa. The rape had traumatised her and she hadn't wanted the child. She had repressed everything so powerfully and so completely that she literally had no knowledge of her pregnancy. When she had delivered the baby on the toilet, she had been astonished. As a result, she was in a state in which she could no longer distinguish right and wrong. She was therefore not guilty of the death of the newborn infant.

In a separate trial, Lackner was sentenced to six and a half years.

Larissa took the tram home. All she had with

her was the yellow plastic bag that the police-woman had packed for her. Her mother asked how it had been in court. Larissa moved out six months later.

After our phone conversation she sent me a photo of her children. She also included a letter, written in her best copybook handwriting on blue paper; she must have done it very slowly. 'Everything is fine with my husband and my girls. I'm happy. But I often dream about the baby lying alone in the cellar. It was a boy. I miss him.'

Justice

The criminal court is in the Moabit district of
Berlin. That part of the city is grey; no one knows
where the name came from; it sounds a little like
the Slavic word for a Moor. It is the largest criminal court in Europe. The building has twelve
courtyards and seventeen staircases. Fifteen
hundred people work here, including 270 judges
and 350 prosecutors. Approximately 300 hearings take place every day, 1300 prisoners from
eighty nations are incarcerated here awaiting
trial, and more than 1000 visitors, witnesses and
trial personnel pass through. Every year roughly
60,000 criminal proceedings are handled here.
These are the statistics.

The officer who delivered Turan said quietly
that he was 'a poor bastard'. He arrived in the
interrogation room on crutches, dragging his

right leg. He looked like the beggars in the pedestrian malls. His left foot was turned inwards. He was forty-one years old, a thin little man, just skin and bones, sunken cheeks, barely any teeth, unshaven, unkempt. In order to shake my hand he had to lean one of the crutches against his stomach and had trouble keeping his balance. Turan sat down and tried to tell me his story. He was serving his term; the sentence had long since started to run. He had supposedly attacked a man with his pit bull, and 'brutally beaten him up and kicked him'. Turan said he was innocent. It took time for him to answer my questions, and he spoke slowly. I didn't understand everything he said, but then he didn't have to say much: he could barely walk, and any dog would have knocked him over. When I was about to leave, he suddenly clutched my arm, and his crutch fell to the ground. He wasn't a bad man, he said.

A few days later the file arrived from the prosecutor's office. It was thin, barely fifty pages. Horst Kowski, forty-two, had gone for a walk in Neukölln. Neukölln is a district of Berlin where schools employ private guards, technical schools have up to eighty per cent foreign pupils and every second person is on welfare. Horst Kowski had gone for this walk with his dachshund. The dachshund had gotten into a fight with the pit bull. The owner of the pit bull got angry, the fight escalated, and the man assaulted Kowski.

When Kowski arrived home, he was bleeding from the mouth. His nose was broken, his shirt badly torn. His wife bandaged him up. She said she knew 'the man with the pit bull' and his name was Tarun. He was a regular at the tanning salon where she worked. She checked the computer in the salon, and found Tarun's discount card and his address: Kolbe-Ring 52. The couple went to the police; Kowski showed them the computer printout. Tarun was not a registered resident of Berlin. The officer was not surprised: Neukölln is not a place where the obligation to register is always observed.

The next day a patrolman failed to find any Tarun among the 184 names on the little signs next to the buzzers at Kolbe-Ring 52. There was however a label with the name Turan. The policeman made enquiries at the State Residents' Registration office; there was in fact a Harkan Turan registered at Kolbe-Ring 52. The officer thought it must be a misspelling—it should be

Turan, not Tarun, so he rang, and when no one answered he left a summons for Turan in the mailbox.

Turan didn't go to the police. Nor did he send an excuse. After four weeks the policeman sent the file to the prosecutor's office. The prosecutor requested a penalty order and a judge signed it. 'If he didn't do it, he'll surface,' he thought.

When Turan received the order he could still have changed everything; all he had to do was write one line to the court. The penalty order acquired the force of law after two weeks. The department in charge of enforcement sent a form for a money transfer to use when he paid the fine. He naturally didn't pay because, aside from anything else, he didn't have the money. The fine was replaced by a term of imprisonment. The detention centre wrote telling him to present himself within fourteen days. Turan threw the letter away. After three weeks two policemen came to get him in the morning. Since then he had been sitting in prison. Turan said: 'It wasn't me. Germans are so thorough—they must know this.'

Turan's deformity was congenital, he'd had a whole series of operations. I wrote to his doctors and gave their case notes to an expert in the field.

He said Turan was incapable of assaulting anyone. Turan's friends came to my office. They said he was afraid of dogs so of course he'd never owned one. One of the friends even knew Tarun and his pit bull. I demanded that the matter be reopened. Turan was released. Three months later there was a hearing. Kowski said he'd never seen Turan in his life.

Turan was exonerated. The court forgot about the charge against Tarun.

By law, Turan had a claim against the state: eleven euros for every day of wrongful imprisonment. The claim had to be made within six months. Turan didn't get any money—he missed the deadline.

Comparison

Alexandra was pretty: a blonde with brown eyes. In older photographs she wears a hairband. She grew up in the country near Oldenburg, where her parents were livestock farmers: cows, pigs, hens. She disliked her freckles, she read historical novels and all she wanted was to go and live in the city. After secondary school, her father got her an apprenticeship in a respectable bakery and her mother helped her look for an apartment. To begin with she felt homesick and went home at weekends. Then she got to know people in the city. She loved life.

After she'd completed her apprenticeship she bought her first car. Her mother had given her the money, but she wanted to choose it herself. She was nineteen. The salesman was ten years older. Tall, slim-hipped. They took a test drive, and he explained the car's features to her. She was drawn to his hands: slender, sinewy, they attracted her. Afterwards he asked her if she would like to have dinner with him, or go to a movie. She was too nervous, so she laughed and said no. But she wrote her phone number on the contract. They made a date a week later. She liked the way he talked about things. And she liked it that he told her what to do. Everything felt right.

They married two years later. In her wedding photographs she's wearing a white dress. She's tanned, she's laughing into the camera and holding the arm of her husband, who's a couple of heads taller. They paid for a real photographer. The picture was to stand on her bedside table forever: she'd already bought the frame. They both liked the reception afterwards, and the solo entertainer on the Hammond organ; they danced, although Thomas said he was not much of a dancer. Their families got on well together. Her favourite grandfather, a stonemason with silicosis, gave them a statue as a wedding present—a naked girl who looked a lot like her. His father gave them money in an envelope.

Alexandra had no worries; everything was going to work out well with this man. It was all

going just the way she'd wished it for herself. He
was loving, and she thought she knew him.

The first time he hit her was long before the baby
was born. He came home drunk in the middle of
the night. She woke up and told him he smelled
of alcohol. She didn't find it that bad, she was
simply telling him. He yelled at her and dragged
the bedclothes off her. As she sat up, he hit her in
the face. She was terrified, unable to speak.

Next morning he wept and blamed the alcohol.
She didn't like the way he sat on the kitchen floor.
He said he would never drink again. When he
left for work, she cleaned the entire apartment.
It took her the whole day. They were married,
she thought, that sort of thing happened, it was a
slip-up. They didn't discuss it again.

When Alexandra got pregnant, everything was
the way it had been. He brought her flowers at the
weekend, he lay on her stomach and tried to hear
the baby. He stroked her. When she came home
from the hospital after the birth, he had tidied
everything up. He'd painted the nursery yellow
and bought a baby's changing table. Her mother-
in-law had brought new things for the child. There
was a wreath of paper flowers over the door.

The girl was baptised. He'd wanted to name her Chantal, but finally they settled on Saskia. Alexandra was happy.

After the birth he didn't have sex with her anymore. She tried a few times, but he didn't want it. She felt a little lonely, but she had the baby and she made herself get accustomed to it. A girlfriend had told her it sometimes happened if the husband had been present at the birth. It would pass. She didn't know if this was true.

After a few years, things got harder. Sales of cars were slow; they had the payments on the apartment to make. They managed somehow, but he drank more. Sometimes in the evenings she smelled a perfume she didn't know, but she didn't say anything. Her friends had bigger problems with their husbands; most of them were getting divorced.

It began at Christmas. She had laid the table: white cloth, her grandmother's silver. Saskia was five; she said where the baubles were to be hung on the Christmas tree. At half-past six Alexandra lit the candles. He still wasn't home by the time they had burned all the way down. The two of them were alone, and after dinner she put Saskia to bed. She read aloud from the new book till the little girl fell asleep. She had phoned her parents and his parents and everyone had wished one another Merry Christmas like a normal family. Only when they asked about him, Alexandra said he was making a quick trip to the petrol station to buy matches, because she had none in the house for lighting the candles.

He did it silently. He had boxed when he was younger and knew how to hit someone so that it hurt. Although he was drunk, his blows were precise. He struck systematically and hard, as they stood in the kitchen between the American break-fast counter and the refrigerator. He avoided her face. On the refrigerator door were the little girl's paintings and stickers. Thinking of Saskia, she bit into her hand so as not to scream. He dragged her across the floor to the bedroom by her hair. When he sodomised her, she felt she was being torn in half. He came almost at once, then kicked her out of bed, and fell asleep. She lay on the floor, unable to move, until at some point much later she managed to make it to the bathroom. The bruises were already showing on her skin and there was blood in her urine. She lay in the bathtub for a long time, until finally she was able to breathe normally again. She was unable to cry.

The first day after the Christmas holidays she found the strength to say she was taking Saskia and going to her mother's. He left the apartment before she did. She packed a suitcase and carried it to the lift. Saskia was excited. As they arrived downstairs, he was standing in front of the door. He took the suitcase out of her hand gently. Saskia asked if they weren't going to visit Grandma after all. Taking their daughter in his left hand and the suitcase in his right, he went back to the lift. In the apartment he laid the suitcase on the bed, looked at her, and shook his head.

'No matter where you go, I'll find you,' he said. In the hall, he picked Saskia up in his arms. 'We're going to the zoo.'

'Yes, yes!' said Saskia.

It was only after the door closed that Alexandra could feel her hands again. She had dug her fingers into the chair so hard that two of her fingernails were broken. That evening he broke one of her ribs. She slept on the floor. She was devoid of feeling.

His name was Felix and he'd rented one of the small apartments at the rear of the building. She had seen him every day with his bicycle, he always said hello to her in the supermarket, and when she buckled over in the hallway once with pain in her kidneys he'd helped with her shopping bags. Now he was standing at her door.

'Do you have any salt?' he said. 'Okay, I admit it, that's a really stupid line. Would you like to have coffee with me?'

They both laughed. Her ribs hurt. She had got used to the blows: she would stick it out for another four or five years, then Saskia would be old enough. She was nine now.

She liked Felix's apartment. It was warm, with pale floors, books on narrow shelves, and a mattress with white sheets. He talked to her about books and they listened to Schubert *lieder*. He looks like an overgrown boy, she thought, and maybe a little sad. He told her she was beautiful, then neither of them said anything for a long time. When she went back to her apartment, she thought that perhaps her life wasn't over after all. She had to spend that night on the floor by the bed again, but it didn't matter quite so much.

Three months later she slept with him. She didn't want him to see her naked, with the blue patches and all the grazed skin, so she lowered the metal blinds and undressed under the bedcovers. She was thirty-one, he didn't have much experience, but for the first time since Saskia's birth a man was really making love to her. She liked the way he held her. Afterwards they lay in the dark room. He talked about the trips he would like to take with her, about Florence and Paris and other places she'd never been. It all seemed so simple to her; she liked the sound of his voice. She could only stay for two hours. She told him she didn't want to go back; she said it just like that, it was a declaration of love, but then she realised that she actually meant it.

Later she couldn't find her stockings, which made them laugh. Suddenly he switched on the light. She clutched the sheet up to her body, but it was too late. She saw the fury in his eyes; he said he was going to call the police, it had to be done at once. It took her a long time to dissuade him, telling him she was afraid for her daughter. He didn't want to understand. His lips were trembling.

The summer holidays began two months later. They took Saskia out to her grandparents in the country; she loved it there. On the trip back to the city Thomas said, 'Now you're really going to learn obedience.' Felix sent her a text message saying he missed her. She read it in the toilet at the rest stop on the autobahn. It stank of urine in there, but she didn't care. Felix had said her husband was a sadist who enjoyed humiliating and hurting her. It was a mental disorder, it could be dangerous for her, and her husband needed treatment. She had to leave, right now. She didn't know what to do. She was too ashamed to tell her mother, ashamed for him and ashamed for herself.

The 26th of August was the last day before Saskia came back. They were going to pick her up and spend the night. Then the three of them were going to Majorca; the tickets were on the table in the hall. She thought things would go better there. He had drunk a great deal during Saskia's absence. She could barely walk. In the past two weeks he had subjected her to anal and oral rape every day, he had beaten her, and he had forced her to eat out of a bowl on the floor. When he was there she had to be naked; she slept on the floor in front of his bed; by now he had also confiscated the bedclothes. She hadn't been able to see Felix. She'd written to tell him it was simply impossible.

During this last night he said, 'Saskia's ready now. She's ten. I've waited. When she comes back, she's going to be mine.'

She didn't understand what he was saying, and asked him what he meant.

'I'm going to fuck her the way I fuck you. She's ready.'

She screamed and flew at him. He stood up and hit her in the stomach. It was a short, hard blow. She vomited, he turned round and told her to clean it up. An hour later he went to bed.

Her husband was no longer snoring. He'd always snored, even during the first night, when they were happy. At the beginning it had been strange; another human being, she had thought, another voice. Gradually she had got used to it. They had been married for eleven years now. There would not be a second life, there was only this man and this life. She sat in the other room, listening to the radio. They were playing a piece she didn't know. She stared into the darkness. In two hours it would be getting light and she'd have to go over into the bedroom, their bedroom.

★ ★ ★

Her father asked me to defend his daughter. I got a visitor's pass. The prosecutor in charge was named Kaulbach, a solidly built, plain-spoken man who talked in short sentences.

'Horrifying business,' he said. 'We don't get many murders. This one's an open-and-shut case.'

Kaulbach showed me the photos of the crime scene.

'She beat her husband to death with a statue while he was asleep.'

'Whether he was asleep or not is something the pathologist can't determine,' I said, knowing that this wasn't a strong argument.

The problem was simple. Manslaughter does not distinguish itself from murder by degree of 'intent' the way you see it in crime dramas on TV. Every murder is a manslaughter. But it's also more. There has to be some additional element that makes it a murder. These defining elements are not arbitrary: they are laid out in the law. The perpetrator kills 'to satisfy sexual urges', out of 'greed' or out of other 'base motives'. There are also words to define *how* he kills, for example 'heinously' or 'brutally'. If the judge believes such a defining element is present, he has no choice: he must give the perpetrator a life sentence. If it's manslaughter

CRIME & GUILT

he has a choice; he can sentence the perpetrator to anywhere between five and fifteen years.

Kaulbach was right. When a man is battered to death in his sleep, he cannot defend himself. He is unaware that he is being attacked; he's helpless. The perpetrator is thus acting with malice. He is committing murder, and will receive a life sentence.

'Look at the pictures,' said Kaulbach. 'The man was lying on his back. There are no defensive wounds on his hands. The bedclothes on top of him aren't disturbed. There was no struggle. There can be no doubt: he was asleep.'

The prosecutor knew what he was saying. It looked as if the base of the statue had been stamped into the man's face. The blood had sprayed everywhere, even onto the photo on the nightstand. The jury were not going to like these images.

'And moreover your client confessed today.'

I hadn't been made aware of this until now. I had to ask myself what I was doing on this case. I wouldn't be able to help her.

'Many thanks,' I said. 'I'm going to visit her now. We can talk again after that.'

Alexandra was in the prison hospital. She smiled, the way you smile at a stranger who visits you

on the ward. She sat up and put on a bathrobe.
It was too big for her; she looked lost in it. The
floor was covered with linoleum, everything
smelled of disinfectant, and one of the edges of
the washbasin had broken off. Next to her was
another woman; their beds were only separated
by a yellow curtain.

I sat in her room for three hours. She told me
her story. I arranged for her broken body to be
photographed. The medical report ran to fourteen
pages: spleen and liver ruptured, both kidneys
crushed, large areas where blood had pooled
under the skin. Two cracked ribs; six others with
evidence of previous fractures.

The trial began three months later. The
judge was due to retire. Gaunt face, crew cut,
grey hair, rimless glasses—he didn't look as if
he belonged in the new courtroom. An archi-
tect had designed it in contemporary style with
bright green plastic moulded chairs and white
formica tables. It was supposed somehow to
represent democratic justice, but it didn't have
any effect on the sentences being handed down.
The judge called the court to order and established that all parties in the trial were present.
Then he ordered a halt in the proceedings while
the public was asked to leave and Alexandra was

taken back to the holding cell. He waited till everything was quiet.

'I'm speaking to you openly, ladies and gentlemen,' he said. His voice was slow; he sounded tired. 'I don't know what we should do. We will proceed with the trial and we will make sure that we comprehend the files. I do not wish to condemn the accused, she has suffered under this man for ten years, and he almost killed her. And his next act would probably have been to assault the child.'

I didn't know what I should say. In Berlin the prosecutor's office would have had the judge removed immediately for bias; such candid comments at the beginning of a trial would be unthinkable. But out here in the provinces it was different. People lived closer together, and everyone had to get on with one another. The judge didn't care what the prosecutor thought, and Kaulbach stayed sitting quite calmly.

'I will have to sentence her, the law gives me no choice,' he said. He looked at me. 'Unless of course something occurs to you. I will give you every latitude.'

The trial indeed only lasted two days. There were no witnesses. Alexandra told her story. The forensic pathologist testified about the autopsy of the victim and, at greater length, about Alexandra's injuries from the abuse. The hearing of evidence took place in closed court. The prosecutor argued that it was murder; he spoke without emotion and there was no way to fault his presentation. He said that the defendant met all the conditions that would apply in a less serious charge. But in cases of murder the law offered no possibility of mitigation; that was how it had been drafted. Thus the only appropriate sentence was life. My address to the jury was scheduled for the following day. Until then the court was adjourned.

Before we left the courtroom, the judge asked the prosecutor and me to step forward to the bench. He had taken off his robe. He was wearing a green jacket; his shirt was frayed and covered with stains.

'You're wrong, Kaulbach,' he said to the prosecutor. 'No, there isn't any lesser charge in cases of murder, but there are other possibilities.' He handed each of us some photocopied sheets. 'Study the decision before tomorrow. I would like to hear some sensible arguments from you.' That last remark was directed at me.

I was familiar with the decision. The Federal Supreme Court had ruled that the sentence in cases of murder is not absolute. Even a life sentence can be commuted in certain exceptional cases. That was the argument I used in my summing up; I didn't have any other ideas.

The court set Alexandra free. The judge said she had acted in self-defence. It's a difficult rule. In order to be allowed to defend yourself, an attack must either be in progress or be imminent. You cannot be punished for defending yourself. The only problem was that a sleeping man cannot instigate an attack. And no court had ever accepted that an attack is imminent when the attacker is asleep. The judge said it was a unique decision, an exception, it was valid only in this one instance. Alexandra had not been obliged to wait until he woke up. She had wanted to protect her daughter, and she was permitted to do so. She herself had been in fear of her life. The court lifted the order of arrest and released her from detention. Later the judge persuaded the prosecutor not to appeal.

After the decision was announced, I went to the café on the opposite side of the street, where you can sit outside under an enormous chestnut tree. I thought about the old judge, the hasty trial, and my stupid address to the jury: I had prayed for a lenient sentence and she had been declared not guilty. It suddenly occurred to me that we hadn't heard from any fingerprint experts. I checked the files in my laptop: no traces had been found on the statue. The perpetrator must have worn gloves. The statue weighed forty kilos, Alexandra barely weighed more herself. The bed was more than half a metre high. I read her statement once again. She said that after she'd done it, she'd sat in the nursery until first light, then she'd called the police. She hadn't showered and she hadn't changed her clothes. Roughly one hundred pages further on in the file were the photos of her clothes: she had been wearing a white blouse. There was no trace of blood on it anywhere. The judge was experienced. There was no way he could have overlooked it. I closed the screen. It was late summer, the very last days, and the wind was still warm.

I saw her coming out of the courthouse. Felix was waiting for her in a taxi. She got into the backseat with him. He took her hand. She was going to go with him to her parents' and take Saskia in her arms, and it would all be over. They would have to be very careful with each other. Only when she felt the warmth in her stomach would she reciprocate, squeezing the hand— squeezing hers—that had killed her husband.

Family

Waller graduated from school with the highest marks of anyone in Hanover. His father was an ironworker, a little man with drooping shoulders. He had managed somehow to make sure his son qualified for the elite high school, although his wife had run away, abandoning the boy. Sixteen days after Waller passed his exams, his father died. He slipped and fell into the freshly poured foundation of a new building. He had a bottle of beer in his hand. They couldn't stop the machine in time, and he drowned in the liquid concrete.

Besides Waller, four of his father's workmates attended the funeral. Waller wore his father's only suit, which fitted him perfectly. He had his father's square face and his thin lips. Only his eyes were different. And everything else.

The German Scholarship Fund offered Waller

a grant, but he turned it down. He bought a ticket to Japan, packed a suitcase and travelled to Kyoto, where he entered a monastery for twelve months. In the course of the year he learned Japanese. After that he applied for a job with a firm of German mechanical engineers in Tokyo. Five years later he became head of the branch. He lived in a cheap boarding house. All the money he earned went into an investment account. A Japanese carmaker hired him away. After six years he had reached the highest position that a foreigner had ever held there. He now had approximately two million euros in his account, he was still living in the boarding house, and he had spent almost nothing at all. He was thirty-one years old. He resigned and moved to London. Eight years later he'd made almost thirty million on the stock exchange. In London, too, all he had was one tiny room. When he turned thirty-nine, he bought a manor house on a lake in Bavaria. He put all his money into bonds. He didn't work anymore.

A few years ago, I rented a small house on this lake for three weeks in the summer. You could see the manor house through the trees; there was no fence between the two properties. I met Waller for the first time on the dock in front of my house. He introduced himself and asked if he might sit down. We were roughly the same age. It was a hot day, we put our feet in the water, and we watched the dinghies and colourful wind-surfers. It didn't bother us that neither of us said much. After two hours, he went back home.

The next summer, we arranged to meet in the lobby of the Frankfurter Hof. I arrived a little late; he was already waiting. We had coffee; I was tired after a day at trial. He said I must come back soon; every morning herons, a great flock of them, flew over the lake and the house. Finally he asked me if he might send me a file.

It arrived four days later, and was the story of his family, compiled by a detective agency.

Waller's mother had married again a year after the divorce, and had given birth to another son, Waller's half-brother Fritz Meinering. When Fritz Meinering was two, the new husband left his family. The mother died of alcohol poisoning as the boy was starting school. Meinering ended up in a children's home. He wanted to become a carpenter. The home found him a place as an apprentice. He began drinking with friends. It wasn't long before he was drinking so much that he couldn't make it to work in the mornings. He was fired, and he left the children's home.

After that the crimes began: theft, bodily

harm, traffic offences. He spent two brief periods in jail. At the Oktoberfest in Munich he drank enough to produce a blood alcohol level of .32. He insulted two women and was sentenced for public drunkenness. He spiralled down, lost his apartment, and started sleeping in homeless shelters.

A year after the incident at the Oktoberfest, he held up a grocery store. All he said to the judge was that he needed the money. He'd still been so drunk from the night before that the salesgirl was able to knock him down with a dustpan. He got two and a half years in prison. He went into a treatment program for alcoholics, which earned him early release.

For a few months he succeeded in staying sober. He found a girlfriend. They moved in together. She worked as a shop assistant. He was jealous. When she came home too late one night, he hit her over the ear with a saucepan lid and burst her eardrum. The judges sentenced him to another year.

Fritz Meinering got to know a drug dealer in prison, a week before they were released. The man persuaded Meinering to carry cocaine from Brazil to Germany. His airfare would be covered, plus he'd be paid 500 euros. The police were tipped off and he was arrested in Rio de Janeiro in a taxi on the way to the airport. There were twelve kilos of uncut cocaine in the boot. He was sitting in prison there, awaiting trial.

This was where the file ended. After I'd read it all, I called Waller, who asked me if I could organise his half-brother's defence in Brazil. He didn't want any personal contact with him, but he felt he had to do this. He asked me to fly there, arrange for lawyers, talk to the embassy, and take care of everything. I agreed.

The prison in Rio de Janeiro had no cells, just barred cages with narrow pallets. The men sat there with their feet pulled up, because the floor was wet. Cockroaches ran over the walls. Meinering was completely dishevelled. I told him that a man who wished to remain anonymous had paid for his defence.

I hired a sensible defence lawyer. Meinering was sentenced to two years. After that he was sent home for trial in Germany. Because a year in a Brazilian prison, given the catastrophic conditions, is calculated as the equivalent of three years' jail time in Germany, his trial was called off and he was released.

Three weeks later he got into a fight with a

Russian in a bar over a half-bottle of vermouth. Both of them were drunk and the barman threw them out. There was a building site in front of the bar. Meinering got hold of a construction worker's lamp and hit the other man over the head with it. The Russian collapsed. Meinering wanted to go home. He lost his sense of direction and kept walking along the fence bordering the site until he'd rounded it completely; twenty minutes later he was back in front of the bar. In the meantime the Russian had crawled some distance, bleeding. He needed help. The lamp was still lying on the ground. Meinering picked it up and kept hitting the Russian until he was dead. He was arrested at the scene.

Next time I was in Munich, I drove out to visit Waller.

'How do you want to proceed?' I asked.

'I don't know,' he said. 'I don't want to do any more for him.'

It was a brilliantly sunny day, with the light glinting off the yellow house and its green shutters. We were sitting down at the boathouse. Waller was wearing beige shorts and white canvas shoes.

'Wait a moment, I'm going to fetch something.' He went up to the house. A young woman was lying out on the terrace. The lake was almost as flat as a mirror.

Waller came back and handed me a photo.

'That's my father,' he said.

It was a Polaroid from the 1970s. The colours had faded at some point and now it was tinged brownish-yellow. The man in the picture looked just like Waller.

'He was in prison four times,' he said. 'Three for fights that he started, and once for theft. He'd taken money from the till.'

I handed back the photo. Waller put it in his pocket.

'His father was condemned to death in 1944 by the Nazis for raping a woman,' he said.

He sat down on one of the chairs and looked out at the lake. Two dinghies were having a race; the blue one seemed to be winning. Then the red one went about and gave up. Waller stood up and walked over to the barbecue.

'We can eat soon. Will you stay?'

'Yes, I'd love to,' I said.

He poked around with a fork in the glowing heat. 'Better nothing after we're gone,' he said suddenly. That was all.

His girlfriend came down to us and we talked about other things. After we'd eaten he accompanied me to my car. A lonely man with a thin mouth.

A few years later there was a report in the newspaper that Waller had died; he'd slipped off his boat in a storm and drowned. He left his money to the monastery in Japan and his house to the local Bavarian church on the lake. I had liked him.

Secrets

The man came to our offices every morning for two weeks. He always sat in the same place in the big conference room. Mostly he held his left eye shut. His name was Fabian Kalkmann, and he was mad.

In our very first conversation, he said the secret services were after him. Both the CIA and German Intelligence. He knew which secret they wanted. This was the way things were.

'They're hunting me, do you understand?'

'Not completely, so far.'

'Were you ever in the stadium during a soccer match?'

'No.'

'You have to go. They all call my name. They call it all the time. They yell Mohatit, Mohatit.'

'But your name is Kalkmann,' I said.

'Yes, but the secret services call me Mohatit. It's what I'm called in the Stasi files too. Everyone knows that. They want my secret, the big one.'

Kalkmann leaned forward.

'I went to the optician. For my new glasses, you know. They drugged me, through my eye. I came out of the shop exactly one day later, exactly twenty-four hours later.'

He looked at me.

'You don't believe me. But I can prove it. Here,' he said, pulling out a little notebook, 'here, take a look. It's all in here.'

In big capital letters it said in the notebook, 26/04, 15 HUNDRED HOURS, ENTER LAB. 27/04, 16 HUNDRED HOURS, EXIT LAB. Kalkmann closed the notebook again and looked at me triumphantly.

'So, now you've seen it. That's the proof. The optician's shop belongs to the CIA and German Intelligence. They drugged me and took me to the cellar. There's a big laboratory down there, a James Bond laboratory all built of high-grade steel. They operated on me for twenty-four hours. That's when they did it.' He leaned back.

'Did what?' I asked.

Kalkmann looked around. He was whispering now. 'The camera. They inserted a camera in my left eye. Behind the lens. Yes—and now they see everything I see. It's perfect. The secret services can see everything that Mohatit sees,' he said. Then he raised his voice. 'But they won't get my secret.'

Kalkmann wanted me to bring charges against German Intelligence. And the CIA, of course. And former American president Reagan, who was responsible for the whole thing. When I said Reagan was dead, he replied, 'That's what you think. He's actually living up in the attic at Helmut Kohl's house.'

He came every morning to tell me about his experiences. At a certain point I'd had enough. I told him he needed help. It was amazing: he saw reason at once. I called the emergency psychiatric services and asked if I could come by with a patient. We took a taxi. We had to go to the locked criminal unit because the other rooms were being painted. The bulletproof glass doors closed behind us, we went deeper and deeper into the building, following a male nurse. Finally we were seated in an anteroom. A young doctor I didn't know asked us to come into his consulting room. We sat down in the visitor's chairs in front of a small desk. I was about to explain things when Kalkmann said:

'Good day, my name is Ferdinand von Schirach, I'm a lawyer.' He pointed at me. 'I'm bringing you Mr Kalkmann. I think he has a severe problem.'